Thomas

A.M.P.D. BOOK ONE

ARTIFICIAL
MILITARY
PROSTHETICS
DIVISION

THOMAS HRAYNYK

MOUNTAIN ARBOR
PRESS

MOUNTAIN ARBOR
PRESS *an Imprint of BookLogix*
Alpharetta, GA

ISBN: 978-1-6653-0249-4 - Paperback
eISBN: 978-1-6653-0250-0 - eBook

Library of Congress Control Number: 2021920943

Printed in the United States of America   1 0 1 3 2 1

∞This paper meets the requirements of ANSI/NISO Z39.48-1992 (Permanence of Paper)

To the loving memory of my fiancée, Michele,
and my mother, Susan.
To my son, Ace, I do this for you.

Prelude

War is a deep and dark place. Men and women put their lives in harm's way to fight for the greater good. Soldiers give their lives for others. The survivors have gratitude for those soldiers who sacrifice body and mind to protect those in need of protection. This story brings into light the question of how humanity could change if we looked at disability and immortality in a new way. This is where AMPD found its life and the world started down a new path of good and evil and life and limb.

CHAPTER 1

A bright sun glares through the dust and debris that flies everywhere. A soldier lies on his back trying to get up. He tries to find some type of shelter. Bomb blasts hit in several spots near him. He is confused and disoriented. He starts to crawl in a direction that feels positive. His hope right now is all he has.

"Keep moving!" a voice screams.

He can't see clearly and suddenly a loud whistle comes close. A massive blast hits a few feet away and sends him in the air before he crashes into the ground violently. His right side feels numb. His left arm keeps pulling on the ground as his consciousness ebbs. He slides his body into a ditch. He doesn't realize it is next to the road where his convoy sits. The convoy is being beaten with artillery and mortar shells. Suddenly he drifts into a blackout and is unconscious.

| | | | |

He starts to come to at the sound of helicopters and voices. Dust blows, and he can barely keep his eyes open. Then a board slides under him. Gunshots and explosions continue as he slips in and out of his foggy state.

"Strap the right arm tight. I don't want him to lose it!"

"Yes sir!"

"Contact Doctor Peck and tell him General Seagar sent you this soldier. He fits the profile. The doctor will take him from there."

"Yes sir!"

The soldier slips into darkness. Two helicopters sit as he is placed on the second chopper. He is separate from the other wounded. In minutes, he is whisked away from the battle area.

| | | | |

General Seagar stands behind an assault vehicle watching the helicopter disappear into the distance. He is a fit man in his fifties, with the typical military grade black shades and rough stubble. With a gruff voice he barks orders at soldiers to round up and evacuate the area. Out of the corner of his eye he sees an enemy soldier cresting the hill to his right. He pulls his pistol and quick-draws to shoot him in the head at forty feet. The assailant falls forward and rolls down the hill to a dead stop. Seagar quickly jumps into the assault vehicle and they storm off.

| | | | |

Meanwhile, in the helicopter, a medic attends to the wounded soldier. "At six feet tall and two hundred and twenty-five pounds he has a solid frame with ginger hair and a trimmed beard. He is of English and German background."

The soldier starts to come to as the medic bandages his side and cleans the right arm, which is mangled and bloody. Small fragments of shrapnel stick out of the skin. Blood smears and drips to the metal floor.

"Where am I?"

"In the medivac helicopter. We are getting you back to base. Doctor Peck can help you. I'm Dell, just keep talking to me. Can you feel your arm?"

"No, my whole right side feels like it isn't there. I feel pins and needles, but nothing for the most part. I don't know Doctor Peck, and I know most people on base."

"We are not going to the mission base. We are going to a separate facility, where Doc can work without distractions or questions."

Concern fills the soldiers face, and he isn't sure he wants to go. "Get me up, I want to sit up. I want to see what is happening."

"You need to stay still. The right side of your body is severely injured and damaged. You may go into shock. What is your name? You can trust me."

"Chase . . . Chase Campbell. Am I going to survive?"

Dell looks at him with a smirk. "Something tells me you are going to do more than that. By the way, my friends call me Surge."

"Why?"

"Because they thought Doc was too 'Seven Dwarfs.' Plus my gadgets are a little more surgical." He pulls his glove off to show a metal hand. It looks almost robotic. He shows off how his fingers move, then, suddenly, one finger rotates and retracts to show a scalpel.

"I don't know if I should smile or freak out," Chase says.

"Just get some rest. The painkillers will probably knock you out." Just as Surge says that, Chase passes out. The helicopter continues on for about an hour.

| | | | |

At the facility where they are headed, Dr. Peck looks

at his computer screen, smiling and making notes. He is a man who resembles Albert Einstein but is balding and a little more plump. He is a genius and medical scholar who wants to change the world. He also has a knack for industrial engineering, which is what makes his project that much more fun. He has worked with amputees before, in his time with the military. Now, his work takes on a whole new meaning.

He is currently waiting for the arrival of Dell. Surge is his assistant and friend. His cell phone rings, and he looks at the screen. He smiles and pushes himself away from his desk. He sits in a wheelchair, and points himself to the door before pushing a button, making the door open. Using a joystick he starts to race his wheelchair out of the room and down the hall.

A nurse moves to the side and says, "Hey, Dr. P."

In his strong English accent, he greets her back—"Hello, gorgeous!"—then disappears around the corner.

| | | | | |

Outside, on the helipad, the medics and Chase arrive. The facility is located in the scenic mountains of Greece. They picked the location because it would be solid, classified, and secure. It is also not a long journey to some locations in the Middle East and Eastern Europe that are of concern.

As terror groups start to develop all over the world, secret projects and highly classified technology are becoming even more important. Dr. Peck and the US Military wanted to build a way to combat the most dangerous of these terror groups. One group in particular poses a major threat. Rumblings of a group called the Plague started to surface out of Romania a few years ago.

Somehow, Chase is about to become a major part of Dr. Peck's program.

As the helicopter approaches the helipad, Chase starts to come to. Surge monitors his vitals, and checks the dressings on his wounds. He can tell that the limbs are going to be lost based on the damage, but he holds that information back, not wanting to create more shock. As Chase starts to wake, he asks where he is.

"We are about to land in Greece."

"Why am I in Greece? Why do I feel so weak?"

"The facility you are going to handles specific injuries and recovery and also has new development programs for the military. You have lost a lot of blood, and the right side of your body has been severely damaged. Once Dr. Peck has assessed you, we will decide what needs to be done. He is aware of your injuries."

Chase groans. He cannot believe he is in this situation. What happened? It was a simple transport convoy that had no significant reason for an attack like that. They were transporting medical supplies to the city of Adana in Turkey. Yes, it's near the Syrian border, but they had a clear operation ahead. He should have had a better idea that something was coming. Chase wants to wake up and have it all be a dream. Please just be a dream.

The helicopter touches down on a helipad, and nurses rush out to unload him onto a stretcher. The sky is clear and blue and the sun is bright and in his eyes. He hears an English accent speak out.

"Get him to the operating room, Surge. Prep the lab, this is happening. We have one shot with this one."

"On my way, Doc. His right arm and right leg, as I messaged you."

"Don't worry about attachments, the arm and leg function is the priority," the doctor makes clear.

"I understand, Doc."

Chase calls out, "Surge? Where are you going?"

"Just relax, Chase, Doc is staying with you. I'll see you in a few."

Doc pulls out a syringe. "When you wake up, you will be all new. Just trust me." He sticks Chase with the syringe and everything goes black.

CHAPTER 2

On a bright sunny day, a woman makes her way to the square in Kraków. The city is one of the most important to the Polish economy. She has black sunglasses to match the dark black hair that drapes down her back. She wears a white flowing dress, with a plunging neckline. A matching white leather purse and pumps complete the outfit. She looks understated but draws attention with how beautiful she is. As she walks across the square a young man notices her. He's twenty-two years young, dumb, and his mind full of cum. He decides to approach and act like he is lost.

"Excuse me, you look like you know where you are going. Can you help me?"

"I'm in a big hurry. Where are you looking to go?" she says with a strong German accent.

"First dinner, then find our way back to your place!" He smiles with a confident smirk.

She smiles back with a giggle. He doesn't notice her hand in her purse. As he gazes at her, she looks deep into his eyes. There is a pause. "I have to ask, young man."

"What's that, beautiful?" His attention is straight at her eyes.

7

"Have you ever had a knife slice into your nutsack?" She smiles with an evil stare. "Because you are a few seconds away from finding out." He failed to notice her quick hands. "I suggest you go try your luck with the easy blonde sitting in the coffee shop."

He starts to back off. "I'll go do that. Sorry to bother you." His eyes are the size of saucers as he backs up and bumps into a huge muscular man looking down at him with a mean smirk.

In a deep German accent, the man asks, "Is this the guy, sis?"

She shakes her head no. "He is nobody. Feel free to dispose of him if you like."

The young guy sprints away. The two chuckle and start walking together toward a monument of a great Polish poet in the square with steps surrounding it. There are statues on each side with the poet in the center, standing high and looking out at the square. Leaning against the corner is a large man in a dark suit. His head is down and he continues to flick a small pistol-shaped lighter in his hand, staring at the flame and then closing it. The woman approaches and starts to talk, but the man speaks first.

"Have you ever thought about how when you flip a lighter, you will never have the exact same reaction?"

She pauses, lifts up her cigarette, and says, "I just want this lit."

He raises his head with a smile on his face. He has a darker tone to his skin and a dark black goatee. The giant X-shaped scar on his face is distinctive.

"Crow, you look beautiful as usual. I don't believe I have met your brother."

"No, you haven't. I am surprised it has taken so long to bring the two of you together." She lights her cigarette from his lighter. "You did say this is a special request, though. Brug is excellent when it comes to the specialty projects."

"Well, I am looking for a team for a very special project. My client is very specific about what he wants. He needs an excellent engineer and weapons dealer."

Brug speaks up. "What type of project are we talking about? I don't go into deals blind. Neither does my sister."

"For now you will report to me and I will provide all the information you need for the deals we are putting together. I have also recruited Sun. He will be joining you on this." Crow looks annoyed by that information.

The man notices her reaction. "Is there a problem with that?"

"No, he just needs to focus on the task and not my assets!"

Brug chimes in. "The Saigon Sun? He is good at what he does. He is the deadliest man I know. Keep him fed with money and women before the job and he will be fine."

"Just remember, you introduced him to me. Now I use him as much as I can." The man pulls a folded paper from his pocket. "I have a suite at the Bonerowski Palace. It is under the name Elodie. Here is your ID for the room." He hands it to Crow. "That will get you a key, and get two extra for your brother and Sun."

"Okay. What about you?" She asks as she flips the cigarette to the ground.

"I have to meet with our client to confirm that you are on board. He is very secluded right now. He is experimenting a lot and doesn't like distractions. I will meet you there afterward. Brug, I need information on bodies."

Brug looks at him in a weird way. "What type of bodies?"

"Our client needs corpses. Anything fit and military grade is best, but a variety doesn't hurt. Have the info for me at the suite."

Crow speaks up. "Why are we meeting in such a public place for this? This isn't your style, Azazil. What is this about?"

He smiles and starts to walk away. "The Plague is coming. Get ready." He vanishes into a small crowd.

Brug and Crow are left standing, wondering what he is talking about. "Do you trust him, sis?"

"You know I only trust you, but something tells me if all of us are being brought together, then it's a big deal. My only question would be who is the client? Let's go get a drink." The two walk away from the monument.

Sitting on the steps is a figure in a black cloak and black hood, grungy and looking homeless. He has a small cup in front of him with change. He collects his things and turns a recorder off that was hidden. In a matter of seconds he disappears and is nowhere to be found in the square.

| | | | |

General Seagar sits at his desk, looking over maps and documents. A knock at the door disrupts his thoughts. "What do you want?"

A young communications soldier walks in. "Sir! Chase Campbell arrived and is in surgery with the doctor as we speak . . . sir."

"Excellent! Is there any information on the others? Is there progress or any developments? Have we had any word from him?"

"Sabu has not checked in yet, sir, but he is due back for inspection with the doctor." The young soldier hands him a file.

"Okay, get a chopper ready. I want to be at the facility when Chase is out of surgery. Also, make sure the others are ready for inspection. Anything else I should know?" He opens the file.

"Sabu was known to be tracking the arms dealer and former Romanian general Azazil between Romania and Poland. His last communication was three days ago, but we did not have a location."

"Have the AMPD files ready for me on the chopper. I have a feeling we are going to need the program fully operational. Much faster than anticipated."

"Yes sir!" The soldier leaves the office and rushes to the communications room. The general sits at his desk and looks at the papers again. He mutters to himself, "I hope this goes as planned."

| | | | |

Back in Kraków, Crow and Brug enter the front doors to the Bonerowski Palace. It is a beautiful building with original murals and architecture. Yellows, crimsons, and golds glisten with the gems on the chandeliers hanging from the ceilings. A massive spiral staircase is lined with a dark red carpet with gold trim. A bright crystal chandelier runs from the first floor all the way up through five floors of the building as the staircase wraps around them. You can see and smell the history of it all in the Gothic Renaissance architecture.

The building only houses eight luxury suites and eight apartments. It's a perfect, quiet location to set up Azazil's meetings.

Crow approaches the desk and hands her ID to the employee.

"You will be staying on the top-floor apartment. I was told a month?" the man asks.

She nods yes, and asks for three keys. The gentleman

smiles and obliges her. "If you have any issues, please call down to us and we will take care of it."

She smiles at him, still sporting the black sunglasses. Brug continues to look around.

He pipes up to the man at the desk, "I need a drink!"

"We have a bar and lounge around the corner. Also, we've opened a night club in the basement. We took the liberty of providing a bottle of vodka and a bottle of fifteen-year-old whiskey. We were told they were suggested options."

Brug smirks as best he can. "I like you! Have someone grab our bags from the car out front. Let's go, sis."

They walk up the winding staircase and Crow observes the one-of-a-kind chandelier. They get to the room, and she unlocks the door. As they begin to enter, Brug stops her and pulls a large handgun out. He moves in front of her and puts his ear to the door.

"Someone is in there," he whispers.

Brug pushes the door open quickly and points the gun straight into the room. Sitting on a love seat with his feet up on the table is an Asian man with a glass in his hand and a cigar. He is wearing a white suit and tie with a blood-red dress shirt, and white dress shoes with bright red socks rest on the table.

"It's about time you got here! I was getting bored. Did you try the ice cream shop downstairs? It's SO good!" Sun's actions are very high-strung with a bit of a high voice.

Crow looks and shakes her head. "You are drunk already, aren't you?"

"Please, you know I can hold my own. Besides, Azazil won't be back here till late tonight or tomorrow morning. He and this scientist have a lot to discuss."

Brug grabs a glass and pours some whiskey. "How did you get in here? And what do you know about it?"

"Please! It's not like this place is a prison, and I can get in and out of all sorts of things. Brug, you know that, and don't forget it." He laughs with an egocentric smirk. He pours more whiskey for himself and takes a big sip of it. "This scientist I don't know, but he has labs in Lithuania and here in Poland. He wants to build an army, and I truly mean build. Our job is to confiscate the dead bodies that can be useful to him. As well as the electronic technology he needs."

Brug takes a shot of whiskey. "He sounds a little sick if he wants dead bodies. Sounds like some Frankenstein shit to me. But the fact that Azazil is his right-hand man makes this legit. This guy must have a huge agenda to be putting this together."

Crow ponders how beneficial this could be for her and her brother.

Sun looks at her. "You know this is a step toward starting a major operation. This isn't peanuts, tootsie. This is big time. This guy has huge plans and does not plan on having problems. We can change the landscape of the world with this shit."

Brug shoots down another few ounces of whiskey. "I love creating chaos, I love creating monstrous technology. I like how this sounds. I know a place here in Poland where we can get what he needs. I just need to contact a few people. I wouldn't mind getting my hands dirty, and bust some skulls in the process."

Sun gets up off the sofa and starts walking toward the door. "Great, go make some calls. I'm going to the club in the basement. Saigon Sun needs some tail." He adjusts his tie and shakes his ass while looking at Crow.

"Don't even think you are bringing them here." Crow looks at him with a *fuck you* face.

"Do I sense jealousy?" Sun flicks his tongue out with

rapid movement. He always had a flare for being repulsive, especially toward Crow. She turns around and walks into one of the bedrooms and shuts the door.

"Your sister wants me!" He looks at Brug.

Brug shoots down a few more ounces of his high-end whiskey. "You make her gag, and not in the fun way." He wipes his chin and pulls his pistol back out. "Just focus on the job. Keep your eyes open while you are out. I got the feeling we were being watched this afternoon."

Sun shakes his head. "You worry too much. I'll bring you a big Polish girl. Nice and round. That help?"

Brug chugs some more whiskey. "I like redheads with big butts. You do you and I'll make some calls."

Sun laughs. "You always did love the taste of ginger!" He heads out of the apartment in a rush.

Meanwhile Crow sits in the bedroom. She turns the lights out and sits at the window, looking out at the city.

She has an uneasy feeling about this afternoon. Scanning through her mind of everything she saw and heard, she remembers a homeless man near the statue, the young punk that tried to hit on her, the crowds in the square.

Growing up with no parents, she learned to be alert, and to watch over her brother. She doesn't trust easily. She sits thinking about growing up in Europe, moving from city to city and country to country. After experiencing personal trauma and turmoil she developed the idea of razor blades in her nails.

When Crow was sixteen, she and Brug found their way to a shelter at a church in Brussels. The priest was kind and attentive, and they felt they could use the situation to build up some money, until they moved on. One evening the priest asked her for some help, and all she wanted was to check the office for valuables. He was in his fifties, and had a gentle demeanor to him, but deep down had serious issues and a dark side. As soon as the office door closed, it latched, and Crow had nowhere to go. The priest got a hold of her arm when she tried to get by him, and she got pinned to the desk. As they struggled, she was able to grab a knife from the desk. It was his letter opener. She pulled her arm free and jabbed it up into his side. As he yelled in pain, she then made a sideways swipe to slash across his throat. She ran out and never looked back.

Since then, she has always carried that knife and a wall that doesn't allow many people to get close. She has anger, and greed, and that's enough for her.

She looks down to the street and sees the hooded figure walking by the palace. He shuffles and moves slowly, but then stops and looks up. He scans along the windows as if he can tell someone is looking at him, but his face is covered by a scarf. He slouches back and continues on his way slowly.

"Brug!" she yells out.

The door opens and he walks in. "What? Why are you in the dark?"

"We are being monitored. A man is posing as a homeless man. Dark, hooded clothing and a scarf around his face. He just walked past on the street. He was at the statue." She grabs her purse. "I'm going to follow him."

"You think that's smart? We don't know when Azazil will show or anything about this. I think we sit tight and wait for him to get back."

"What if the hood knows things? You and I need to cover us. We've always made sure we look out for each other. I'm going for a walk, and it will get him away from here."

"Okay! I don't agree, but you have always been intuitive about things like this. Message me if you have any issues. I will be here calling my contacts."

"I can handle myself. You know that. I think I have proven that."

She walks out. Brug grabs the bottle of whiskey and drinks from it. He nods his head, knowing that she can handle almost any man or woman that she comes across. He wonders who this hooded individual could be. They have encountered many people in their lives. Traveling throughout the world together, fending for themselves and doing anything to survive, you deal with many people. Saigon Sun being one of them, and the reason Crow is so dangerous. Sun trained her, and sparred with her for years. That was while Brug sat in a German military prison, the prison Sun broke him out of. He has gratitude, but is cautious.

Crow steps out into the street and turns right, the direction the hooded man went. With a deep breath, she pulls her purse up on her shoulder and begins to walk. The streets are not crowded, but they are not empty either. She is very perceptive, and keeps an eye on her surroundings.

People are getting ice cream at the shop Sun spoke of. There are people heading to the basement area for the club. They don't concern her, and so she continues down the street. Yellow and pink lights line the umbrellas of the outdoor patio. There is laughter and voices, music from the basement of the building. She moves into the center of the square. She places herself in clear sight of anyone following, wanting the hooded man to see her. Draw him out, get his attention. She has no fear of being where she is. She wants to see him, even desires it. She continues on, with no reaction from anyone.

| | | | |

The hooded man is watching, aware of her ploy. He is smart, and knows of her ways. He considers getting close, but the current risk of that action is not worth the information it may provide. Based on what he heard at the statue, there is too much unknown to make that move. It's time to check in and report what he knows. He backs down a small alley and disappears.

The people are still laughing and talking, and music still plays.

CHAPTER 3

Puddles of blood are on the floor, with rags and towels sitting on a metal side table. Chase lies on an operating table, unconscious. The steady beep of the heart monitor repeats as he rests. The door opens and Dr. Peck wheels in with Surge at his side. A nurse enters behind them and starts to clean up the side table.

They move next to the table and Peck starts to examine Chase. He puts his hand on his forehead to check for fever.

Chase softly speaks, "I feel like death ran me over a few times!"

Peck chuckles and responds, "How would you know that if you have never died before? You are fine but need to recover from the procedure. We are going to move you to a comfortable room. I'm surprised you are awake, to be honest."

"What did . . . you . . . do to me?" Chase mumbles.

Surge moves to the other side as Peck gestures for Chase to squeeze his left hand. He is able to squeeze the hand easily. Peck asks him to move his left toes and he does, again, with ease.

"What I ask may cause some shock. I want you to wiggle the fingers on your right hand."

Chase suddenly realizes his arm feels different. Metal fingers start to move by his side. He rolls his head to the right to find a metal arm attached at the shoulder. He then realizes his right leg feels different as well. Just below his hip starts a metal, robotic leg. It starts to move with his thoughts and fear of what has happened.

"You need to rest. I know you have questions, and yes, we have answers, but you were in bad shape. We had to act fast. Thankfully, I was able to make the connection points and stabilize you. You are about to become part of something incredibly special."

Surge turns to the nurse. "Move him to the room with Bull. They can get acquainted while they recover."

A few more nurses enter and they transfer Chase to a mobile hospital bed. They wheel him out as he wonders where he is going next. The bed rolls down the hall and they take a right. It enters into a room with another bed and a muscular Black man lying in it. He has a neck-stabilizing halo on that seems to run behind him down his back. It's difficult to see, as his sheets cover his body. Chase feels relieved, in a sense, that he is not the only one in a hospital bed. He still has a lot of questions and hopes this guy may have some answers.

"Finally, I have some company. Streaming movies only gets you so far when you're stuck motionless in a bed."

"How long have you been here?" Chase says quietly.

"They rushed me here a few days ago. After the blast, medivac picked me up and brought me here. I was part of security teams in Istanbul. We were evacuating a crowd from a bus terminal. Suicide bomber got close and I shielded a mother and her son. Took debris in my back, my neck, and lost my hands at the forearm."

"I'm sorry." Gratitude hits Chase. "Can you feel anything?"

"Not sure what this Peck guy did to me, but it must have worked. I know I can move my toes, and he says I'll walk. I hope I can walk. What about you?"

"Was on a medical supply caravan and got ambushed. I was hit with an explosion that sent me flying into a ditch. Then I woke up with a metal arm and metal leg. I'm still trying to figure this place out." Chase groans as he gets his body adjusted.

"Well, I can help with that. I've known about this place for a while. A few years back the military wanted to see if there were ways for injured soldiers to get back into military duty. Dr. Peck helped his now assistant with his hand amputation. I only know that because Surge and I studied chemistry in university together. He went medicine and I went chemical warfare and engineering."

"So we are lab rats? Our accidents put us into a military experiment?" Chase says in an annoyed voice.

"If you want to look at it that way, then go ahead. Keep in mind, if they didn't see something in you and I, we would be lying in a medical tent somewhere, wondering what is going to happen."

"Are you saying this is my golden ticket?" Chase says, still annoyed.

"No! I'm saying we could be in a lot worse than this. There is more to come, I just don't know what."

Dr. Peck rolls into the room as Bull finishes his comment. Surge walks in behind him with a smile and looks at Bull and nods at him. Dr. Peck moves his wheelchair between the two beds.

"Yes, there is more to come. I'm very excited about what we have in store for you. I know Dell has filled you in on some of this operation."

"You can call me Surge," he quips quickly. "I prefer Surge."

"Of course, I guess I can fill you in on the rest," Dr. Peck continues. "Several years ago I studied and practiced medicine back in London. As a hobby, I also liked to build machines and robots. After working with children with amputations, I started to research the possibilities of nerves and electric currents. The US Military had heard of my research and wanted to work with me. I met Dell and he impressed me, so we started working together on it. Thanks to his accident, I had a sudden chance to try the procedure on him."

Surge shakes his head and jumps in. "It wasn't ideal, but sometimes things happen for a reason. He had to amputate my hand, and it worked. The gadgets came after." Surge raised his hand, moving the electronic fingers.

"Gentlemen, welcome to the Artificial Military Prosthetics Division. We call it AMPD in short form. Basically, the top military members who have been involved in severe trauma in action get brought here. We perform immediate surgery when needed. It takes split-second decisions to get the nerves and electrodes bonded the right way. If you wait too long, the opportunity is gone."

Chase and Bull look at Dr. Peck like he is some mad scientist. Chase pipes up, "Do we get a choice?"

"No, your injuries were so bad they brought you right to me. I just saved your life, by the way. I have also given you a chance to use the most advanced and technical prostheses in the world." Peck puts his hand on his legs.

Surge suggests in a quick response, "Doc, maybe we should let them rest a bit, and then we can introduce them to the others."

"There are others?" Bull asks.

Surge responds to his reaction. "We have three others here. One is out on a recon mission. He had both legs below the knee amputated and both forearms. He was our first major patient. He saved children from a hospital that had been bombed. He turned to go back into an area that was burning and one of the oxygen tanks blew up. He also experienced severe facial trauma. Since we worked on him, his gratitude gave him the determination to help us and help build this program. He started doing recon to test out his new limbs. He should be back here by tomorrow."

Chase asks, "What's his name?"

Surge looks at Chase. "Sabu. Why do you ask?"

"I knew a guy that did security detail around the world. It was great money. I heard he was killed in an explosion at a children's hospital. I guess he wasn't."

Doc and Surge both smile, before Doc responds, "No! No, he wasn't." Doc then continued. "We kept his records as deceased. He wanted it and we felt, for the program, it was best he stay dead on paper. People in the world want what we have, and the more they can track us, the worse for us it can be. That's why we are here in Greece. It's a perfect location for us, and Greek government knows they have military assistance from us."

Chase is puzzled but happy. He met Sabu a few years ago. They were both in Afghanistan but with different outfits. Sabu was an independent contractor of security for specific companies. He was usually hired with others to secure items or people in areas where others didn't want to go and where military were not allowed to go. He was an adrenaline junkie. It wasn't about the money, although that helped. He loved the feeling of going into hostile situations and helping people. He was also really good at it. Chase had a lot of respect for him.

Bull reaches out to Doc. "Who are the other two?"

The doctor smiles. "I will have Salene and Kitch come

by. We can properly introduce them." Doc looks at Surge. "How should we introduce them?"

Surge looks back at Doc. "We need more space to show off the upgrades they have. I will have the nurses wheel them to the hangar."

"Be sure General Seagar is there. I think we need him to outline some things as well."

Chase's head rises with concern. "General Seagar? Is he in charge of this?" He shakes his head in frustration.

"I know you have lots of questions, but we can't cover everything right now. It will all be explained when we bring you to the hangar. Just be patient, and you will see what this operation is and why we have it. At the moment, you don't have control of your new limbs and attachments. They have to take time to bond and I have to make sure the charge I give the attachments doesn't hurt the nerves."

Surge walks over to Chase and puts his hand on his chest. "Trust us, Chase. I know this is overwhelming, but we can help and change the world. We can protect people like we never believed before. With some sacrifices, we have developed new ways for injured soldiers to contribute." Surge and the doctor walk out of the room, leaving Chase and Bull lying in the beds with question marks floating around in their heads.

Chase believes Surge for some reason, but he has no trust in Seagar, even if the general did get him the medivac that got him out of the ambush.

"For some reason, I can sense your thoughts, Chase," Bull says. "What's wrong? You didn't seem too thrilled at the name Seagar. I only have a little bit of experience with him, but I know he's a hardass."

"Not just a hardass, he always has motives and I don't always agree with him. We have had a few moments of tension. Don't get me wrong, I'm grateful I'm lying here and not dead in a ditch. But at what cost, is my question?" Chase pauses. "I need some rest. Wake me when they come for us."

"I will, and I understand your feeling."

CHAPTER 4

A zazil sits in the back seat of a black luxury SUV as it pulls up to a large mansion in Cluj-Napoca, Romania. It's in a secluded area and part of the Transylvania region. The gated land has a medieval feel. Wrought-iron gates with gargoyles and Gothic symbols present themselves at the front of the property. It's a wet night with a dark tone to the sky. The only lights you can see for miles are some of the dim flickers of lanterns at the mansion. Those who travel to the area would feel dead themselves just by the heavy air that weighs on the surroundings.

The driver gets out of the car and approaches a keypad at the side of the gate. He presses in five numbers and the gates begin to open. He is a large, muscular man in a black suit and has a military haircut and an olive complexion. He gets back in the car and pulls into the property. A long, single-lane gravel road leads to an empty fountain at the front entrance. The castle makes you feel like Dracula would be waiting in the shadows. It doesn't draw attention to itself, but anyone not from here would be curious of the story behind the building.

The SUV pulls up to the front and shuts off. Azazil sits

and waits for his driver to open the door for him. They both walk up to the front door, a large oak door. The door-knocker looking like a hellhound stares at them. The driver grabs the ring and taps it three times, pauses, and taps three more times with pauses in between. A latch unlocks and the door releases. They enter into a large entrance area that has two stairwells arching up around and meeting in the middle on a second-floor landing. A shadowed figure in a black hooded robe appears on the landing. The room is lit with lanterns and a giant Gothic chandelier.

"You have news for me?" The hooded figure speaks in a deep accent, but it is followed by a wheeze.

Azazil responds quickly. "I come with answers from the others and with a gift."

"Who is this with you?"

"My driver, Asher. I thought he may be handy to you?"

Asher looks over at Azazil, a little curious. He has worked for him and been at Azazil's side for a few years now. This is the first time he has entered the mansion.

"He looks very fit, strong," the hooded man says. "Is he able to fight?"

Azazil nods. "Yes, he is one of my best fighters!"

"So how can he be handy to me? He is an asset to you. You talk highly of him, yet you are handing him over to me?" The figure starts to walk down the left staircase slowly, a burn-damaged hand grasping the rail.

As he comes closer, Azazil starts to fill him in on the progress. "Crow and Brug are both interested but have questions. Sun is all in, as long as the money comes with it."

"Yes, I figured Sun would have a price, but all we need for him is cash and loose women. Crow is the one I am concerned about. Will she follow? Will she stand by us and not deviate for her own benefit? She is the smart one. A smart woman with an evil way can be very dangerous."

The figure walks up to Asher and inspects him. Asher can't see under the hood. A subtle mumble of "I like him!" comes from the hood. There is a pause. "Kill him."

Azazil pulls a knife from his jacket and slashes Asher's throat. Asher grabs his throat, staring at Azazil with disbelief as he drops to his knees. Blood sprays and pools on the floor. Asher's body falls limp.

"Thank you, Azazil, he will make a wonderful addition." The man rings a bell. Two more hooded figures come out of the shadows and grab the body. "Take him to the lab and have him hooked up for the procedure," the wheezing voice speaks.

"I will meet with Crow and Brug again to be sure they understand how important it is they stand by what we are doing."

"The Plague will rise and change the world. Do you know Shakespeare? Mercutio speaks of a plague—'a plague on all thy houses.' I will bring that plague to life, and the world will burn. It will fall as I rise." The figure turns and starts to walk back up the steps. "Do you need a new driver?"

"No, Velnias, I will be fine without one. I have plenty of replacements." Azazil turns and exits the house, wiping the leftover blood from his hands on a handkerchief. He pulls his cell phone out.

In Kraków, Brug answers his call.

"Azazil, thank you for the suite. It has been very relaxing!"

"I'm glad it is to your satisfaction. Where are Crow and Sun?"

"Sun is in the club downstairs being himself. Crow went for a walk; she had this feeling a homeless man was following us earlier. She has gone to scout it out."

"Have your sister call me as soon as she can. Our employer wants to make sure that the both of you are committed and on board one hundred percent. He is skeptical of your loyalty. Also, let me know about who may be following."

"Azazil, I will come through for you. She will call. I do have some information about a US Military project operating in Greece. My contact works in the Greek government and saw documents giving approval for military contracts with the US."

"Why would I want to know this?"

"General Seagar is the one overseeing the operation personally. His name was on the documents. I happen to know he pushes very hard for experimental practices. It is not far away, and if we have someone following us, they could be linked. We need to be cautious with our moves."

"I will send some scouts to set up in the area. Get Sun back to the room. I can't have authorities putting attention on us. Not now!" Azazil's voice raises. He is a man who has a temper that rivals and surpasses the highest-regarded psychopaths. To be on the world's top five terrorist watch list takes a very smart but dark personality. Crow is not far behind him on that list. She has a very clear and straightforward approach regarding other people and what she wants in her life. She uses her sexuality against people and gets what she wants. Azazil is more aggressive, and brute force is what has made him the shining star of terror that he is today.

| | | | |

Crow finds herself walking the streets with attention on everyone. She has not seen the homeless man in about an hour. There are still plenty of people out at the square and enjoying themselves. Seems like the crowd has grown the later it has gotten. It is a cooler night, and the moon is almost full but missing a sliver.

Crow starts to think that she is wasting her time. The hooded man is long gone, and with luck, will not be back. She starts to make her way back when her cell phone buzzes. Brug sent her a text message:

> **Azazil called, he wants Sun back to the suite. Can you go get him? He messaged me that he went to a gentlemen's club around the corner called DIAMOND.**

She is not amused, and it's not the first time she has had to round Sun up. They know it's best if she goes. Sun has had a thing for her for a long time. She started as his student, but over time, developed an arms business. She has no interest in him, but he will follow her to the suite like a puppy wanting a biscuit.

She texts back:

> **As usual, and if I have to crack someone's skull, you owe me one.**

Brug messages back an emoji sporting a middle finger.

Crow approaches the entrance to the club, where a large Polish bouncer stands at the door. He is wearing a tight black T-shirt with the word *obsada* on the chest. Its translation is *staff* or *casting*. He has on a leather jacket with a large diamond on the chest. He has blond hair to his shoulders and his eyes get hooked on Crow as she walks toward him.

"*Dobry wieczor,*" he says with a smile. It means *good evening* in Polish. She smiles at him and stops in front of him.

"Hi, is this where the fun is?" She gives him a wink.

"Yes! You speak . . . uh, English." He speaks in broken English. "I need . . . check . . . bag, jacket?"

She pulls some lipstick out and presses it to her lips.

"No, you don't." She smiles and winks and starts giggling. Her two fingers slightly touch his forearm. He pauses and looks at her with a grin and not much else going on in his head.

"Go ahead! Have a good time." He opens the door for her. She puts her lipstick away and struts in with her ass swaying from side to side.

All he can do is continue staring. All she can do is laugh with a big grin on her face. "What a dumbass!"

Crow enters the main club, where pink lighting glows on the old red brick of the building. Behind the bar is a bright blue-and-pink display. The bottles glow as the bartender mixes drinks.

"The Devil's Bleeding Crown" by Volbeat plays over the speakers as a busty brunette dances on stage wearing a neon-green G-string. She swings herself around the pole with force and energy. Crow can hear Sun's obnoxious voice through the music cheer the dancer on and give suggestive vulgarities at her. "I like your cheeks!"

Crow spots him and starts to walk toward the stage where Sun sits. As she approaches, a large man wearing a business suit and tie steps in front of her.

"I like your style, baby! How much for a night with you?"

Crow looks him in the eye, pissed off. "Excuse me?"

He chuckles. "How much for some private time? You got it going on, baby. I bet you're a beast!"

Crow laughs at the comment. "Did you just call me a beast? Honey, you have no idea what a monster I can be. I can make men like you cry just with the flick of my wrist. Have you heard what 'eunuch' means? How's that for beast, honey?"

The man smiles with a shocked grin, which is not a good idea for him. "Baby, relax!" He puts his hand on her shoulder, and that is *definitely* not a good idea. Crow looks at him and licks her lips. She puts her hand on his and wraps her fingers around his index finger. She smiles at him while removing his hand off her shoulder. She holds his finger tight.

"I have a firm grip, I have been told."

He keeps smiling idiotically as she tightens her grip on his finger. She stares into his eyes. "Want to see something special?" He is silent but nods his head in excitement. He has no idea the club patrons are watching intently. She keeps smiling while she suddenly flicks her wrist viciously. His finger is instantly snapped out of joint, the fingernail now in line with his wrist. "Instead of showing you that you are an asshole, I'm going to make you feel like one!" she states with aggression.

His face shows pain and fear. Crow pushes him toward a table and bends him over it. She undoes his belt and pulls his pants down. With his bare ass facing everyone, she pulls his arm between his legs. Holding one wrist, she punches her other hand at his elbow, breaking the joint and positioning his injured hand toward his own ass.

"Now you can fuck yourself and know what an asshole feels like!" She shoves the injured hand into the man's ass.

He squeals and whimpers. "I'm sorry!"

"It's a little too late for that!" She turns in Sun's direction, who is dying from laughter. "You want to be next, Sun? Get your ass back to the suite."

He knows not to test her when she's that angry, as the other man found out so intensely. The bouncer with the blonde hair runs in, and sees the patron in his position. Crow walks and passes by him. "Like I said, you didn't need to frisk me!"

The bouncer watches her walk away as he sees two

other bouncers standing in the club with shocked faces. They all have no words. The club dancers go back to work while the bouncer pulls his cell phone out trying to figure out what to do. The DJ cues up a new song as Crow walks out the doors in an aggressive and confident way.

Sun scurries after her like a puppy chasing a stick.

CHAPTER 5

hase sits in a wheelchair as a nurse pushes him down the long hallway. Bull sits in a larger wheelchair riding next to him. A door in front of them opens to the right and a tall, slender blonde woman walks out, putting earbuds into her ears. Only her left side is showing, but Chase notices the incredibly sexy profile she has. She turns and starts to walk ahead of them. Her blonde hair has amber highlights that lead to fire-red tips.

The headphones are plugged in to her phone and she starts to listen to Halestorm's "I Am the Fire!" She stops and pauses for a second, realizing there are people behind her. She turns her head looking over her left shoulder to see who is behind her. She catches Chase staring back at her.

"Take a picture, they last longer! If you need a paper towel, the bathroom is to your left."

Bull starts to laugh as Chase realizes how long he was staring at her.

She pipes up again. "You can call me Salene. Are you coming? We have a lot of work to do." She continues straight with an assertive walk. Her music continues as she focuses on what she is about to show off.

She enters the delivery hangar where General Seagar is standing at a table. A large black briefcase sits open on the table with files stating CLASSIFIED showing. Surge and Dr. Peck are with him, waiting. Salene walks toward the table and turns around.

As Chase and Bull get wheeled into position, Chase sees the right side of her face. A portion of the side of her head is shaved and has a metal plate. It connects to what looks like the laser-scope sight you would see on a sniper rifle.

Covering where her eye would be is a red reflective lens, as well as a laser pointer. She takes off the camouflage jacket she is wearing, revealing both arms are metal and were fully amputated to the shoulder joint. A nurse pushing a covered cart enters the hangar and approaches Salene. She removes the cloth from the cart to show rifle parts and clips. Salene starts to assemble the parts for two sniper rifles.

Dr. Peck wheels over to Chase and Bull. "As you can see, Salene has had both arms amputated but was outfitted with a sniper scope that is programmed to both amputated arms. The smaller modified sniper rifles attach to the forearms of the amputations."

Salene grabs one of the rifle modifications and clicks it in place to the out portion of her forearm. The back end lines up with her elbow perfectly. Her arms move fluidly and she looks completely mobile. Chase starts to look down at his right side, seeing his right arm and hand. He still can't feel anything. He thinks about squeezing his hand. All of a sudden his right hand clenches closed. Dr. Peck notices and smiles.

"How did that feel?" Chase isn't sure, but it felt good in his mind. He looks at Dr. Peck in astonishment.

"Try to stand," Peck suggests.

"But how can I do that? I lost my leg, like you said."

Chase is scared, which is unusual for such a strong and able-minded soldier.

"Think about just getting out of a chair like you are home. The technology and the procedure help the limbs and the human tissue to bond as if normal. It reduces the recovery time and keeps the body strong."

Chase puts his hands on the armrest of the wheelchair, and suddenly his body is getting up and out of the chair. He turns and looks at Bull. Chase smiles like it's a miracle. He looks at the hand again and starts to wiggle his fingers.

Dr. Peck motions to two nurses to the side to go to Bull. "Remove the neck stabilizer and any restraints." Peck is smiling with excitement.

Bull hasn't turned his neck or body in a few days. The nurses start to unscrew the frame that surrounds his head and rests on his shoulders. They remove it and Bull feels relief.

"Oh wow. Now that feels good."

Dr. Peck looks at him. "Bull, I had to fuse the two broken vertebrae in your back, but with our back-brace contraption, we have supported your back. It extends and connects to the nerves in your legs. Basically, we have created an exoskeleton, to an extent. It allows the nerves to bypass the fusion location and keep you mobile. We also amputated your forearms."

Bull stands up, and he is amazed at what is happening. He starts to put his right foot forward, realizing he can walk. He examines his forearms and sees slots in the same spots as where Salene attached her rifle modifications. "Does something attach here?" he asks with a kid-in-a-candy-store grin.

Dr. Peck smiles with even more excitement. Like a kid playing with new toys. "I have been waiting for you to ask. Bring his hardware out."

The two nurses grab another cart that was covered from the side of the hangar. Through all of this, General Seagar stands at the table watching, sunglasses on and without even a smile, just all business in his mind. He has a large file sitting on the table in front of him. He whistles to get everyone's attention.

"Before we start with the demonstrations, I have business to discuss. Yes, Bull, you are about to become . . . upgraded. If everyone could gather over here at the table. I need everyone to understand what this is and how they will be a contributing part of this operation. We have a situation developing in this region of the world, and I intend to contain it."

Salene stands near the table adjusting her customized rifles on her forearms. She doesn't know if she fully trusts Seagar, but she has been given a second chance. She has at least developed some gratitude toward this second chance by being alive and still being able to serve. Her laser scope starts adjusting as she calibrates the sensors on the rifle. Whatever the scope sees, the rifle sees, and matches the trajectory.

Chase walks over with a quiet excitement that he can walk. The fact that Seagar was part of that doesn't sit well. He has been used by Seagar before and knows how he manipulates people. He has used his position to influence a lot of people and a lot of political events. Chase can't help thinking, *I have a new leg and arm, but at what cost?*

They all surround the table and Seagar sits with a large file in front of him. "Where is Kitch?" As he states that, the large bay doors to the left side start to lift. Sunlight beams into the hangar as a human form takes shape. As the door rises higher, the full-figure silhouette appears more clearly and stands with a large wing outline.

"What's up, dudes?" a young voice speaks out. "Sorry I'm late, was out practicing. These things are the shit!"

He walks up, and before he takes a seat the large metal-plated wings retract into a pack that is fused to his back. He has both forearms amputated and semiautomatic machine-gun attachments built in. He also has his lower legs below the knee amputated and small thruster engines secured to all four extremities. "Kitchener Williams. My friends call me Kitch!"

Seagar looks at Kitch with an annoyed look. Everyone gets seated as Seagar opens the files to a specific page. "All of you have been selected to be part of a specific and especially experimental program, the Artificial Military Prosthetics Division. We take the best soldiers who have been severely injured and provide the tools and equipment to keep you in service. Why? Because you are considered the best, and we need the best!"

Chase speaks up quickly. "So what makes us so special, and why the urgency in your voice?"

Seagar looks at him seriously. "We have a new enemy developing and we need to be prepared with the most advanced projects. You are one of those projects."

He throws a few files on the table.

"So what are we? Are we the new-age superhero team that the military decided to create?" Bull pipes out loud in a sarcastic and mocking way. "Are we expected to fall in line just because you throw some fancy prosthetics on us?" He gives the general an agitated look.

Seagar isn't amused. "I think once you see what I'm about to show you, that tone will change. The facts are that we have information indicating a terror cell forming in Romania. These individuals are now believed to be in Kraków, Poland. Our first member is currently on recon in Kraków and has confirmed that. Romania's former general Azazil has been known to use the army for war profiteering and smuggling. We have word that a new group is forming and has hired him to recruit. The individual in charge is unknown."

Chase grabs Azazil's file and starts to go through it. "We don't have much personal information on him, but being a general in Romanian government allowed him to recreate himself. A very tall, strong man who sports an X-shaped scar on his face."

"He disappeared shortly after the Romanian government discovered his extracurricular activities," Seagar states. "He's very resourceful and has had help from one arms dealer from Vietnam in the past."

Seagar opens a new file. "Also a part of the terror group is Brug, a German arms dealer who loves a good fight. He supplies terror groups and militias with what is needed and relies on his sister for negotiations. Pure muscle, but he knows his weapons, and can build anything you can come up with. He was discharged from the German army after he disagreed with orders from his commanding officer. To make his point, he hung him from the flagpole by his feet. He then positioned a tank with the cannon pointed at his midsection. He was arrested immediately."

Seagar throws that file on the table and pulls out another. "Crow is Brug's sister and an expert manipulator and negotiator. She's not afraid to use her assets and is also deadly close up, and can snap your neck when you least expect it. She has the tendency to have razor blades added to her nails. Crow is probably one of the most dangerous women in the world."

Chase starts looking at her file while the others look at Brug's and Azazil's. He feels uneasy about all of this, as he is going into a situation he does not know much about with new tech on his right arm and leg. *How were we selected when he rescued us from the situations we were in?* That seems a little odd in his mind. Now they're sitting at a table like one big family planning to protect the world from these misfits on paper? That's another question mark for Chase. Seagar, in his military career, has done questionable things.

Chase examines his new right arm and looks over at Dr. Peck. He and Surge look like genuine people, and you can tell they are close. They have a bond and the program is important to them.

"Chase," Seagar interrupts Chase's thoughts, "are you paying attention? I need focus!" With a new file in front of them, he continues. "Sun is a martial arts expert from Saigon. Some people call him the Saigon Sun, and he loves money and women. He ran several businesses and was approached by Crow to run the weapons they sell. He was hired to be the assassin for Azazil. His parents put him in a school to learn the arts and discipline, but he has a greedy dark side. Crow would be his weakness, and he courts her at times."

Chase stands up and looks at Seagar with a *fuck you* look in his eye. "This whole thing feels very weird to me. You say 'selected,' yet you rescued me from an ambush on my convoy. Sounds like the others were rescued from similar situations. I don't trust you, and you will need to give me a good reason to start. How do I know you didn't set up the ambush? Based on our past, it wouldn't shock me."

Seagar stands up and faces him with a cold and irritated look. "Looking past your insubordination, yes, you are right, you don't know! That's fine, because if you don't take what is in front of you seriously, then this world could change dramatically. Then you will be on your back in a pile of rubble somewhere in the world asking yourself one question: What if I had just listened?"

Seagar turns and signals to uncover the equipment to the side. "Kitch, stand up and show your attachments fully."

Kitch springs up and smiles with excitement, stepping back and throwing his arms out. His wings release from the compartment attached to his back. "It's like hang-gliding right now, but we are working on different types of thrusters to attach to my prosthetics. I was in the Air Force and got shot down during maneuvers. There was an issue with my ejection, and even though the chute deployed, I hit the ground faster than I should have. Broke my back like Bull and had my forearms and feet amputated. They were burnt and mangled pretty bad. Thankfully I still had feeling throughout my body, and have an upper-back brace that houses the wings. I didn't have nerve damage, so I didn't need the full kit Bull has. I can attach guns to my forearms and shins. Once I master the thrusters and compressors, it should be a lot of fun. Like Iron Man, but without a full suit." He keeps smiling.

Salene stands up and has her custom rifles hooked up to her arms. She starts to fiddle with the dial located on her right temple next to her scope. It's an SWFA tactical rifle scope but has been customized and digitally modified to correspond with the rifles on her arms. Off in the distance there are five metal targets located at different ranges. It is a very large hangar and the farthest target is five hundred yards away. She has her rifles loaded and now the scope starts to move on its own, but she is controlling it.

She looks at the table and blows a kiss toward Bull. The smile disappears and she raises her arms straight out. She starts firing, sending off five rounds of alternating shots between her forearms. She throws the right arm out, aims at the table, and fires without looking. A bullet screams through the water glass sitting on the table in front of Bull. Quickly over the next ten seconds, off in the distance, the metal targets fall to the ground with a perfect hole in the center bull's-eye.

Bull looks at her and looks at the broken glass in front of him. He chuckles and looks at Chase. "We need to stay on her good side!" Chase smirks and nods agreeably.

Seagar pipes up, "Well, Bull, I guess we can show you what we have in store for you."

The cart that was moved toward the table is a large one. It's tall, like someone is standing underneath it. The nurses pull the sheet off to reveal what looks like a backpack.

"This attaches to your back brace and leg supports. I wanted to give you the heavy-duty stuff. So your arms lock into the weapons that are secured to your pack. All ammo is in the backpack compartment. If you notice, on the backside, we have attached two forty-one-pound lightweight modified M134D miniguns. You can reduce a terrorist to mush in five seconds."

Bull gets up and walks over to the outfit. His eyes look like Ralphie's from *A Christmas Story*, but he just received a lot more than a kids BB gun. "This is cool as hell."

"Chase, we have some ideas for you, but obviously, we will take your input as to what we can do for you," Seagar states. "The fact is, I need all of you working with our man doing recon as soon as possible. Sabu has been following leads for a while, and I need all of you knowledgeable with your new AMPs so we can get started. We have to get more information on why those four are communicating and who is hiring them. Chase, you are the highest-ranking officer of the group. I'm putting you in charge, and I know you have a connection with Sabu, so I don't think that will be an issue."

Chase is looking around like he just got dropped into a compost heap. "Sir, what if I don't want to?"

"Son, you are still a soldier, and your new gear is the property of the United States Military. You can fall in line and follow orders, or we take your arm and your leg and put you out on your own. I don't think you really have a choice. Sabu will be in contact with you in the next few hours. Hopefully he will have something more for us."

Seagar storms out, without any other words. As he heads toward the door, he pulls out a cigar and lights it up with a large gray puff of smoke.

Chase watches him and doesn't say anything. He turns to Peck and Surge.

"Can you get me a KS23 shotgun and attach it to my thigh? I also want a drone that I can control from my arm. Maybe another smaller gun in my forearm? Once we get that sorted out, we can go to Kraków and meet with Sabu." Chase's face looks somewhat disheartened and frustrated.

Dr. Peck wheels over to Chase and places his hand on Chase's forearm. "There should always be a choice. I saved your life because it's what I do, not for what we get from you. I don't know everything that man does, but I can tell you have a good idea about it. You can trust me and Surge. I promise."

Chase looks at him. "I know I can, and I needed them to know about Seagar." He points at Salene, Bull, and Kitch. "It's kind of unreal to go from a convoy to an ambush, to a medivac, to having cybernetic prosthetics. Now I'm being told to lead a team with these amazing prosthetics and weapons, and I don't get a choice. In a matter of days, my life changed. It's messing with my head a bit, to be honest."

Dr. Peck looks at him. "Walk with me. Let's talk." They start to move out toward the targets Salene shot down. "When I started my research, it didn't fully make sense. I just had a thought and idea. As I developed it, I looked at it as a medical breakthrough to help people. Seagar and the military approached me about disabled veterans. From that point, it grew, and then the AMPD program was presented to me. I thought this could be a great opportunity, and it has been. It has also been at a cost, though. I devoted so much time and energy to it, my wife and son eventually left me."

"I'm sorry to hear that about your family. Seems to me like you don't really have a choice anymore."

"We all have a choice, and it's what we do with it that provides us with the path of what our life can be. When I was paralyzed, I felt what knowledge I had could be used for a greater good. The mistake I made is that I allowed it to take over my life. I wish I knew what happened to my son and wife, but there is no record of them, and they disappeared. I put my family second and it cost me."

"I'm sure you will find them. It'll work out and you'll be able to hold your son and say you are sorry. I hope life won't be so cruel that you don't get that chance. You made a mistake, and it's clear you recognize it."

"Thank you, that means a lot. I know the last forty-eight hours have been a whirlwind, but you have a chance to do something special with this group. Clearly you don't trust Seagar, but maybe some good can come out of this, and maybe you are right and I can find my son and wife, and rebuild. To have that chance would be everything."

Chase nods but doesn't say anything. He moves his right arm around and flexes his new hand. "I'm still amazed at how you did this. How am I able to move an arm and a leg and support myself like this? How is that turnaround possible?"

"Don't think it's easy!" Dr. Peck chuckles. "I have been experimenting and trying all sorts of things. Some experiments I did were with cadavers. I focused on understanding the nervous system and how it works. We developed a human growth hormone that helps you heal and bond your body with the amputations. I had to learn the wattage and how the body relates. After putting Surge's hand in place, we found we could do a lot. The possibilities are greater than we think. A shotgun and a drone is a good start."

Dr. Peck smiles at Chase. "Maybe we can come up with some interchangeable options? Come see me in an hour. Surge and I are experimenting with something." He wheels off in a hurry.

Chase walks back to the table, where Kitch sits with his feet up. Salene stands next to it fiddling with her rifle attachments. Bull is walking around testing out his new attachment and back brace. He starts to move toward Chase and the others.

"I have full movement like I had before the accident." Bull throws his arms behind him, and suddenly two loud clicks are heard. He pulls his arms forward with the rotating Gatling-style machine guns under his forearms. "I gotta test these out!" He turns over toward the shot-down targets.

Over to the side is a large six-foot-by-six-foot target that is used for larger-scale target practice. Bull smiles big and closes his new hands to a fist. The Gatling-style guns start to rotate and a flurry of bullets fly toward the targets. Smoke and bullet shells fill the air as Bull reduces the target to nothing but splinters of wood and paint. The guns stop rotating and Bull's face looks like he orgasmed.

Salene chuckles. "You need toilet paper, big boy?"

He looks over at her. "I just might! Damn, that felt

good. So what do you think, Chase? We just got dumped into a whole new situation that we didn't ask for. Considering what happened to us, there's not much of a choice, right?"

"I don't know, dude. This is kind of fucked up. The fact that I'm alive is because of Seagar, but on the other hand, it feels like he owns us. That doesn't sit well with me. Am I wrong?" Chase looks at the others.

Salene walks toward Chase. "I don't know you and don't know if you have family, a dog, or if you just live by your own rules. I'm following in my father's footsteps. I became a member of the US Military to make a difference and honor his memory. I have a second chance, and I'm going to use it."

Kitch pops up with enthusiasm and a smile. "My parents hated that I became a pilot. They wanted me to go to an Ivy League school, get a 4.0, and make money in business or as a lawyer. That's not me, I love an adrenaline rush. I'm still alive and can make a difference. I can't say much more than that. The way big boy over here just unloaded, I'm guessing he is on board. You missed a spot." He points at his pants.

Bull flips the middle finger at him. "Don't worry, junior, you'll learn what it's like to touch a girl one day!" He turns to Chase. "You have three willing and able bodies ready to follow someone. The question is, are you that person?"

CHAPTER 6

After a long night of phone calls and trying to keep Sun under control, Crow and Brug sit in the suite's living room. Sun is passed out in the main bedroom feeling more of the effects from his partying. It's now 10 a.m. and they expect to hear from Azazil at any time with his first instructions. Crow still wonders about the hooded figure she thought was following them. She also wonders how the money works for this project. She needs to see some money.

"We need to get paid if I'm going to continue this. I'm not getting taken advantage of," Crow says.

Brug responds, "I think Azazil is taking care of that. He knows you are more direct when it comes to the terms of things. We should hear from him soon."

A loud and hard knock sounds from the door. Brug gets up and puts his hand on his sidearm. He checks through the peephole to see the distinctive X-shaped scar on Azazil's face. He opens the door to see four armed men standing behind Azazil.

Azazil enters the suite and starts to look around. He has a black briefcase in his left hand. He says nothing and walks toward Crow, throwing the case onto the table in front of her.

"This should help with any blocks you have. Check it!"

He walks toward the bedroom and throws the door open. A passed-out Sun lies facedown on the bed, his ass pointing up in the air under the covers. A slight groan comes from the pillow. "Unless you're naked and admiring me, Crow, you can go away!"

Azazil clears his throat and pulls his pistol from his holster. He cocks it quickly so the loud snap is heard. Suns eyes open wide, showing bloodshot redness. "I don't remember coming back here! Where am I?"

Azazil clears his throat. "I've had my suspicions that you were not what I needed on this project. So get your ass up and prove me wrong."

Sun struggles to roll over. He climbs out from under the covers and gets to his feet. His hair stands up in a floppy bedhead mohawk. His eyelids flutter as he tries to get his bearings.

"Good morning, Azazil! Sir!" Sun stands in front of him still wearing the same white suit from the night before. He brushes his jacket and pants. He tries to look presentable, but the impression has already been made.

"Be aware that I just slit my driver's throat. I could consider doing the same with you. However, your connections and talents are needed at this time. Don't fuck it up!" Azazil puts his pistol back into his holster, turns, and walks back toward Crow and Brug.

Sun stands with a look of relief on his face. He lets his guard down. Azazil stops suddenly and looks at Crow then back at Sun. "Actually, on second thought, I think Velnias could use you more than I could."

He puts his hand on his knife, the same that slashed Asher. He turns and looks at Sun and grins, pulling the knife and throwing it straight through his heart. Sun's face turns blank as he drops to his knees. Two of the men with Azazil walk over and catch his body before it hits the ground. Azazil grabs the handle of the knife and pulls it out. He wipes the blood off on Sun's white suit, leaving the blood-red X swipes on his left shoulder.

"That is what you call a business decision. Use the assets that you have in the right way. Wrap him up and take him to the truck. All of us are heading to the castle. That includes the two of you," he says, pointing at Brug and Crow. "That money should cover the deal. I included Sun's amount, but he doesn't need it anymore."

Crow and Brug look stunned, both unsure what to think. Crow opens the briefcase to see what looks to be six million in American dollars.

Brug looks over at it and nods his head in approval. "So where are we going? I have my contacts working on a location in Kiev. They should have a hundred dead soldiers ready to ship within the hour."

Azazil looks pleased. "Have them go to Cluj-Napoca in Romania, and from there more instructions will come. Feel free to head down to the trucks. We leave in ten minutes."

| | | | |

Sabu stands on the roof with a wire attached outside of the window. He has recorded the whole sequence and now knows that they are headed to Romania.

While he is listening, four large men in black suits emerge on the roof and notice he is up there. He senses they are approaching him and stands with his back to them. Loosening his jacket and hood, he throws it off to the side with his arms up in the air, revealing prosthetic arms. Long dark hair runs down to his shoulders. He turns to face them, sporting a black face mask that resembles the old-school goalie masks. The lower section connects to his throat like a respirator.

Suddenly he speaks with a voicebox sound. "Is there a problem, gentlemen?" The men start to walk toward him. "I guess so!"

He takes a defensive stance with his arms up and his right leg back, then throws his right arm out in a quick punch. One man drops to the ground despite the fact that they haven't even reached him. The other three look down to see a ninja star stuck between his eyes. They look back up and the figure speaks out. "You sure you want this?"

The three men spread out and surround him. The figure steps forward to challenge the one in front of him. The goon to his right approaches and the figure throws out a side kick. His foot extends from his leg, kicking the man's chest like a battering ram. He can hear the sternum crack, his leg hit so hard. The man drops to the ground in a crumpled mass.

The other two converge on him and all three start fighting in a flurry of kicks and punches. The figure is fast and is getting the best of the other two. He grabs hold of an arm of each of them. Suddenly, with a piston-like burst, his body jumps into the air as he backflips and his extended feet connect to each thug's jaw. The hit is so powerful it dislocates the shoulders of the arms he holds. He lands on his feet and the compressors in his lower legs move back into place. One of the radios from the thugs goes off.

"Perimeter! Report! Is the roof clear?"

The figure looks up and checks his escape options. He grabs the recorder from the bug he set. He checks the distance to the building across the street and gives himself a running start before taking a giant leap. With a burst from his legs, he is propelled farther.

| | | | |

Azazil, Crow, and Brug stand down on the street with six men in black suits as well.

Brug notices the figure in the air. "What the fuck?"

Crow shouts, "That's the guy who followed us yesterday."

Azazil points to three of his goons. "Track him! Don't let him get away." The three thugs run into the building the figure jumped onto. Azazil pulls a radio to his mouth. "Get the jet ready at the airstrip. I need a drone in the air right now tracking someone on the roofs near the square."

| | | | |

The figure lands, catching himself on the gray slanted roof. He pulls himself up to the top of the building. He hears voices down below and realizes he was seen. He needs to get out of the area fast. He starts running across the rooftops, along a stretch of colorful buildings. The roof heights vary and are slanted. He works his way quickly across the roofs, realizing he needs to get down to the street.

He stops a second and turns to see three men following him. Then, he takes his right wrist and twists his forearm by 25 percent, noticing a pink building to his right. It's too far to jump, so he points his right arm at a chimney stack on the roof and fires a grappling hook–like arrow attached to a metal cord. The arrow penetrates the chimney and the slack retracts into his arm. He leaps off the side of the building and swings to the other. The pistons in his legs propel him as he swings to the side of the building.

The three men pull guns from holsters and start shooting. Screams are heard as people in the square start to scatter.

The figure squeezes his hand and the cord detaches from the arrow. He falls to the street but again is cushioned with the pistons in his legs. He sees a dirt bike and quickly grabs it. The guy standing next to it yells in Polish, "*Co do cholery?*" *What the hell?* He tries to get a hold of the man but can't. The bike speeds away down the street. The three thugs regroup and radio to follow with the drone.

On the bike, the figure speeds down the street and starts to work his way out of the city. He needs to get to the rendezvous point that he and Seagar agreed on, an abandoned military airstrip about thirty minutes south of the city. That's where he's headed, but he wonders if that's where Azazil and his men are following. He stops the bike and looks around. He sees a white balloon floating in the sky. He ignores it, not realizing it's the drone following him. He pulls his cell phone out and sends a text.

Headed to rendezvous point. Found Azazil and have been spotted. They are possibly in pursuit.

He revs up the bike and continues on.

| | | | |

Back at the square the three men report to Azazil and what the hooded man was able to do. Crow is on the Bonerowski Palace roof looking at the four victims of the man. "Azazil, this man is a pro and has some special gifts, from what I am seeing," she says over the radio.

Azazil responds, "Collect the bodies and bring them. Nothing is left behind."

The bodies get wrapped up and brought down to the entrance. A black van sits and they load the bodies quickly. The van speeds off quickly as a woman in a blue dress walks toward the entrance. She has a large white hat and sunglasses. She stops and picks up an envelope from the sidewalk. She looks inside to see a key and enters Bonerowski Palace. She makes her way to the second floor and disappears to a separate suite.

| | | | |

In the lead van Azazil sits with Crow in the backseat. He keeps his head pointed straight while he speaks to her. "We will be in Romania at our destination in about six to seven hours."

"Was it necessary to kill Sun?" Crow asks in a frustrated tone.

Azazil looks at her. "I thought you found him obnoxious and trite."

"I did, but I also know he was an asset from a connections and martial arts standpoint. I don't plan to be seen as expendable." She looks at him with a blunt face.

"Trust me, my dear. Very soon you will see how valuable we all can be. No matter if we are dead or alive, we are all assets."

Crow looks back at him curiously. "There is a lot of secrecy with this, even with those involved. I don't like being kept in the dark. I want more information, or you can have your money back."

"Maybe I should just kill you now, then? If you don't trust me. Why try to convince you?"

"You killed an ally in front of me, and I have shown no problems to this point. A project that seems this big needs trust. Give a taste of what we are doing."

"My dear, we are changing the way armies are built. We are developing a technology that will make even a dead soldier valuable. You will see for yourself at the castle."

"Stop calling me *dear*, I don't like it. As for this science project that seems to be world-changing, it sounds interesting." She pulls her compact out and starts fiddling with her makeup as if she is indifferent to what he told her.

"Tell me, Crow, what impresses you? Are you impressed by someone strong and firm? Does something powerful impress you?" He looks at her, intrigued, but she seems more annoyed now.

"Now you really remind me of Sun when you talk like that. I thought you were better than that, General. A man and his mini pencil do not impress me. Frankenstein-like dead body experiments do not impress me. Sounds kind of sick to me, but, when I know what I get out of it and can profit, that is what grabs me. Give me opportunity, success, even some power, then I will be impressed. Up until now, you have intrigued me but not impressed me. Don't ruin it."

Azazil smiles for a second, and turns back forward, pulling his cell phone out. He types a quick text and sends it.

Make sure the plane is ready, we are 5 minutes away!

| | | | |

As Azazil and his crew head to the private jet waiting for them, the hooded man heads to the abandoned airstrip to wait for Seagar's extraction. He pulls the bike up to a broken-down utility shed and ditches the bike in some bushes. He notices the white balloon in the air from earlier. He realizes he has been followed and breaks his way into the shed. He pulls out his cell and messages:

I was followed. Need assistance as soon as possible.

A reply comes through.

Extraction team is headed your way. Find cover. ETA forty minutes.

Knowing he may not have forty minutes, he starts grabbing tools off the wall. They are old and rusted, but he can use them. From his black duffle bag, he pulls out two Uzi machine guns and five clips.

He doesn't know how many could have followed him. Azazil has access to the Romanian army, so any number could be possible. He hears trucks pulling in. He needs to get out of the shed without the drone seeing. Throwing the tools and Uzis into the duffle bag, the hooded man pulls up a section of the floor to see if there is space under the shed. He decides he can fit and slides under the shed, quickly crawling commando style through the heavy grass. He stops and stays low to see what they do.

Five black trucks arrive and move close to the shed. Five men get out of each truck, one dispersing the others. He sends three men over to the shed where Sabu is hiding.

Only ten minutes have gone by when Sabu decides he has to do something to stall until the extraction team arrives. Behind the shed are two large drums with chemical symbols on the side. He starts to adjust his left forearm and rotates it one hundred sixty degrees. Pointing his arm at the drums, a device shoots out from an opening at Sabu's wrist, sticking to the drum.

As the three men open the door to the shed, the drums suddenly explode, sending the three men flying and disintegrating the shed to small pieces. The other men still outside get on the ground to protect themselves.

This allows Sabu to get to the wooded area on the other side of the runway.

The man in charge signals to grab the bodies and get back to the trucks. He looks around the area and doesn't see anyone. Sabu is hidden well. The trucks disperse and Sabu is left waiting for his rendezvous.

CHAPTER 7

Velnias makes his way down the long, dim, lantern-lined corridor toward a large wooden door. The air is thick with age and dust, with a slight dampness. As he reaches the door, the burn-scarred hand reaches out and pushes it open.

He enters a huge, brightly lit room that resembles an operating room. On the far side is a huge glass wall with darkness behind it. In the center of the room is an operating table, a body covered by a sheet lying on it. Two male individuals stand in the corner, still with no movements. They both have medical scrubs on. At the center of each of their foreheads, a metal device runs over their heads to the back where the spine connects to the brainstem. From there it wraps around both sides and enters their skulls right behind the ears. There is also a metal collar that lies on their shoulders and wraps around their necks. At the brainstem a small USB clip is inserted into the device.

Velnias speaks out. "Awake and assist me with the procedure!"

The two individuals step forward and stand next to the operating table. They await instructions from Velnias.

"Doctor Kalinko, grab the new head device. Doctor Nash, take the cover off of the body."

They both follow the instructions without words. They move normally, without hesitation. When the sheet is removed, Asher's body lies on the table, his slashed throat covered by thick towels but soaked red.

"Remove the towels, Doctor Nash." He pulls the towels away to show Asher's neck has been stitched back together.

"Begin attaching the device to our subject." Velnias walks over to Asher's head and stands at the end of the table. With his hands, he lifts the head as Nash and Kalinko stand on each side attaching the device.

Kalinko takes a power drill and starts to tighten a pin into the front of Asher's forehead. It is the same device and same pin on Nash and Kalinko. The two work with quickness and precision as they would in the operating room. They don't speak, and work as if they were programmed to do so. They drill openings behind the ears and plug in the side prongs of the apparatus. They flip the body over and start to work on the port for the USB clip.

Velnias approaches with a clip in hand and inserts into the device. It clicks and makes a connection to the skull and brainstem. A generator and a computer are wheeled over. The device is hooked up to the computer and programs start to download. The generator is turned on with a slight hum. The body twitches and the computer registers a brainwave. A dial on the generator is turned up and a stronger charge pulses into the body. The hum is louder and the body has a little more vibration to it. The dial is turned up to max and the body drastically twitches, the flat-line brainwave starting to show raised and lowered lines.

There is activity, and Velnias gives a slight chuckle. They turn the body back over and Asher's eyes are open. Velnias stands at the computer and starts to open up programs and boxes with lists of information. The computer continues to download data into the device and the USB clip.

He turns to Asher. "Stand up!"

Asher's body gets off of the table and stands.

"Walk five steps!"

Asher takes five steps and stops.

"Join the others in the storage bay!"

Asher walks to the door, opens it, and exits to the left, disappearing. Velnias turns on a switch next to the big glass window, illuminating what is behind it.

Hundreds of soldiers stand in a large room in precise rows with an opening in the front. Asher enters the room and takes his place in the opening. The two doctors stand in the room with Velnias.

"Back to your post!"

The two walk back to the corner they originally stood in. Velnias exits the room and disappears back down the hall.

| | | | |

Azazil, Crow, and Brug arrive and enter the front gate. Five black SUVs enter the complex and pull up to the castle. Azazil orders his men to spread out and secure the entire perimeter. He keeps five to help carry the dead bodies inside, including Sun's body, which is very important to Azazil and his hooded counterpart.

Crow and Brug walk up to the front door with very curious eyes. The door opens as they approach and the hooded figure stands in the entranceway. "Please enter quickly!"

They all gather in the large front foyer.

"Please follow me," the hooded figure says. "The bodies need to be tended to as soon as possible."

Azazil speaks up. "We have Sun's body with us."

The hooded figure stops and turns. "This I did not request. Why?"

Azazil answers nervously. "His actions in Kraków were unacceptable and he showed his liabilities."

Crow and Brug had never seen Azazil act nervous like that. It is new, but also shows that he is human to an extent. He is capable of emotions and weakness. This is the type of information Crow feeds off, and can use in the future.

The hooded figure turns and continues to walk down a dark corridor. "It is what it is, but we can enhance his true skills, and not worry about the liability of his attitude and personality. This is why I am doing this. Why I am developing an army technology that eliminates the attitude, and allows countries to continue use of a soldier after death. To program a military vessel to openly become a human suicide bomb and not have the conscience get in the way. I am building the future of this world."

They reach a metal elevator door after a long walk down the dark corridor. The burnt hand touches the button and doors open to a bright metal interior. It is a large enough service elevator to fit all of them. It starts to move down and feels like a long drop deep under the castle. The doors open to a long hallway. Torches line the walls as another dim hall stands in front of them.

The hooded figure moves forward and they come to the doors that lead to his operating room. "Place the bodies in my work room. Come and see my work, Azazil!" He turns right and they enter a large dark room.

The motion automatically lights up the warehouse-like room. Hundreds of soldiers stand still in front of them without reaction to the light. Asher stands up front in the center, and does not react to Azazil standing in the room.

"Asher, step forward," Azazil calls out with hope of a reaction.

Asher steps forward, with no reaction toward Azazil. He stands still as if awaiting instructions.

Crow and Brug examine the device on Asher's head and the technology created. She moves her hand up and down in front of Asher's face. Asher turns his head and looks at her with a blank stare as if he is processing why she did that. There is no emotion, and it is as if his soul has been ripped away from him.

The hooded figure steps forward. "He is completely obedient to our requests, and the clip on the back of the head is programmed with skills and knowledge to be able to react to combat situations. Operation manuals for weapons and machinery are also programmed. In a matter of minutes, a soldier can be born." The hooded figure removes his hood to show a man in his midthirties, with short dark hair. On the left side of his head there are burn scars instead of hair. His face has burns as well, running down his neck. He can speak and breath but has moments of struggle.

"Brug and Crow, this is our employer, Velnias."

"The Lithuanian word for devil," Velnias says. "My mother was Lithuanian, and my father is English. My mother died in the accident that scarred me. It was a fire in our high-rise building in Dubai. I got my scars trying to save her. I made a vow that I would find a way to bring her back. Through some of the work in my past, I started experimenting, and finding subjects to test ideas. I had willing participants, and some not as willing. I have found a way to raise the dead, and now I shall use it and build my army, build a new world that the Plague will control."

Crow looks at him in amazement. "Where is your mother? Did it work on her?"

Velnias smiles mildly and turns away to go to his operating room. "She is exactly in the right place. In Kraków! Come, we need to look at Sun, and decide how to program him. With his skills, I am thinking an exhibition and maybe assassination of some sort."

Crow steps forward and follows him. "I may have the perfect option for that." She turns and looks at Brug with a smile. "Brother?"

He looks at her curiously and then realizes what she is talking about. "That would be a bold move, sis."

Azazil chimes in, wanting to know. "Can you two explain what you are talking about?"

Crow has always had a talent for creating chaos. "I believe we should use Sun to kill a key leader of a terror group or country and make it public. Show the world how you have developed a major development in war."

"Who do you have in mind? It has to be a major figure or group," Azazil says, flicking his lighter as he thinks.

Crow responds quickly as if she has always known the answer. "Moscow! We make a statement to the world by action. An assassination to gain influence on major military countries. These surrounding countries are making decisions on policy. Is our goal to dominate or to sell? How do we maneuver the International Military Security Council? An action like this will create questions in the world, create chaos in certain political groups. Suddenly you will have control without even leading a country."

"If we assassinate the Russian leaders," Azazil counters, "we could gain control of one of the largest military surpluses in the world. It would also allow us to develop the connections of those around Russia. Brug, we need to put together a meeting with the leaders in Ukraine, Poland, Belarus, and Kazakhstan. Use our connections in those countries and tell them we have something new for them to see. When this plays out, we could have World War Three."

Azazil starts to pull down on his goatee with his fingers. He has a smile as he thinks more deeply on this. The others follow him as they go with Velnias to the operating room.

CHAPTER 8

Chase sits in a bedroom looking down at his new arm and hand, moving the fingers and squeezing the hand into a fist. He is amazed but still scared and confused. How does a large, physical soldier become as scared and confused as he is? Why did he lose his arm and leg like he did? He doesn't trust Seagar, but he has gratitude for Dr. Peck and Surge.

The bedroom he sits in is a stale military quarters that he will now call home, at least for the near future. *Is it home?* He gets up and looks into a small square mirror that is attached to the wall. He turns sideways and looks at his profile. A large metal shoulder is where his prized sleeve used to start. "My Vegas tattoo that took months to complete is now gone. That fucking sucks!"

There is a knock at the door and Chase reaches to open it. His hand touches the doorknob but he can't feel it. He pauses and has a second of frustration. Then, he grasps the knob and opens it. Salene stands in the hall, a little more cheerful than she was at the meeting.

"Hey, I just wanted to check and see how you are doing. It's a process. I was really frustrated when I realized what had happened to me." She pauses and looks at him with a smirk. "Not feeling doorknobs. Fucking sucks! Now that I understand what I can do, it's really cool. It's nice to know how you can make a difference in the world."

Chase smiles and nods his head. "I can understand that. It's why I joined the army, and why I was on that convoy leading them. But at what point do they turn to us and say, 'You can't go home, you are ours now'? My parents have no idea what happened to me. When do they get to find out? When do I get to talk to them? Share the news that I may be an amputee, but they gave me this really cool weaponized amputation! When can I share that? Have you?"

Salene shakes her head. "My mom never wanted me to follow my dad and do what I do. She was afraid of this happening. She accepted it and loves me, but doesn't understand me. We haven't spoken since I was deployed. She focuses on my little sister she had with my stepdad. I will let her know, but not now."

"I'm not against this project and fighting whatever we need to fight, but I believe that we need to be able to have choices. That's my concern with this. It just feels like it was made for us."

Salene nods her head. "Okay, let's make a deal. I have been here a month and it's been a positive development for me. Give me and the program a month, and if you think you want out, I will support you." She puts her hand out.

"I can do that." He puts his hand out and they shake on it. "Okay, I can't feel anything and I'm guessing you can't. From now on, can we just fist-bump?"

She laughs. "I'm totally good with that. Some things are a bit weird with these."

They walk out to the hall and Dr. Peck greets them. "You were supposed to come and see me and Surge."

"I'm sorry, Doc. I was talking with Salene. She was helping me. I can come with you right now."

"It's all right, it's not the first time I had to wait because a girl got in the way. I know how things work." The doctor turns his wheelchair and starts down the hall. Chase looks puzzled and turns to Salene. "Is he implying?"

She stops him from finishing. "Yes he is . . . and no you don't! Let's go check out what he has for you."

Chase smirks. "Gee, first you ask me to stay a month, and now you toy with my emotions. Reminds me of a movie a girl made me watch."

Salene turns and looks at him. "You wouldn't last my interview process."

They walk down the hall and enter into a huge metal shop. Surge and a few technicians are talking on the far end in front of a table full of parts. The doctor sits in his wheelchair to the right, next to another table full of weapons and gadgets. He smiles and waves Chase over.

"This is your chance!"

"This is my chance for what?" Chase asks, walking over.

"To put who you are into the amputations. Make them your own! Show all of us who you still are." Dr. Peck points toward the tables at all of the weapons, and Chase looks at them and his arm and leg.

"Do you still have my arm and my leg? I want to see them."

Dr. Peck is puzzled "Yes, but why?"

"I want my tattoos back!" He starts looking at his arm. "This isn't me without my tattoos. Without those, I'm not myself."

The doctor looks at him in amazement. He didn't expect that response, and had not even considered something like that. He doesn't have tattoos, so he doesn't know the connection a person can have with one.

"What does it mean? The tattoo you are speaking of? I have to figure out a way, but that doesn't mean we can't do it. I will see if we have any imaging techs."

"It was done by an amazing Japanese tattoo artist. He did a Japanese sleeve depicting a koi fish turning into a dragon. It represents the transformation and sacrifice that it takes to change."

"There is a lot more to you than I expected. It will take some time, but we will think of something. For now, let's look at your weapons options."

Chase nods in agreement and starts looking at the table, which displays small versions of rocket launchers, rifles, and shotguns, and even a mini flamethrower. As he looks through all of the great gadgets, he goes back to the flamethrower. He starts thinking about the tattoo he had and the storyline of a koi turning to dragon. He looks at Dr. Peck and smiles. "I want to throw fire. Fireballs, a stream of fire, or even fire connected to my punching fist. Can we do that?"

Surge starts to chuckle and smile. "Now that sounds cool. The main thing we need to figure out is the fuel, but we can do it."

Chase looks at the doctor and in a split second makes a decision that to some may seem extreme, but he feels makes sense. "If I'm doing this, I have to be all in. I have to be complete. Do the other side!"

The room suddenly stops and there is a pause of silence. The Doc and Surge both look at Chase with amazement that he just said that.

Surge looks at him in shock. "You realize you are asking me to take off a perfectly good arm and leg to be fully amputated? We did what we did to save your life."

"It's changed my life forever. To have one side metal and the other side not, it doesn't make sense. There is a

Japanese proverb that says, '*Doku kuwaba sara made,*' which means, '*When poisoned, one might as well swallow the plate.*'"

The doctor smiles, because he knows what he is talking about. "Go big or go home?"

"You got it, Doc! I don't feel right the way I am; it feels like I'm two different people. And yes, I know it sounds crazy, but maybe that's what the group needs. I need to lead and I need to show that I'm committed."

The doctor just smiles with some amazement and disbelief. In reality, no one would do this, but this man would? He turns to the nurses. "Get the operating room ready." Dr. Peck turns to Surge, and nods his head to go. Surge exits the room quickly and the Doc exits a different way.

Chase stands there holding the flamethrower. No smile, no expression, just a calm that he is about to make a sacrifice and change himself completely.

As the doctor quickly steers his wheelchair down the hall, he turns the corner to see the general standing in front of him. His arms are crossed and he looks as if he knew the doctor was coming his way. Seagar doesn't look happy, but that's usual for him. He chews on the unlit cigar in his mouth. "Am I hearing correctly? Chase wants the other side amputated? When did this come up and who approved it?"

Dr. Peck looks and smiles. "He just asked me to do it. It's such an amazing decision for someone to want go to that level for the program and his development."

"I don't know why you are happy! I don't approve it. I get the final say on these things. I write the checks. Tell him to get his current AMPs weaponized and we will be getting a debrief from Sabu shortly. Nothing is to be done further on Chase unless I say so! You can tell him that."

Seagar walks away and disappears around the corner.

The doctor sits for a moment, taking in what he was

just told. Why would the general not want him to do the surgery? He has a willing participant who wants to be more complete.

A nurse approaches with a clipboard.

"There is no need for that," Dr. Peck says. "The general has shut it down, so hold off on the prep. Get Surge for me. Thank you."

The doctor continues down the hall and disappears around the corner.

CHAPTER 9

In the large dark room, Sun and Asher stand still with all of the other altered corpses Velnias has worked on. The room is dark and cold with a silence that would put a fearful thought in anyone. There are no thoughts or actions or feelings to be known or felt among the bodies. They all stand facing the glass wall that displays the surgical room where they were altered. All of the blank faces gaze at Velnias and the group as he shows them how his work gives these dead bodies an afterlife, a cause or reason to still be.

Asher stands still with his stitched-up throat, and Sun with a heart that was pierced by Azazil's knife.

They don't blink, breath, or speak, but with the charge to the brain and nervous system, they can respond to any commands programmed. Specific words can trigger the charge. As the group watches Velnias demonstrate the process, he walks over and flips a switch to a microphone that transmits to speakers in the other room. The echo of the speaker runs through the large room.

"With specific words, I can activate and shut down the Surgical Cybernetic Zombies. We can use any name or code word. With our two men here, I embedded their names because I deem them as more valuable than the others. Asher! Sun! Come to the window."

The two respond and walk forward to the window. They stop with full awareness of the window in front of them. They stare straight with no acknowledgment of what is on the other side of the window. With blank faces, they wait for instructions.

Velnias shows no pleasure in what he has created and has the same blank face as the pair hidden behind his hood.

Crow walks closer and starts to observe them more.

Velnias interjects, "Crow, please step back. I have more to show you. As you can see, through radio or loudspeaker, they can respond and take orders."

As she starts to turn away, Sun looks at her briefly. His eyes turn in her direction and gaze at her for a split second, only to return straight. It surprises and startles her. Brug notices that she reacted to him.

"Sis, what's wrong?"

"Sun looked at me!" She steps back a few steps and turns to Velnias with surprise. Her demeanor changes, not knowing what to think. "Is that possible with what you have imbedded?"

Velnias walks over, seemingly unpleased and unamused. "No! They are obedient and listen and act. There are no feelings left, no self-thought or decisions. It's like a robot but with a human body. With the right code or command, they simply do and complete it. I'm sure you are seeing things. He did not look at you."

Azazil steps forward toward Crow. "I have you and Brug taking Sun and Asher and a squad of SCZ troops to Moscow. There you will wait for orders and carry them out. I have a contact that will provide you support and details."

"How are we supposed to transport a squad of these over the borders to our destination? And not be detected?" Crow seems skeptical.

"You have clear path from here to the Russian border. You will meet the contact at the border at Haradzec."

Brug looks over to Azazil. "Who is our contact?"

"Alexis Grim. He will provide you with all of the support you need. He also has transport to a warehouse outside of Moscow for you to operate out of. As we discussed, we should target high-ranking officials and take control of the Kremlin in Moscow. The squads are to provide cover and chaotic diversions. We also have a second target outside of Moscow. I will give you more details on that before you leave."

Crow turns and starts to walk to the door. "We need to get prepped, Brug. Come on!"

She walks out quickly with Brug following her, and they head toward the elevator that brought them down.

Azazil stands in the operating room with Velnias staring out the window into the eyes of Sun. He turns and the dark hood faces Azazil.

"I'm not sure I trust her," Velnias states. "Do you still trust her?"

"That is why I have Alexis. He is one of my most trusted colonels. Just let the man with the money know that everything is going as planned." Azazil turns and walks toward the door.

Velnias raises his burnt hand. "You make sure that if either of them dies, preserve them and bring them back to me."

As he says that, Sun's eyes turn and look at Velnias. As he blinks, he returns to the state he was in.

Azazil stops and answers, "Understood." He continues out the door and goes the opposite direction away from the elevator.

Crow and Brug stand on the elevator as it heads to the main floor. "Do you have a good feeling about this, brother?"

"The pay is good and I know this Alexis guy. He is a paid assassin and was colonel to Azazil in the Romanian army. He does trafficking between Russia and Belarus right now. He is very deadly and the right person to get into Russia with no problems or detection. I know you have a good sense for good and bad deals, but I feel good about this." The elevator stops and they leave walking down the hall.

"I didn't get us this far in the arms game to get double-crossed by a corrupt military soldier and some wrinkled-up druid with a science project. We need to be on the ball with everything. Why don't we have our target yet? Why a small squad? I *know* I saw Sun's eyes move. We need to watch our backs. Be ready and moving in two hours."

"I got it, sis! You have been on guard a lot lately. I will be down looking for the arms room. Figure out what these things can use." Brug goes back on the elevator and heads back down to the operating area.

| | | | |

Azazil stands at a computer in a small room. The screen boots up and a man with dark hair in a fauxhawk style appears. He has tattoos on his neck and shoulders. The word *Grim* is etched in Gothic script on the front of his neck. Azazil knows that the word *Reaper* is on the back of his neck. As a colonel to Azazil in the Romanian army, Alexis built a long trust and relationship over a ten-year span. Now working as a rogue mercenary, he is called upon by Azazil when needed. He is known for his large pair of Bowie knives he named Black and Sabbath. Over time he gained the nickname "The Grim Reaper" for his work as a contract killer.

"Reaper! They will be leaving and headed your way in two hours. They will meet you on the Belarus side of the border in eighteen hours. From that point we need you to get them over the Russian border. After that, we carry out the plan as discussed."

Alexis replies, "I am all set and prepared to do what is needed. If there is any trouble, I have backup prepared. We also have the troops you requested and twenty doctors."

"Brug will have further instructions for you about the troops and doctors. They need to be stationed with you at the border. All are to be transferred to an air base near Moscow when we have the first tasks completed."

As he is completing his instructions, Velnias walks into the small room. "Azazil! We have a problem!"

Azazil turns from the screen. "What is it?"

"We have three objectives to fulfill in Russia, and then I can start the full-scale production of the Plague Army. I feel like Crow could be an issue. She is a survivor, a fighter, but can she create anarchy? Her brother can, and I can see it in his eyes. We need to watch her closely."

Azazil pauses and responds, "What happens to her brother if we have to eliminate her?"

Alexis chimes in from the screen. "You leave that to me! If we have multiple targets, then we need to divide them. Send her to Moscow and the Kremlin, and send Brug to the air base. It gives you the opportunity and ability to cover yourself."

Velnias slowly responds, "Azazil, he is right. Pair her with Sun and send Asher with Brug. Alexis, I want you with Crow and Sun the whole way. We will be in touch with you before the rendezvous. I want to be on the air base within the next forty-eight hours." He moves toward the door, and before exiting, pauses then continues. "The Plague is something I have wanted to build ever since my accident. Nothing and no one is going to stop this. Kill anyone who gets in the way." He exits and disappears.

Azazil turns back to the screen. "Stay in straight communication with me while in Moscow. As soon as the job is done, I will be there to take control. Have the doctors and the soldiers delivered to the air base. Is your Spanish counterpart available?"

"Yes! Bautista is still with me. Since his brother died, Bautista has been focused on work and finding the asshole who shot him. What do you need from him?"

"Bautista is not to be with the rendezvous. Have him follow and watch Brug and Asher at the air base. Only watch and do not intervene. I know that Brug can handle the job, but if I have you in Moscow, I want someone at the base as well."

"I understand. How will I know if I need to take action against Crow?" Alexis asks.

"I will let you know. Just provide progress reports. I will be in touch." He shuts down the communication and leaves the room. He can see Brug wandering down the hall toward him. "Are you looking for something?"

Brug nods. "I would love to see the arms room. Is there an armory in this place?"

Azazil nods, stops, and checks the lock to the door. He gestures to come with him. "Follow me! It is part of the wine cellar."

He leads Brug down the hall farther, and turns a corner to a short hall with a big wood door that looks hundreds of years old. A digital pad is on the wall to the right. Azazil punches in eight numbers and a loud unlocking noise sounds. Azazil lifts the handle and the door swings open and inward.

A large dusty room of wine bottles and barrels sits in front of them. Azazil walks to a barrel to his right that has ten bottles sitting on top of it. He lifts the center bottle and then pulls down on the third bottle on the left. Glass starts to rattle and chatter as the large wall of wine in front of them splits down the middle and opens up to a huge room filled with weapons. Brug has a big smile on his face.

Azazil looks at him. "Take what you need and anything special you want the squad to have. Make sure it's programmed. I'm pairing you with Asher and Crow with Sun. We have two targets. So we will divide and conquer, the start of a new world."

"Cool! I will have us up and moving in the next ninety minutes. Make sure these things are ready and can take orders. For the record, Crow and I don't usually work separate like this, but it makes sense with two targets."

"We will be ready to go. You have my word." Azazil turns and walks away.

CHAPTER 10

C hase enters a meeting room to see Kitch, Salene, and Bull sitting at a table together. Dr. Peck comes to the door. "General Seagar will be with us in a moment. Sabu is back and has a lot of info for us."

Chase takes a seat with the others. The general enters the room and all four rise to their feet and salute.

"Be seated!" Seagar says.

Behind him Sabu walks in and looks up to see Chase. In his electronic voice he speaks out. "Chase? I didn't believe it when he told me."

Chase stands up and walks toward him. "I thought you were dead."

Sabu shakes his head. "No, just recreated, I guess. It's good to see you. The circumstances suck, but it is good to know you are part of it."

General Seagar chimes in. "We can get reacquainted later. We have a severe situation developing. Sabu was able to get close to the entire group in Kraków."

Chase and Sabu sit and Seagar continues. "All four players, Azazil, Crow, Brug, and Sun, were all at the Bonerowski Palace in Kraków, Poland. Sabu can also confirm that Azazil killed Sun with a knife to the heart. The body was taken with them to Cluj-Napoca, Romania. I have sent a contact to the area where they are receiving them and many other bodies of soldiers. We also know that the one hundred Ukrainian soldiers were procured by an individual named Alexis Grim, a.k.a. the Grim Reaper. My contacts in the Ukraine confirmed he is headed for the Belarusian border of Russia."

Sabu raises his hand to interject. "When I was listening, the original order was for the one hundred to go to Romania. That moment is when I was spotted on the roof. They may have changed the plan."

Chase raises his hand to jump in. "Why would a guy like Azazil kill one of his assets just like that? That makes no sense to me. Unless they have some experiment happening as well."

Sabu turns to Chase. "Before Azazil killed Sun, he said Velnias would know what to do with you!"

Dr. Peck pulls his wheelchair forward. "Did you say Velnias?"

Sabu nods. "Yes! That was clear, and I had heard the name before."

The doctor shakes his head. "My deceased wife was Lithuanian. I know the language well. It is the word for 'devil.' Clearly someone with Lithuanian ties is the one leading this movement or creating something."

Salene jumps into the conversation. "We need to figure out Lithuanian scientists with ties to biological research. Doctor, could the research and work you do be used in the same way with cadavers?"

The doctor becomes stressed. "Theoretically, yes! I never had success with regeneration of the nerve system. To bring a body back to life was never worked on. The cadavers I worked on were to understand the connection of a nerve to an electrode."

Chase jumps in with a thought. "If one did the research, could it be possible to develop a way to make a nervous system active?"

Seagar stands and takes the cigar from his teeth. "With science, all sorts of things are possible. It all depends on the mindset of the individual creating the research. This Velnias person is working out of Romania. That area of Cluj-Napoca is part of Transylvania, a place with a dark history and a dark culture."

Chase stands up and starts to walk around. "Okay, so we have dead soldiers, a Lithuanian scientist working in Romania with arms dealers, and a tech-savvy German psycho and his sister. If Alexis is going to the Belarus border of Russia, we need to go to that point."

Seagar doesn't agree. "Romania is the right move. Go and find the location they work from. That is an order. I want all of you ready in one hour. You will fly to Cluj-Napoca and investigate."

Chase agrees hesitantly. "Okay, but we need Surge to go with us. As we get information, I think we might need him on site. Because he knows Doctor Peck's work. If this is tied to it, he may be able to decipher it."

Salene stands up from the table. "I agree. Plus, he can help with any glitches we may have. All of our prosthetics haven't been field-tested. We need him."

Chase looks at Seagar. "I also need to see the file on Alexis Grim. We didn't have that before. We need to know what he is capable of."

General Seagar nods his head and starts to leave the room. They all stand and salute as he exits.

The doctor rolls his wheelchair over to Chase and grabs his wrist. "I'm worried someone from our operation has branched out and taken it to the level of using dead soldiers. I will look into any files of men and women who have worked on my research. See if I can minimize the list."

"Don't share it with the general. I want to minimize some things myself. Thank you, Doc. I know I can trust you."

"Good luck! Oh, and go see Surge. He has the fully weaponized arm and leg ready for you." The doctor has smile on his face. "I think you will like what he has for you."

"Okay." Chase walks out of the room and heads down the hall. He sees Surge standing in the hall waiting for him with a big smile on his face.

"You never mentioned the tattoo on the back of your calf."

"My Mr. Hyde tattoo? Yeah, it goes with my Dr. Jekyll on the other calf."

Surge looks at him. "Well, I made sure it was taken care of."

"What do you mean?" Chase looks puzzled.

"Just follow me. Tell me what you think of this." Surge brings Chase back into the room with all the weapons. A sheet covers a table to the side. "You asked for the tattoos back, you got it."

Surge pulls the sheet back to display a weaponized arm and leg sporting Chase's original tattoos. On the back calf of the leg is an old-school Mr. Hyde tattoo with the face reflecting in the mirror. On the arm is a full sleeve tattoo of a dragon moving up the arm with smoke and flames. Behind the dragon is a koi being hit by water but fighting through it. The lines are etched into the metal with metallic coloring filling specific spots.

Surge has Chase sit in a chair to the side of the table. He starts to remove the current arm, detaching it at the shoulder port where it plugs in. It looks like a metal plate but with small holes and connectors to sync the nerves with the electrons of the arm. Surge grabs the newly designed arm and begins to attach it to the port. The outer rim of the port locks into a seam of the arm and pulls it into place.

"How does it feel?"

Chase moves the arm around and raises it above his head. "It's doing what I want it to do."

Surge starts connecting the leg to the port at the upper thigh, right before the joint. The same rim locks into place and pulls the new leg into position. "Go ahead and stand up. Walk a little bit to see how it reacts."

Chase starts walking around, beginning to feel comfortable. He hops and jumps a few times. "This feels good. What about the weapons you put in?"

"Think 'flaming punch' and make a fist."

Chase follows the instruction. Near the wrist, a few openings are created. Suddenly his whole fist is engulfed with fire.

"You asked for a fire punch, you got it," Surge says. "Flamethrower is on the side of the forearm and on the top of the forearm I worked in an Uzi outfitting. Basically, you can put a clip in the bottom side of your forearm and it will fire from the top. Now, as for your leg, you didn't really say much, so I took the liberty of designing something special. At the thigh, parts detach and assemble an M79 mini grenade launcher. You also have a hidden pistol inside your calf for the right moment."

Chase looks at Surge and finally starts to feel like himself again. "This is awesome, and exactly what I was looking for. You ready to go?"

Surge looks at him, confused. "What do you mean?"

"I requested to take you with us. We need your knowledge on Dr. Peck's work. We think a former worker here is connected to the activity in Poland and Romania. Possible ties to Lithuania."

"Shit, I was worried about that. Where are we starting?" Surge looks concerned.

"Seagar wants us to find the base in Romania, but my gut is telling me to find Alexis Grim in Belarus."

Surge thinks for a minute and looks at Chase. "So once we leave, let's figure out a way of dividing up. Once we leave, we are officially following orders. If we have to make choices toward our investigating, then you can do so."

"I was thinking about you, Salene, and Kitch going to Romania while Bull, Sabu, and I hunt down Alexis. Why was Seagar so adamant about going to Romania and not trying to find Alexis?"

"You really don't trust him, do you? It's pretty clear, from what I can see. I got your back, Chase. You can trust me."

"I have seen soldiers die because of his decisions and actions. I joined the military because I wanted to make a difference and defend people who need it. Have you ever just felt like you can't trust someone? I have always had that with him."

"I guess with time we will find out! As long as I have been here, he has saved lives and brought them here. He did save your life. All I can do is judge from what I see."

"Yeah, it was pretty lucky he was close with that squad." Chase pauses and starts thinking about his assignment. "It was a delivery convoy with medical supplies. It was also a safe zone that we were attacked in." He pauses again with questions in his head.

Surge sees the wheels in Chase's head turning. The concern on his face is clear. "Chase? What's wrong?"

"How did you end up on the helicopter with me?" he asks Surge, puzzled.

"Seagar had requested I go on patrol with his group to provide medical assistance if needed. At the time, he had not brought in any new recruits since Bull, which was an unusual situation. Kitch was the last one, and it was about a month before. So I guess having me close by was in his best interest."

Chase shakes his head. "That seems convenient. I never did hear who attacked us. Like I said, that area was marked as a clear zone."

Surge shows empathy and sorrow. "I'm guessing it isn't now, since you got attacked."

"That's a good point! I should look into that. It would have to be marked as a combat zone now. Thanks, Surge, I appreciate the information. By the way, great job on the tats!" Chase smiles and offers up a fist-bump.

Surge happily reciprocates the bump. "No problem! I could tell how important they were. I will see you in the hangar for departure."

Surge walks out and Chase starts looking at himself in a mirror off to the side. Seeing the metal where his flesh used to be, he opens and closes his fist. The ability to touch is gone and his motor skills have now changed. He doesn't want it to be real, but the cold reality is that it is real.

Chase exits into the hallway and starts walking down the hall. He sees a communication officer walking toward him. He decides to stop him for a second. "Excuse me, sir, do you have a second?"

"Sure! What can I do for you?" He stops and looks at Chase, eager to help.

"Can you tell me the current status of the area in Turkey I was air-lifted from? It must have been changed to a combat zone. It was close to Adana."

"The last I heard was the general deemed it clear with no threats to be aware of. We also do not have confirmation of what group it was that attacked the convoy. I have to get to my post. If I have any new information, I will let you know."

"Thank you!" Chase gestures his appreciation before continuing down the hall. He starts to feel like there is more to what happened in Turkey.

CHAPTER 11

A long the Belarus–Russian border, five large military trucks drive in line down a long dirt road. They are headed toward Haradzec to rendezvous with Crow and Brug.

Alexis grabs the radio and calls out to his associate. "Bautista! When you see the body of water on the right, remember to pull over to the old farm on the left. Crow and Brug should meet us in the next few hours."

"Copy that," the voice responds with a smooth Spanish accent. As the trucks barrel down the rural road, Alexis grabs a cell phone from his pocket and dials a few numbers and waits a second.

"General! We are almost at the rendezvous and will be heading into Russia within the next few hours. Do you have any further instructions I need to be aware of?"

The phone on the other end pauses and hangs up. This doesn't faze Alexis and he puts the phone back into his jacket pocket. As he does so, the driver pulls the truck into the farm Alexis spoke of. Bautista pulls the lead truck into the huge barn that sits ahead of them. All five trucks pull in and the door shuts behind them.

Bautista jumps out of the first truck. He is a muscular

six-foot, 230-pound man with caramel skin. Sporting a military flat-top cut and tribal tattoos on his arms, he is an intimidating individual with no smile on his face. Alexis walks toward him and starts to point to the large transport truck parked outside of the farm.

"The refrigerated truck outside has the one hundred soldiers and twenty doctors we need to transport to the air base near Moscow. I want you to move ahead with that truck and two smaller trucks. Once Brug and Asher take control of the base, you move in and deliver. If they have any struggle, you can insert yourself with the team. I want you out of here as soon as they arrive."

"I got it! Do we anticipate any other factors I need to know? Like what happened in Turkey?" Bautista says with anger on his face.

Alexis puts his hand on Bautista's shoulder. "I know your brother was shot and killed during the job in Turkey. That was not anticipated, and I assure you we will make it right."

"He was shot after we were instructed to pull back. I just want to be the one who pulls the trigger." He clenches his hand.

Alexis nods. "You will get that, but for now, head out with that truck. I will contact you after we depart from here."

Bautista grabs a handful of guys standing next to the trucks and exits the building with them. They prep the trucks they are taking and leave quickly as Alexis walks through the building. He pulls the phone out of his pocket again and dials the same number and waits. The phone rings but there is no answer. He puts it away in his jacket and escapes to an office at the far back corner of the building. The remaining men stay with the trucks.

As Alexis waits, Crow and Brug drive down the same

road headed toward the farm. In the back of the large box truck are Sun, Asher, and the other SCZ troops they have with them.

Crow notices the lake to the right and realizes they are close. "The farm will be on the left after the lake." She points out with her hand.

Brug can see the large building and pulls in. He stops and flashes the front lights three times. A man sitting in a chair next to the large door stands up and pulls the big door open. Brug pulls the truck in and parks next to the three military-green trucks already inside. Alexis walks out from the far office with his arms open in a welcoming fashion.

"Crow! Brug! Welcome, so good to see you. What about our favorite Saigon Sun? Where is the rude and trite little bastard?"

Brug chuckles and points back to the truck. "He is in the back of the truck with the other SCZs."

Alexis looks at Brug with a confused face. "The what?"

"Azazil's new soldiers. Surgical Cybernetic Zombies! It's actually quite ingenious what they are doing." Brug smirks and chuckles.

Despite being confused, Alexis is quite intrigued. "Is that what they are doing with the bodies? So you are saying Sun is dead?"

Crow steps forward and takes the gloves she is wearing off, putting them in her handbag. "Yes, the lovable little throat slicer got a dagger to the heart, compliments of Azazil. To be honest, he seems much more obedient now."

"Well, let's bring them out and divide up," Alexis says. "Once we get to Smolensk in Russia, we will separate and use choppers to get to the targets. I will accompany Crow and Sun. Brug, I have some insurance for you if you need it. Bautista also has the dead soldiers and doctors we discussed a few days ago."

"How are we crossing over the border?" Brug asks. Crow stays quiet and continues to take in all of the information.

Alexis starts to walk toward the truck. "We have a backroads route that heads into the wooded terrain. I developed it about a year ago when I was smuggling weapons out of Russia for small militia groups. So let's see these SCZs, as you called them."

One of his men opens the back of the truck. The SCZs all sit on benches down the length of the truck bed. Brug grabs a headset and puts it on. He clicks a button that powers it up.

"Stand and exit the truck with arms in hand!" he orders out. The SCZs all stand and turn to the back of the truck. In unified formation, they move and jump down to the ground. After all have exited, Asher and Sun stand on the truck looking down at Alexis. They jump down and join the rest in formation.

Alexis chuckles. "Damn! Do they speak? Can they fuck?"

Crow rolls her eyes. "I'm pretty sure they don't give a fuck!"

Brug smirks a little. "Not that we can tell, but I'm looking forward to seeing them fight."

Alexis smiles at him. "Shall we test it out before we leave?" He starts to chuckle. "Don't you want to be sure they work? It sounds like they are sending you in as experimental rats, into uncharted waters. I would not want untested fighters suddenly clucking like chickens."

Crow steps forward. "I like that idea! I want to see Sun against three of your men." She pulls a headset out and puts it on.

Alexis starts clapping and moves toward a group of his men standing next to the trucks. "You three are up. I want you to attack Sun. No guns!"

Crow speaks into the microphone. "Sun! Defend yourself and eliminate threats."

Sun steps forward and moves his head, scanning the area. He sees the three men spread out to surround him. Two have large knives and the third has a large crowbar. Sun moves forward more and surveys the three men again. The one with the crowbar in front of him charges forward. Sun crosses his arms and throws them in the air to block the crowbar as he front-kicks the man's groin.

The other two move forward and Sun twists to his right, removing the crowbar and swiping it across the aggressor's face. He then continues to turn and drops to a split as he smashes the crowbar into the other man's ribs. The force of the blow creates a giant grunt and buckles the man to his knees. His ribs are broken for certain.

The first attacker gets up from his knees and tries to grab the crowbar, but Sun shifts his legs to his knees and elbows the man. He jumps up to his feet and sidekicks him to the ground. The man behind him is about to stab Sun with the knife, but Sun quickly throws his right arm out to the side. A large blade protrudes from his jacket sleeve. He turns, and with a quick swipe decapitates the man, his head falling to the ground next to the body. The blade then retracts back into the sleeve and Sun moves back into position.

Alexis is stunned, and quite impressed by the display. "Well! That sucks for Vladimir, but that was fun to watch. Do we know that these other minions work?"

Brug shrugs and bellows out an order. "Troops, detain all armed soldiers in the building!" Suddenly the SCZ troops wield the rifles in an alert way and spread out. In the span of a minute, each one has a rifle aimed at a soldier or is positioned to take one out. Two SCZs stand with rifles pointed at Alexis, leaving him a little annoyed.

Alexis shakes his head. "You can call them off now."

Brug gives his weird brutish smile. "Maybe I won't! This is kinda fun."

Crow steps forward. "We need to get moving. Velnias and Azazil are both expecting us to be on time."

Brug calls the SCZ troops off and instructs them to load into the three military trucks. Asher is instructed to follow Brug and Sun to follow Crow. Alexis jumps into the third truck.

Through the radios they have, Alexis instructs Crow and Brug to follow his truck and keep up. He has an uncharted off-road path that allows him to traffic back and forth between countries. It will take them to Smolensk to fly out to Moscow.

Crow asks, "How do you not get monitored or caught going back and forth?"

"It is a heavily wooded area and there's not a lot of activity along these parts. Plus, I have some Russian connections that help out. We should get to Smolensk in about two hours. My associate Bautista will be providing assistance if needed. I like to have backups. He is on standby."

Crow responds, "How long till we get in the air at Moscow?"

Alexis responds back. "I have a crew that works at the airfield. They will have everything ready for us. Load up and go."

They travel down a rough, beat-up, man-made road until it all of a sudden runs into a heavy dose of brush and trees. The path is still visible, but it is hard to see the sky.

Alexis leads with Crow following in the second truck. Brug tails them both and has his usual Rammstein heavy metal playing. Crow has no music playing as she focuses on the truck in front. Sun sits next to her looking straight ahead with no ounce of emotion or actions. She looks over at him, amazed that he is so quiet and proper. This is the same man who showed up to a meeting with his penis hanging out to show how much she motivated him. Even though for years she despised him, she suddenly misses some of the banter. She decides to try something.

"Do you remember our meeting in Budapest a few years ago? I could not believe the nerve you had showing up like that." She looks over, but he has no response. "That's a shame, to not remember something like that. I can't imagine not having a memory of such a rude and vulgar gesture."

As she continues to drive, the left corner of Sun's mouth starts to twitch, almost as if he is smirking and laughing inside. Crow looks over in time to notice the quick twitch. It surprises her, but also gets her even more intrigued. "Do you remember what you did?" she says, shaking her head.

Sun sits quietly without saying or doing anything. The road is quite bumpy, so it's possible the twitch was nothing.

Crow goes back to focusing on the truck ahead. As she continues to drive, Sun's hands start to shift and rise to his legs. Without Crow noticing, he slowly unzips the zipper on his pants. When she turns her head, she sees him flip his penis out in front of her and put his hands back next to him. A slightly bigger smirk is on his face. She starts to laugh and realizes he does have some memory left.

"So you do understand conversations?" she asks.

Sun puts his thumb up but still in a robotic way. He shifts his head to look at her, still smirking and with his penis out. Crow can see the original Sun in front of her, but not quite the same.

"Can you speak?" she asks him.

He shakes his head back and forth. She is amazed that she can get responses like this.

"How do you feel? Do you feel anything?" She has no idea what to do.

Sun looks straight at Crow and flips the middle finger at her. She looks back at him, shaking her head. "Cute. Zip yourself up!" She turns her attention back to the road. Sun listens to her command and zips himself up. Crow asks another question. "How are you able to remember things?"

Using body language, he shrugs and continues to sit still for a second. He then turns and points to her. She looks over at him again. "Me? What the hell do I have to do with you remembering anything?" Sun points to his temple and then makes a breaking action with his hands. He then opens his hands and points at her.

"The memories are broken open by me?" Crow shakes her head again, not understanding what that means.

Sun nods, and goes back to sitting and looking forward. Crow sits and continues to drive, but there's so much going through her mind. Not knowing what to think or what else to say, she just focuses on the truck ahead driven by Alexis. She suddenly throws a question out.

"I can trust you, right?" she says seriously.

Sun sits for a second and then puts his left hand up and puts it to his chest before raising his thumb. Crow looks at him for a second. "With all of your heart, I can trust you," she says, suddenly believing him.

He nods a firm confirmation.

Crow then has a thought and throws another question out. "Can I trust the others?"

Sun turns to her and shakes his head no. Crow then wonders how much of this is accurate and true. She turns her attention back to driving and doesn't say another word.

CHAPTER 12

C hase sits on the small cargo plane heading to Romania. He keeps to himself, going over the last few days and months. Thinking about that day in Turkey, and why the whole attack seemed so wrong. There had been no communication of rebels of any kind in that area. Chase was not even given any radio communication from headquarters or his scouts.

Surge walks over and sits with him. "I wanted to make sure you were alone when I came to talk to you."

Chase looks at him curiously. "Why?"

"The area of Turkey you were attacked in is all clear. It has been for the past six months. US and British forces did a full sweep in Turkey; any rebel groups related to terror ops moved to the north. That area was clear and always was. Right now, US communication has it as clear."

"That makes no sense. Several soldiers were killed, and that was a heavy attack on us. Even with it being a few days later, an attack like that goes on record and would not be marked as clear."

"There is another weird thing about the report from the attack. It has twenty-four soldiers killed and missing in action," Surge divulges to Chase.

Chase looks at him, shocked. "What do you mean missing? Medics were all over the place."

Surge continued. "We headed back to the Greece facility. Everyone else disappeared. Including attackers! I was instructed to focus on you. Seagar looked after the rest."

Chase starts shaking his head. "I knew I couldn't trust him! We need to figure out where the other soldiers went."

"I'm thinking if we are splitting up, Salene, Kitch, and I will find out in Romania. Based on the intel we have, there has been a lot of activity at a castle that has been abandoned for decades. At first it was reported that it was being restored, but that stopped a few months ago. People are going back and forth, but the outside is still the same."

"How far are we from there?" Chase asks.

Surge looks at his watch. "Ten miles from our drop point."

Chase thinks for a second. "We don't have time to tell the others, so you, Salene, and Kitch need to find a link between the castle and that attack. I'm wondering if the soldiers were taken from the attack site."

Surge looks at Chase, concerned. "But if that's the case, then General Seagar would have been involved. Are you saying General Seagar was behind the attack?"

Chase looks at him seriously. "I don't know, but it could be possible. Why would the soldiers disappear? He was there, right?"

Surge nods. "Yeah, he was there. After you were loaded onto the helicopter, he instructed that you go to Dr. Peck. We took off and he remained to control things. Some thought it was odd that a general would be present for something like that, but everyone was following orders."

"It is because he is only to be in front-line situations in absolute emergencies. What if he planned the attack for the purpose of gaining me for the AMPD program?" Chase says as aggravation shows on his face.

"That's pretty fucked up if it's true. So the others and what happened to them could have been planned as well?" Surge says, unable to believe what he is saying.

"It's a possibility, but until we know for sure, I don't think we should say anything to the others. Sabu, Bull, and I will go to the Kremlin, and you go with Salene and Kitch."

"Okay!"

Suddenly the red lights start to beep for preparation. A voice comes over the intercom. "We are two minutes from the drop point. Please prepare to depart."

Surge gets up and checks the harnesses on his parachute pack. Salene walks over already wearing a pack. "Ready to go?"

Surge nods and tightens one more belt. Chase stands up and looks to Salene. "We need as much information on these experiments as we can get."

"We will get it. We need to be in contact at all times. Let me know what you need from there." Salene starts walking to the back of the plane. Surge follows and Kitch heads back to join them.

Chase yells out at him. "You don't want a parachute?"

Kitch turns and looks at him. "It's built in! Besides, I got these!" He throws his arms out and his giant wings deploy from his back. "Young, mean, and to the extreme!" he laughs out loud.

Chase just smiles and shakes his head. "Just be careful! Watch each other's backs."

Kitch gives him two thumbs up. "You got it!"

The back loading ramp of the plane starts to open as alarms start to sound. A sixty-second call sounds on the intercom. Surge and Salene prep to jump and Kitch stands behind them with his wings in full position. Sabu and Bull walk over to Chase to watch the others jump. The countdown continues to the last second.

Bull yells out, "Good luck! Kick some ass if you have to!"

Kitch turns and smiles at them. Salene and Surge give thumbs-up and jump out of the plane. Kitch lunges out after them and takes flight with his wings. The thrusters in his prosthetics engage. As Surge and Salene pull the parachute cords and start to float, Kitch scouts out landing spots. There is a farm near the castle for a target landing. Once they land, their focus is to get to the castle and figure out what is happening.

Now, Chase, Bull, and Sabu head to the Russian border with the hope of finding Alexis or any trace of activity. They have some intel that he has a personal crossing but do not know the exact location. The pilot is unaware that they are still on the plane. Chase signals Sabu and he heads to the cockpit.

"Bull! Do we have anything in the Alexis files that show connections or hideout information?"

Bull sifts through the documents looking for anything that previous work has dug up. "The most I can see is that he is well known for running weapons and drugs back and forth from Russia and Belarus. He has been spotted in Smolensk, Russia, on a number of occasions."

"Then forget the borderline, we need to go to Smolensk. We can land at the airfield or strip there."

Sabu walks back and approaches Chase, saying, "Pilot is wondering why we are here and wants a heading. He has gone dark on communication, but cannot stay dark long."

"Tell him Smolensk, Russia, and to create an emergency landing, if he can do that." Chase feels confident in his decision.

Sabu nods his head and goes back to the cockpit.

Chase and Bull continue through the files trying to find the smallest information that can get them closer.

| | | | |

Meanwhile, on the ground in Romania, Surge and Salene land safely in the field and gather up the equipment. Kitch is still in the air looking for the castle and how they can get to it quickly. He motions to head east on the main road. They follow his direction and start walking.

About two miles down the road is the entrance to the castle. It's in the late evening, so they are hidden by the dark sky and lack of lights.

Kitch flies ahead to check out what is happening and can see multiple vehicles being loaded up with hooded figures and what look like doctors. Kitch radios down to Salene and Surge.

"A lot of movement happening. They have a couple of large trucks and a few black SUVs, one in front and one behind like a convoy. They are moving out in a few minutes."

Salene responds, "Can you get close enough to see anyone?"

"I will try! I'm trying to keep distance so they don't see me. Maybe if I land I can get closer. I'm going for it." Kitch commits and dives.

Salene is concerned. "Kitch, wait till we get there. Don't go alone." She looks at Surge. "We need to hurry." She starts running and Surge starts after her.

Kitch notices a wooded area along the perimeter's stone wall. He aims to land that way. Using the thrusters, he controls his descent and gets to an opening in the trees. His wings retract and he checks his forearms and the built-in guns. Loaded and ready, he makes his way along the stone wall toward the castle, making sure he doesn't get noticed.

Salene and Surge are easily ten minutes away and the trucks are being loaded quickly. Kitch decides to get closer and slowly walks up the grassy hill at the front of the castle. It is about two hundred yards to the dirt-road driveway. He notices a narrow stone walkway to his left that leads to the front door. Before it reaches the front, there is a small wall that separates the grass and the path. Kitch quickly runs to the small wall and gets down on his stomach, crawling toward the driveway until he reaches a spot where he is hidden and can hear someone speak.

A man speaks into a radio. "Yes sir! The trucks are loaded and we can leave when you and Velnias are ready, sir!"

A voice comes back from the radio. "We are on our way."

The men in black suits start to scatter and get into positions near the door. A few seconds later Azazil and the hooded figure come out. A third SUV pulls up to the door. The driver stays in while two other men jump out with machine guns. The two start walking down but the hooded figure stops.

"I have what I need from here. Leave no evidence. Blow it as soon as we are gone." The hooded man gets into the SUV. Azazil turns to the two men who got out of the SUV.

"You heard him! Set up the self-destruct and set the time for twenty minutes. I don't want us near here when it goes." Azazil gets into the SUV with the hooded man.

"Yes sir!" The two run into the castle and the convoy starts to pull out. The last SUV sits waiting for the two who ran in.

Kitch lies still. They will only have about ten minutes once the others get there. He can't radio them for fear the others may hear him. The two men run back out and jump into the last SUV. As they pull away, Kitch jumps up and runs to the door. He quickly radios Salene.

"We have less than twenty minutes. Hurry! They set up a self-destruct. We may have about fifteen minutes to get what we need. Azazil and this other guy just cleared out."

Kitch runs into the castle and starts looking for doors or passages. He sees a hall that leads to an elevator for downstairs, running down it until he finds the elevator. He checks his watch trying to time how long he has. He gets on the elevator and heads down to the bottom floor. There he sees an operating room. He runs in and sees no one. Over on a side table are a headset and a USB. Kitch grabs them and quickly sees a computer.

Salene radios to him. "We are running up the driveway. Where are you?"

Kitch responds back, "I am in the basement in an operating room. I'm grabbing what I can. No time for you to come in."

Surge responds, "Is there a computer?"

"Yes, I'm at it," he calls back.

Surge gives him instructions. "Try and pull up procedures or programs."

Kitch struggles to find anything with links to those. He quickly puts the USB clip from the headset in the computer. Suddenly the screen shows data and skill listings. He takes it out of the computer and puts it in his pocket. A flash drive sits on the desk. He grabs it to download information.

Looking at his timer, Kitch quickly grabs the flash drive from the computer. "I found a flash drive. I'm heading out, not much time left."

He glances at his watch again and realizes he may be out of time. He starts running for the elevator and hits the button until the doors open. Red warning lights start to sound off.

"One minute until self-destruct."

The elevator slowly moves upward. Kitch is getting nervous not knowing if he is going to make it.

The speakers call out, *"Thirty seconds until self-destruct."*

The doors open and he starts running down the hall as the speaker starts counting.

"Ten . . . nine . . . eight . . ."

He throws his arms forward, shooting the doors ahead. The thrusters in his feet engage and shoot him through the front doors as the castle begins to explode. The blast throws him out over the old empty fountain and down the grassy hill.

Salene and Surge stand on the driveway keeping distance and see Kitch hurtle through the air. The castle continues to explode as debris flies everywhere. It becomes nothing but fire and rubble. Surge and Salene run over to Kitch, dodging the debris to check on him.

Salene calls out to him. "Kitch! Are you okay?"

Kitch is on the ground in a mound, scorch marks covering his back brace and attachments. Little bits of smoke flutter from his body.

Surge gets down and carefully rolls him over. As Kitch rolls to his back, laughter breaks the tension.

"What a fucking rush! Wooooooo! That was awesome!"

Salene shakes her head. "You scared the shit out of us!"

Surge looks at her. "Maybe you, I figured he was all right."

Salene looks at Surge, saying, "Fuck you!" She then turns and starts walking away. "Let's go! We need to get in touch with Chase and the others. This turned into a waste."

Kitch jumps up. "No it didn't! Check these out. A flash drive and . . . whatever this is?"

Surge looks shocked and reaches out for the items. As he takes the USB clip, he takes a deep gulp. "This can't be!"

Salene looks at him, puzzled. "What is it? Why can't it be?"

"When Dr. Peck and I started on the program of amputations, we had to work on regeneration of the nerves and how it reacts with the technology. In order to do so, we had to work on cadavers. We also had to work on stimulating the brain to see if it could control the technology. We came up with this to measure the data of the brain and the nervous system. It clips into a headpiece that we attached to the skull. Someone from the project is working with them."

"We need to radio back to base and let the general know." Salene starts going through the bag she is carrying.

Surge quickly interjects. "We can't do that!"

Kitch looks surprised. "Why not?"

Surge takes a breath. "Because it could be him. Chase and I figured out that Seagar could be behind the attack in Turkey that put Chase with us. Seagar may have preselected him. He may have preselected all of you."

"That man saved my life!" Salene belts out with frustration.

Kitch reciprocates. "Me too. Without him being there, I would be dead."

Surge looks at them both. "I know. He is *always* conveniently there. It's pretty cool that a general happens to show up and save specific people to be put into a program. We also found out all of the soldiers from the attack in Turkey have been recorded as missing in action. I'm sorry."

Salene gets even more frustrated. "When was this going to be shared?"

"Chase and I were talking about it on the plane. Right before we jumped. We didn't have time to pull everyone together when we started to piece it together. I need to look at this flash drive."

"We also need to contact Chase and the others." Salene gets the radio out. "Find out where they are headed. If the general is behind this, it makes sense why he was so insistent on coming here. He knew it was being destroyed."

Kitch looks at Salene. "We need transportation. I can get up in the air, but I can't take both of you with me."

"Let's get moving then. I will contact Chase and see about a rendezvous." Salene takes the lead and they move back toward the road.

| | | | |

Meanwhile, on the plane, Chase, Bull, and Sabu are gearing up for when they arrive in Smolensk. The plane starts to turn and a voice on the intercom speaks out.

"My apologies, gentlemen. General Seagar has requested we turn around and head back. He is aware you are still on board and that you requested to go to Russia. We cannot accommodate that request."

Chase looks at Sabu and Bull. "It looks like we need to jump, unless either of you can fly?"

Both Bull and Sabu shake their heads. Chase starts thinking and trying to figure out options.

Then Sabu gestures to Chase. "We may be close to Kraków. I have a contact that can help us. He was at my safehouse."

Chase nods at him and goes to the phone that transmits to the pilot and cockpit. "What is our location? Are we turning west or east?" He pauses. "West and will have to loop over Poland! Are we anywhere near Kraków?"

The pilot responds, "We are just south of Kraków now."

Chase grabs a parachute and moves toward the others. "We need to go now. We are just south of it. Bull, grab two chutes, you will need them."

Bull looks at him, irked at the notion, but realizes the weight of the guns and back assembly do need it. He grabs the second chute and straps it to his front. Sabu has his ready and Chase is set. The three walk to the back of the plane. As they do, the two security officers from the front of the plane come to the back.

"Excuse me, gentlemen, but we have been instructed to detain you."

Bull shouts back, "For what?"

"Not following orders and going rogue! Now turn over all weapons and gear!" They move closer.

The three of them start laughing. Chase steps forward. "You want our ARMS? Come get them!" He makes a fist with his right hand and it engulfs in fire. Bull steps forward and nudges Chase to the side.

"No, he doesn't want that! He wants these." Bull puts his forearms behind him and attaches his Gatling-style guns. He pulls them forward and they start to rotate. "Are you going to open the bay doors, or do I need to make my own?" The security officers are frozen not knowing what to do. "Times up, dipshits! Make my own it is." He turns to the back and lets loose a barrage of bullets, tearing an opening in the back tail of the plane. "After you, gentlemen!"

Sabu goes out first and Chase follows. Bull walks forward.

"It's not big enough!" He opens fire again and makes a bigger hole. Looking back at the officers, Bull salutes to them before jumping out of the plane. In the air, all three men free-fall in the dark trying to find a light source on the ground. Sabu signals the other two. They position themselves and dive to the left to get closer to the targeted area. It is a giant construction zone south of the city. They start to control the free-fall and gauge the altitude.

Bull being so big and carrying so much weight is the first to pull his chutes. Chase and Sabu pull it next and the three float down to a flat next to the large crane. They quickly detach the chutes and start running for cover behind some large equipment and concrete tubes.

Sabu pulls out a cell phone and starts messaging his contact. In a few minutes he gets a response back:

Ten minutes next to the train tracks.

CHAPTER 13

G eneral Seagar walks down the hall toward Dr. Peck's office. He has files with him and two armed guards following behind him. He arrives to the closed door and knocks.

The doctor's voice responds. "Come in!"

The general enters the office and approaches Dr. Peck's desk sternly. "We have a problem, Doctor. Three of our specimens have decided to go rogue. We have also received a report of a castle in Romania being destroyed. It is believed to be the one that they were supposed to investigate. What do you know about this?"

The doctor maneuvers his wheelchair out from behind his desk. "I have no idea about any of that. Why would I? Did they decide to split up?"

"Whether they decided that or not, it was not the orders they were given. I need to know what you know. Go with these gentlemen." Seagar points to the door as two officers enter.

"Why can't we talk here? Am I being arrested?" Dr. Peck challenges.

"No, we just have information that needs to be discussed, and you may be able to help figure out the

Plague's plan." The general gestures for him to accompany the two officers. The doctor obliges to follow and grabs his bag from the table near the door. They move out into the hall and the doctor notices people gathering bags and belongings.

"What is going on?" Dr. Peck asks. "Why are so many people gathering belongings?"

"I need to contain the rogue soldiers, and although this has been a success from a technical aspect, we are going to move the operation to a new location. I am also setting up a new crew at that location. These men are going to transport you."

The doctor is confused and concerned. "This is crazy! You can't just move years of data and experiments to a new location. And what new crew? Everyone here has given so much to build these six miracles who have not even had a chance to show who they are and what they can do."

"They did by blowing a huge hole into the back of a plane and parachuting out over Poland. This is after refusing to cooperate and come back here. They were supposed to all be at the castle. As far as the other three, they are gone, and all the evidence from the castle with it. This is a disaster and I need to keep things on track." The general chews on an unlit cigar.

The doctor can't believe what he is hearing. "Okay, so where am I being taken?"

The general holds the cigar between two fingers. He looks down at the doctor. "Follow these two. When you get on the plane, they will give you what you need to know. I will follow behind once I have this taken care of."

Dr. Peck follows, but he knows something is wrong. Trusting the general has just become an uncertainty.

The men guide him to the main hangar, where a small private jet sits ready for his arrival. Next to it is a lift to get the doctor up to the entrance of the plane. To the far side of the hangar is a giant cargo plane with the back loading ramp down. A full army of soldiers continues to load equipment and computers onto the plane. Boxes labeled MODIFIED WEAPONS sit on pallets waiting to be loaded. "What is going on? Why is everything being moved?" he asks, uneasy.

One of the officers turns to him and repeats, "The project is being moved. The general has made a new agenda."

"What kind of agenda? This project was developed to help injured soldiers and rehab veterans to greater things."

"We are just following orders. We don't make the rules," the officer states in a professional tone.

Dr. Peck is really worried and starts to think he needs to contact Surge. He pulls his cell phone out, and starts to type a message. One of the officers notices and stops him from completing the message. "No communication outside is allowed. I'll take that."

He reaches over and grabs the phone, shaking his head at the doctor.

They get to the lift and load Dr. Peck on. The lift raises them to the entrance of the small private jet.

They radio to the general, stating, "We have reached the private bird." There is a pause.

"Proceed as planned and I will be there momentarily." The officer puts the radio away and nods to the other, who moves the doctor into the plane.

As he stands behind the wheelchair, the officer pulls a small needle out and inserts it into the doctor's neck. The doctor struggles for a second before he finally passes out. The officer straps him to a wall in a back section of the plane's cab.

The two officers start to get the cab set up and prepared for the general. Over to the side is a small bar. One officer grabs a glass and pours an ounce and a half of high-end black-label whiskey. It's placed at the large leather seat close to the front. On the small pull-out table sits a large black book with a file folder under it. The two officers stand at attention waiting. Two minutes later General Seagar enters and acknowledges the officers.

"Get comfortable, men, we have a long flight. I assume the tranquilizer will last the duration?"

"Yes sir. We may need to dose him around landing though. How long would you like him out?" the one officer asks.

Seagar thinks for a second. "I would like to wait till we get to the new facility. I want to introduce him to my new lead when he wakes up. This project is about to take a very big turn."

"Yes sir! You won't be disturbed during the flight."

The general nods and takes a seat, grabbing hold of his glass. He takes a good sip of it before opening the black book. He pulls out a cell phone and presses a number. After waiting a second, the other end answers.

"Yes, Mr. Secretary. Everything with the AMPD project is going well and moving forward," General Seagar says. "We have six active and in-the-field troops with enhancements. I will keep you notified of progress." The general listens for a moment. "Yes, I will have the full budget to you by the end of the week." He pauses for another second. "I will be back on US soil very soon. I have a few more stops to make. I will contact you in a few days." There is another pause. "Yes sir!"

He hangs up the phone and puts it back in his right pocket, then begins going through the black book and the files in the folder, which document all the bio information about Chase and the crew put together. He pulls a cell phone out of the left pocket and pushes a number to auto dial. "Is everything set to move in on the air base?" He listens for a moment. "Let me know when the base is ready. Any issues, you tell me." He hangs up and drinks the rest of the high-end whiskey, sitting back and thinking about what he is doing. He starts to relax and closes his eyes.

| | | | |

Velnias and Azazil are traveling to an old, run-down landing strip about ten miles from the castle. Knowing the castle has been destroyed, they are calm and relaxed about what has been left behind. Now they are transferring the remaining SCZ troops to the air base outside of Moscow.

"Azazil, so far everything is going as planned. The air base will give us a large enough location to increase our production. I want the twenty doctors to be programmed first; after that they are to do the procedures on all soldiers brought in or killed at the base. All nations interested are to send the deceased to the base for the procedure and programming."

"Understood. Do we know where we want to demonstrate the skills of the troops?" Azazil asks.

"The AMPD program is trying to stop any assassination attempt at the Kremlin. Inform Crow that we need her to initiate a solo assassination on the Russian president. We will coordinate Alexis with the troops. Crow will be expendable, and Sun will be instructed to take her out."

"I thought Alexis was going to take care of Crow?" Azazil is surprised by that information.

"My first goal is to gain the business of the surrounding countries. This needs to be a quick demonstration on how reliable the SCZs are. We also need to make sure Seagar is unaware of any deals we have with other countries. He may have provided the backing to do this, but I don't want him to know our dealings with anyone else. We also tell him that Crow tried to follow her own agenda and we had to stop her. As long as he believes this is a Russia and US deal, then we don't need to worry about him. Soon all soldiers around the world will be serving their country after death, and we will profit from it."

"And if countries object to it and create problems?" Azazil asks.

"Once we have enough soldiers under the device's command, that won't matter. We will be able to take control of any soldier in the world. We will have access to them all."

CHAPTER 14

C hase and Sabu sit in the front cab of Boris's truck while Bull sits in the back under the protective cover of the truck bed. Boris is Sabu's safe house contact in Poland.

Sabu instructs his contact to take them to the Bonerowski Palace, where he had investigated before. Boris informed them of a major investigation currently happening because of some murders.

Boris explains, "Apparently the night manager and a room attendant were killed. A woman in a blue dress who had stayed there for a while went crazy."

Sabu responds. "It could not be Crow; she left when I was found."

Chase asks Boris, "What else can you tell us? How were they killed?"

Boris pulls the car toward the crime tape, where police officers are holding press and spectators back. "They were mutilated; that's all that is being said. I wish I knew more. I don't know how much information they will give you."

Chase looks at Sabu. "Stay here, and let me see what I can find out. I don't want to draw attention." Sabu agrees.

Chase hops out of the truck and walks over to the police barrier. He waves an officer over and the officer comes close to see what he wants.

Chase asks, "English?"

The officer stops what he is doing and motions with his finger up to give him a second. He walks over to a man with a suit. The officer points to Chase and the inspector looks annoyed. He walks over to Chase.

"You want to speak English to someone?" He takes a drag of his cigarette.

Chase nods his head. "Yes, I'm with the US military, and we have been investigating someone who stayed here recently."

The inspector looks at him, interested. "Who is that? Do you know what happened here?"

Chase shakes his head. "No, I just know an international terrorist was here and we need to find her."

"Tell me her name and maybe we can talk more." The inspector takes another drag from the cigarette.

Chase thinks for a second. "Show me the crime scene and I will give you a name." He has a jacket on hiding his metal arm, but the inspector sees his hand. Chase looks at him and nods his head at the inspector. The inspector's mood changes.

"Come in, let's talk!" He shifts the barrier and Chase enters.

Chase walks with him side by side. "Why the change when you saw my hand?"

The inspector smiles. "Something tells me you want to see this. By the look of that metal hand, I may be out of my league here. I'm Detective Bosko." He hands Chase a rubber glove. "You only need one, right?" The detective shrugs and drops it into Chase's hand. "It is a crazy scene in here. The woman bit the victims!"

Chase stops suddenly and looks at the inspector. "Did you just say *bit*?"

The inspector nods his head. "Yes! She bit the neck, the arm, the forearm, and even some of the face. I have not seen anything like this, but when I saw your hand, I thought maybe you knew something I need to know."

"I'm First Lieutenant Chase Campbell. I'm with a special unit looking for a group that may be experimenting with dead soldiers."

"You think this woman is one of them? What we know is she didn't talk, stayed in the room all the time, and never left." He directs Chase to follow him.

They enter the front entrance and the body of the night manager lies on the floor. Blood is pooled up on the floor and smeared on the railing to the stairs. He has bite marks and flesh torn from his face and neck.

The inspector looks at Chase with concern. "Are you a *Walking Dead* fan?"

Chase smirks. "Has he changed yet?"

"No, it's been several hours. We are about to move them now." The inspector looks at the body, not sure what to think.

"No, I don't think it's zombies in the traditional horror movie sense," Chase states. "The woman we are looking for goes by the name of Crow. She has a brother named Brug. They are German weapons dealers who stayed here. One of my associates followed them here a while back. Do you know what happened to this woman?"

"No, but she has to be in the city still. We have a warning out that she is very dangerous. The problem is if we tell everyone to stay inside, she may just go into hiding."

"Thank you, Inspector. This has been a big help." Chase turns to leave.

"Take my card! If you need anything else or have any information, call me."

"Thank you. I don't have a card, but I will message so you have my information. If you find her, let me know." Chase puts his metal hand out to shake the inspector's hand. The inspector obliges and Chase heads out of the building.

As he walks back to the truck, he thinks more about the victim and the bite marks. The inspector said she never left the room, so how did she eat? It didn't make sense.

He gets back in the truck, and his phone buzzes. He looks to see Surge sent a message.

The castle has been destroyed, but Kitch was able to get a device and a flash drive before it was destroyed. It's linked to someone who worked with us.

He types a reply back to them saying to meet them in Smolensk, Russia, that they had to bail out in Poland, and to not trust the general.

Surge replies back:

Agreed!

Chase puts the phone away and turns to Boris. "We need to get to Smolensk, Russia, as soon as possible. Do you have any contacts who can get us to the airport there?"

Boris thinks for a minute. "Yes, my cousin Jakob is a pilot. He has a plane and should be able to take you. But what about security?"

Chase looks at him seriously. "We need to be snuck in. Security is not going allow us anywhere."

A deep voice from the back of the truck speaks. "I

know I'm the big guy and that I have pretty heavy military weapons on me, but can we speed this up? I'm lying on my back in the rear bed of a truck waiting on you guys. The best way for us to get on the plane at the airport is to get in with a fuel truck or mechanics truck."

Boris nods. "I will call him and have him meet us near the airport. He will know how to get you to the plane on the tarmac."

Bull's voice comes from the back of the truck again. "What happened here?"

Chase responds back to him. "A woman was here in the same suit as the others. She decided to kill the two employees by biting them and eating some of the flesh."

Sabu looks at Chase like he is crazy.

Bull shouts back, "You are joking, right?"

"I wish I was! I saw the body of the night manager. His neck and face were ripped up. Whatever is being done to the bodies they are collecting, it is creating some sort of rage reaction. I'm going to guess that they may not know this happens."

Boris looks at his phone. "Jakob can meet us in an hour. I suggest we go that way now." He starts the truck and pulls away from the scene. As he drives, Chase messages Surge about the victims.

| | | | |

Surge looks at the text and stops walking. Salene and Kitch stop and look at him.

Salene asks, "What's going on?"

Surge looks at her. "Whatever this device does, it caused a woman to attack and bite two hotel employees, killing them. What if they figured out how to revive the brain and body to operate under military commands?"

She looks at him with a weird face. "What do you mean revive? If you are dead, then you are dead! It's crazy."

Surge looks at her while thinking about the experiments they did. "When the doctor and I first started, we had to revive some brains to get a reaction. Whoever is reviving the brain has created a device that acts as the brain with the ability to allow the body to respond to it."

Kitch starts chuckling. "So basically they revive it, program it with military information, and give it instructions to destroy things. If they get hungry, they bite people."

Surge nods his head. "That's what it looks like, but until we see for ourselves, we don't know for sure. I tried messaging the doctor, but he isn't responding. Chase needs us in Russia."

They continue down the dark road looking for a vehicle. Kitch stops for a second. "Are we being followed?" He turns, but it's too dark to see. He clicks the light on his left arm to see what is there. The road is full of military troops walking in formation. They all have machine guns propped on their left shoulder. Salene grabs clips from her backpack, inserting them into her rifle attachments. She asks how many.

Kitch takes a second to calculate. "More than a hundred. Where did they come from?"

Surge responds back. "We need to get moving and figure out if they are following us." He starts to jog and the other two join him. After a few minutes Kitch checks behind them, seeing that the troops reacted to the pace.

"They started jogging as well. We need to try and hide or fight."

Salene points to a clearing down the road. "I think there was a church that way." They cut through the field and realize the troops are in a full run after them. "Kitch, can you get into the air?"

He yells out, "Yeah!"

As they get closer to the church, he takes a hard run and jumps to the lower roof section. The thrusters in his feet boost him, allowing him to land on it. He turns and starts firing his machine guns, hitting several troops in the front.

"Get inside, I got you covered." The troops keep moving forward and start firing back. Kitch is caught off guard that they did not go down. "Oh shit!"

Salene and Surge bust the door in and get inside. Surge shuts the door and hinges the lock while Salene pushes a large bench over to block it. "I need to get into a spot with a clear sight where I can start picking them off." Surge motions to go. He has a machine gun with him but not much else.

Meanwhile Kitch makes his way behind a gargoyle. Gunfire sprays all around him. He knows he needs to try something he has not done before. He waits for the next pause of reloading and fires his machine guns again, taking a few more out. As he throws his arms to the side, his wings deploy and he starts running along the low-roof section of the church. The thrusters burst on and he rockets off the roof and into the air. Machine-gun shots follow him.

Suddenly individual troops start dropping to the ground. Salene made her way to the third floor of the church. Standing at an open window, she starts picking off troops one by one. The scope on the right side of her head can see each one. It automatically dials in on one and she uses her right arm to fire. She picks another one and the left arm fires. Gunfire starts to rattle toward her as well.

On the main floor Surge takes cover as windows break and debris flies all over the place. The blocked door gets blasted open and troops start entering. Surge begins to fire the machine gun from behind a pillar. Twenty troops get in the door and start moving toward him and he keeps firing as he makes his way to the stairs. He looks behind him to see lit candles and starts grabbing and throwing them at the zombie-like troops. They start to catch on fire as well as the benches. He fires off a few more rounds and runs for the stairs. The troops shoot but are hindered by the fire building up.

Kitch soars in the air, shooting down at the walking troops. They struggle to keep up with his speed and ability to change direction. He launches a grenade from a thousand feet in the air.

"Open wide!" After several seconds it hits the ground and explodes, dispersing body parts all over. "Wow, this is cool." As he maneuvers to turn, he gains speed and starts to dive toward the remaining troops. He puts his arms straight out and shoots as he dives. As he gets low to the ground, he is able to use his wings to cut through troops standing in his way. He gains momentum and heads back up into the sky.

Salene fires a few more shots and heads back to the stairs to see Surge running up. "You okay?"

"Yeah! The church is engulfed in flames. I had to use candles to start it."

Smoke starts to billow up the stairwell. Salene checks out the window to see how many are left. There are a few scattered troops remaining. Kitch has landed in a clearing away from them. She starts to climb out the window to a thick ledge. Surge fires off a few shots at the troops coming up the stairs. Even though they are burning, they still move and function. Surge takes them out with quick shots to the head. He goes out the window and joins Salene on the ledge. They both look for options to get to the ground.

Kitch continues to fire at the remaining troops, drawing attention. The church becomes fully engulfed in flames as the sound of collapsing wood builds. Kitch flies to an old beat-up truck in the field. His wings retract and he jumps into the cab, then realizes he has to hot-wire it. It takes a second as he tries to spark the wires. Suddenly the engine kicks in and starts. Kitch puts it in gear and hits the gas. He quickly steers it toward the church, where Surge and Salene are standing. They will have to jump down to the back bed of the truck.

While he drives, he sticks his left arm out of the window, firing shots at the remaining attackers. He skids the truck to the corner.

Surge continues to fire shots as Salene carefully jumps down to the truck bed. She starts firing as Surge jumps down. Salene uses her right eye scope to find an escape route. She sees a dirt road past the field the truck was in, then starts banging on the cab and pointing for Kitch to head in that direction. As he drives, the two in the back try to shoot the remaining troops. As they drive off, the church crumbles and collapses to the ground. Salene and Surge sit back and look at each other.

Surge takes a second and a deep breath. "We need transportation and fast. We have to get to Smolensk, Russia."

Salene speaks out. "We need to find a safe place to regroup. Then we contact Chase for what we need to do." To Kitch, she says, "Stay on the side roads. Look for any abandoned buildings."

The truck continues and disappears into the dark.

CHAPTER 15

Alexis, Brug, and Crow pull the trucks into a large hangar at the south end of the Smolensk airport. It is a small airport, meant only for civilian use. Two medium-sized jets sit on the tarmac at the end of the runway. A large white building sits halfway down the runway. It has a small control tower at the far end of the building.

It is very quiet with only a few people on site. They quickly unload the trucks and order the SCZ troops to board the jets. The majority of them get on the first jet while the rest get on the second jet. Two pilots stand at the jets waiting. Both are employees of Alexis and his operation.

Alexis walks over to Brug. "Azazil and Velnias are headed to the base. You need to go as soon as possible. My man Bautista is also headed that way with the Ukrainian soldiers."

Brug nods and walks over to Crow. "Okay, sis, I'm on my way."

She looks over to Alexis for a second before replying to Brug. "Can we talk? Something isn't right."

Brug puts his hand on her shoulder. "Stop being paranoid. Everything is good. Alexis has your back. I know him and trust him. As soon as you hit the Kremlin, and I get to the base, everything will be on point. We got this!" He hugs her and kisses her cheek. "Besides, you're the toughest bitch I know."

He turns and walks out of the hangar to the first jet, where Asher stands waiting. He points to the steps and Asher walks up and into the entrance. Brug follows and the pilot closes the door.

Crow walks over to Alexis and grabs a bag off the ground. She looks at Alexis. "When are we taking off?"

Alexis shrugs. "Within the hour. Your brother needs to get to the air base before the others. Did you get the schematics of the building?"

"Yes, and they have been loaded into Sun and the other SCZs as well. Sun and I need to be able to get to the complex section that the president lives in. We also need the troops inside the main wall. Sun and I can maneuver more quickly alone. The troops need to take the rest of the complex and lock it down." She puts the bag on her back and starts walking to the plane.

Alexis pulls a phone out and makes a call. After a ring the other side picks up. "Azazil, it's Grim. Where are we with the Russian president?"

Azazil on the other end responds. "He has agreed to cooperate, and anyone planning action against him must be detained."

"Understood." Alexis hangs up and puts a headset on. "SCZ Troop Two! Exit the plane and surround Crow. She is now a threat!"

As Crow walks toward the plane, the SCZ troops start to exit with weapons in hand. Sun exits last and joins the twenty soldiers surrounding her. She stands with her arms out wondering what's going on. She turns to see Alexis with the headset on.

"Do you really think I am the type to be used as a pawn? My brother didn't believe me, but for some reason I knew. This plan has been so scattered and never made sense to me."

Arrogantly, Alexis puts his arms out and shrugs. "They wanted some of the more known criminals to be the face. These new troops capturing them and making major headlines can show how valuable the technology is. I get to profit in the background."

"So is this happening to my brother?" She shrugs the bag off of her shoulders.

"No! Once you are dead and boxed, he will only know what he is told. You didn't follow the plan and they had to take you out. We know you are the smart one."

She stretches her arms out and rolls her neck around to loosen up. "So are you going to just shoot me? Or do I get to make this interesting?"

"I highly doubt twenty-to-one odds are favorable! After talking with Azazil, I knew this part would be tricky. You are and always have been a psychological work of art. Soft and beautiful at one moment, and lethal the next. How can you kill something like that? However, it is what it is!"

She gives him a *fuck you* smile and laughs. "Twenty on two are great odds for me!"

He laughs. "Babe! Little brother is on a plane. It's just you!"

She smiles. "Come on, big boy. Help a girl out," she says in the sexiest voice she has.

Immediately Sun throws his arms out, displaying his blades, and decapitates the SCZs on each side of him. Crow pulls pistols from her back holsters and starts shooting the others in the head.

Alexis runs for cover and calls for his men to retaliate. The SCZ troops start to fire. Sun goes on the attack, kicking and swiping with the blades. Crow runs toward the jet and, as she gets to the belly, rolls under it. She turns and takes out two more soldiers. Sun is fighting with three in the open space.

She fires a shot and takes one out. With two left, Sun quickly takes them out with spin kicks and plunges his blades into their skulls. The blades retract and he takes a stance. Glancing to the plane, Sun sees Crow come out with pistols in hand. She stands next to Sun for a second looking for Alexis.

"Let's go!" She runs into the plane and Sun follows. A second later a gunshot is heard before a dead pilot is thrown out the door, the door closing behind him.

Crow jumps into the pilot's seat with Sun in the copilot's chair. They start the engines up and in a few moments they are ready for takeoff. She pulls back on the lever and the jet starts down the runway.

As it takes off, Alexis emerges from the hangar. He has a cell phone with him. He dials and after a few rings there is a click.

"Sun helped her! Somehow he reacted to her and the two of them took the jet. They killed my pilot."

Azazil answers on the other end. "How the fuck did this happen? Do we know where they are going?"

"Out of nowhere, Sun had his blades out and was attacking the other SCZs. I don't know where they are going. They took the jet," Alexis says nervously.

Azazil pauses. "Come to the air base. With the Russian president on board, we can start production and not waste any time."

"Yes sir!" Alexis hangs up and looks around for vehicles. He can see a pickup truck in the distance.

| | | | |

As the tarmac sits quiet and bodies lie on the ground, a small beat-up plane approaches and lands. It has a Polish flag and is rusted on the body. The door opens and Chase exits to the ground. He is alert once he sees the bodies on the ground.

Sabu and Bull exit the plane and they disperse. A bag sits on the ground. Chase rolls one of the bodies over, recognizing the face as a fellow troop from his convoy.

"Seagar, you motherfucker!" He rolls him back to look at the headgear and chip on the back of his neck. Chase then pulls his phone out and takes a picture of it, typing a message and sending it to Surge.

Is this what you found? This soldier is from my convoy!

Bull walks over, picking up the lone bag. "This bag has schematics of the Kremlin and information from Azazil."

Sabu looks at the decapitated bodies. He points to them. "This is Sun's work!"

Chase looks confused. "You said he was killed! Could Sun be one of these things? Why fight against the others? It makes no sense, especially if he was killed and turned into this experiment."

Bull looks around at the gun shells. "I think he was protecting Crow. I studied forensics, and if you look, the two are side by side with no heads. A space in between means that is who did it. The bag is centralized and must have been surrounded."

Chase is frustrated and annoyed. "This is getting worse as we go. Hopefully Surge and the others can get here soon. I don't know what to do next!"

"Contact the secretary of defense maybe. If Seagar is involved, then he has an agenda. We have to let the secretary know," Bull says.

Chase agrees and pulls his phone out. He messages Surge and notifies him that they need to meet up as soon as possible.

CHAPTER 16

Brug prepares on the jet as it approaches Kubinka Air Force Base. At the back of the plane are large metal chests full of semiautomatic weapons and grenade launchers. He gives instructions and the SCZ troops grab weapons from the chest. As they load up Brug is buzzed from the cockpit. He makes his way forward and checks in.

"We just got radio confirmation. Russian government is going to cooperate and work with the program. We are landing in a few minutes."

Brug is confused and wonders what is happening. He suddenly feels like his sister was right. He turns to go back to the cab of the plane. All of the SCZ troops are armed and ready, looking at him. The pilot speaks over the intercom again.

"Security! Please disarm the prisoner!"

Suddenly the rifles are aimed at him, and Asher approaches with shackles. Four SCZ troops take Brug's guns away and Asher places the shackles on his wrists and ankles. He has no options and there are too many troops to fight off. He sits and waits for landing.

| | | | |

As the jet approaches the Kubinka Air Base, Azazil and Velnias stand with several Russian military police and a high-ranking member of the Russian army.

"We have Brug in custody. Crow was able to get away, but we believe we can get her in custody very soon. We promised help and development in return for the use of this base," Azazil explains to the official.

In a strong accent, the official replies, "Yes! We will take Brug into custody. We'll need a team to hunt down Crow as soon as possible. We are impressed that your troops are so efficient."

Velnias starts to walk toward the main buildings. He pauses. "I would like to get started in my new lab."

The official graciously responds. "Yes, the facility is all yours."

Velnias disappears from the dark hangar and into a large building.

"We can build an excellent army for you and develop the resources to use them after death. General Seagar will be here soon to finalize the US portion of this deal. Do we expect any issues from the International Military Security Council?" Azazil pulls on his beard.

The official shakes his head. "No! There will be no problems. They are focused on establishing new international protocols for dealing with war criminals. Trial procedures and a united group like Interpol."

The jet lands and pulls toward the hangar they stand at. All SCZ troops stand from their seats with rifles ready. They motion to Brug to get up and exit the plane. He is not happy and now understands why they wanted to divide him from his sister as he walks down the steps to see Azazil and the Russian official waiting for him.

"You are now being handed over to Russian custody

for planning an attack with your sister on Russian soil." Azazil smiles and points to the Russian officers. The SCZ troops guide him over to the Russian officers.

"Pawns! Nothing but pawns the whole time!" Brug spits out and grumbles. "Where is my sister?"

Azazil chuckles. "On the run! But she won't get far. We have SCZ troops in many places. We have been developing these troops and other experiments for quite a while. In order to get the Russians on board, they wanted major arms dealers like you and your sister out of the way. Capturing you was a major part of the agreement."

Brug spits at the ground but gets punched in the stomach and hauled away by the Russian officers.

A second jet lands on the runway. As it pulls to a stop, the door unlatches and the metal stairs roll to the open door. General Seagar appears with an unlit cigar in his teeth with a smile.

"Gentlemen! It is so nice to see you again." He walks down the steps with an arrogant strut.

Azazil walks toward the steps and greets Seagar as he walks down. They shake hands and the Russian official greets him with a handshake.

Seagar looks at both the Russian official and Azazil. "I have news. An unexpected issue. My experimental soldiers have gone rogue! Split up into two teams." He lights his cigar.

Azazil looks displeased. "What do you mean rogue? We needed them under surveillance at all times."

"All six did not go to the castle as I instructed. Three stayed on the plane. They're trying to get to Smolensk. When my officers tried to bring them back to our facility, they shot up the plane and jumped near Kraków." Seagar puffs on his cigar, not worried about what he is sharing.

Azazil looks at Seagar, angered. "Why did you not let me know earlier?"

"I just got all of the details. Besides, I have a feeling this can give you the chance to really test the troops. Which is the whole reason for this first phase of the operation anyway. Troubleshoot and problem-solve, right?"

Azazil understands what he is saying and feels the need to share his news. "Crow got away."

General Seagar suddenly looks displeased as he puffs on his cigar. He raises his hands. "How did that happen? You had a full group with her! What the hell happened?"

Azazil turns to the Russian official. "Sir! I already filled you in on this. If you don't need anything else from us, feel free to go if you need to."

The official nods in agreement. "That is fine. Please keep me informed on when Crow will be apprehended. The IMSC will be interested in that as well as the soldiers. We need to have all details in line."

Seagar and Azazil shake his hand and he leaves in a black sedan with tinted windows.

Azazil looks at Seagar. "Let's talk in the plane. Somehow Sun helped Crow escape. That part I did not want them to know."

Seagar looks at him. "I thought Sun was programmed? Under full control with the chip."

"Sun was able to react to Crow's request for help. She had mentioned at the castle she noticed him look at her briefly," Azazil explains with concern.

Seagar motions for Azazil to come onto the plane. He follows and Seagar continues his questions. "Sun still has an ability to think on his own? Even with the chip and the control it should have?"

Azazil responds while they walk up the stairs. "It should not be the case, but he acted without a direct order. Yes, they are programmed with the skills they had when alive, but the fact that Sun attacked the other SCZ troops without a direct order seems like he has put Crow in a hierarchy."

"Well, that is a concern. But I do have a surprise for Velnias!" They enter the plane and Azazil finds Dr. Peck unconscious in his wheelchair.

Azazil laughs out load and nods his head. "I like your style, General. Bringing the doctor with you is just ruthless. Creative! Opens the door for a lot of possibilities."

"You think Velnias will appreciate it?" Seagar keeps puffing away, smugly.

Azazil laughs even louder. "Oh, I think he will love this! Like I said, it opens up possibilities. I think we need to get moving on finding Crow and your soldiers. As soon as Bautista arrives, we will send him and Grim out in groups to hunt them down."

Seagar agrees and pours Azazil a drink of expensive scotch. Azazil smiles and takes the glass from him. Dr. Peck sits in the chair, still unconscious. Seagar walks over to his files and flips them open.

"The International Military Security Council is the only concern I have. They are looking to establish an Interpol version in the military. Like our Russian friend stated, we need all details in line. Now that both programs are operational, we can start putting them together. Both my government and the Russian government have full intentions of having our soldiers work for us in any state. The main form of making money will be on the black market."

Azazil takes a long sip of his drink and looks at Seagar. "When I first joined the Romanian army, all I wanted to do was fight and represent my country. As I moved up the ranks, I started to see I had to look out for me, and I did. I had to do things I never thought I would do, but I did them. Now it's about changing the world, my way and his way. I don't care if the world burns, as long as I have a view to watch it."

Seagar pours some more scotch. "You will and so will I, and over time, we will build our countries the way we see fit. In alliance!" He gulps his drink in a quick shot.

There is the sound of a large transport truck pulling in, and when Azazil checks out a window, he sees that Bautista has arrived. "Good, the shipment is here." He puts his glass down and makes his way outside.

Bautista jumps out of the transport cab and slams the door closed. "I thought this place would be crazier!"

Azazil approaches him. "We changed plans! I need the truck pulled into that hangar and all major doors shut down. Then you and Alexis will be given teams to go hunting. We need some individuals hunted down and brought to us."

"Hunted? I'm in the mood to hunt. I have a little hunting of my own I would like to do." Bautista stretches out his arms and trimmed muscles.

Azazil replies with curiosity, "Who might that be?"

"The American asshole who shot my brother. The job in Turkey on the convoy was a bad idea from the beginning. I never understood why his team took it. Is Grim coming here?" Bautista remarks with anger.

"Get the truck in the hangar and set up a meeting with Grim. We have to find these people soon. Especially Crow," Azazil orders. "I have no time for resentments!"

"Yes sir!" Bautista jumps back in the truck and pulls it into the quiet hangar. A few Russian soldiers close the door behind him.

Seagar walks out of the jet and down the steps. Azazil looks at him. "You may want to stay on the jet."

"I heard him from inside the plane. His brother charged at me. He is lucky I made it quick."

"Well! I'm sending him to meet with Alexis. They will take two teams and hunt down all of them. I think I will send Asher as well, as insurance. Now, shall we take Dr. Peck to his new host?"

Seagar grins and blows a smoke ring. "Hell yes! Have some fun with this."

| | | | |

Velnias stands in a large operating room with dozens of operating tables set up. His two assistants Nash and Kolinko stand to the side, still with no movement. Velnias moves around making sure that all the stations have what they need. A Russian soldier walks in and gets Velnias's attention.

"Pardon me, sir. The truck shipment is here. Twenty doctors, and the rest are male soldiers. Ready for processing."

Velnias acknowledges him and turns back to his tables. As he preps the stations Azazil walks in.

"Is everything as needed?" Azazil asks.

Velnias turns to him. "It is functional. Getting things started is very important. We have no time to waste."

Azazil responds, "We have something for you. *General Seagar* has something for you."

Velnias waves his hand in annoyance and speaks up. "No! No! I don't want anything. Just let me work!"

Azazil takes a second to stop him. "Sir, you want to see this. It is Dr. Peck from Seagar's program. Seagar brought him here as well."

Velnias is quiet, looking at Azazil. He starts to walk around. "Did he come willing or unwilling?"

"He was knocked out with a tranquilizer. Unknowingly," Azazil says arrogantly with a smile.

Velnias starts rubbing his burnt hands. He walks over to a small mirror on one of the tables. He picks it up and looks at himself. His image is reflected back at him. Anger sits in his eyes. "Bring him! Let me see him."

Azazil turns and motions for the two men with him to bring Dr. Peck in. A moment later they wheel him in, still unconscious, the tranquilizer starting to wear off as little movements in his fingers occur. He takes in a deep breath as he shifts his head. He groans briefly, putting his hand to his head.

Velnias acknowledges him. "Welcome! I'm guessing you have a headache."

Dr. Peck looks up to see the hooded man in front of him. He squints his eyes to get them to focus. "Where am I?"

Velnias paces back and forth, pondering what to say. "It has been so long. So long since we have been in the same room."

Dr. Peck, still feeling the effects of the tranquilizer, is confused and can't figure out who the hooded man is. "Where am I?" he asks again, his voice rough.

Velnias gets frustrated. "You don't know me, do you? You can't figure it out? Do you have any idea how that makes me feel? It is upsetting and angering, and all I wanted was for you to see me and accept me for who I am." He pulls his hood back, showing his full face and head. He puts his hands up for the doctor to see the scars, walking forward and kneeling to get close. "Look into my eyes, deep like a father looks into his son's eyes."

Dr. Peck looks deep into Velnias's eyes. He starts to see who he is—his own son kneeling before him. "It can't be! Lukas?"

Velnias gets up. "Yes! Yes, Dad! I'm the flesh and

blood that came from you. The pride and joy of the Peck name! I go by the name Velnias. I am the Devil, and I have taken what you developed and created something greater." He stops and stares at the doctor.

The doctor keeps looking at his son in shock and disbelief, not knowing what to do or say. He lowers his head and tears fall from his eyes. He is happy to know his son is alive, but to know that his son is behind this is heartbreaking. He looks up again and stares at his son once more.

Velnias points to the man standing behind the wheel-chair. Dr. Peck then feels a needle in his neck. Suddenly he feels weak and the room turns black.

CHAPTER 17

A young man runs along a sidewalk while breathing heavily. Every few blocks he stops to catch his breath. The more he runs, the more he coughs and spits up crap from his throat. He is not out of shape, but he is so late that he has to run as hard as he can.

The sixteen-year-old can see the building he is running to. He needs to get to the back of the building and up the ramp to the back entrance. He was scheduled to be there at 6:00 p.m. but it's 6:20 p.m.

He checks his tuxedo pants, black shirt ,and black vest. His tie is a bit crooked. He starts running again. Sweat drips down his forehead as he runs. He bolts across the street, aiming for the entry that leads to the back. A car honks and screeches to a halt as he dodges it. He gets through the opening and turns the corner. At the top of the ramp waits a beautiful woman.

"It is about time you got here. I hope you don't stink like a gym!" the woman shouts.

"Sorry, Mom! I got held up!" he yells back with a deep breath. He runs up the ramp and stops adjusting his vest and tie, brushing off his pants. With wide eyes he looks at his mother with a smile, feeling bad about being late.

"I'm really sorry, Mom. I just lost track of time. I should

have left earlier." He shakes his head and pins her with sorry eyes.

She smiles and chuckles. "Oh baby, you are on time. I told you a half hour early so you would be on time. I know my son better than you think."

His mouth opens. "Seriously, Mom?" He pauses and thinks for a moment. "Moms really are brilliant." He shakes his head and opens the big metal door to the inside.

They enter a big kitchen with staff running around frantically. Appetizer trays are on a table next to the prep lines ready to go. The mom walks over and starts checking them. She looks up and waves her son over.

"All I need is for you to keep up the appetizer passing for a few hours. I knew I would be short-staffed, and this event may be good for you to see." She hands him a tray.

"Why do you think that?" he says, puzzled.

With a big smile, she responds. "Because it's a military event honoring veteran soldiers and the medals they have earned. The guy I am dating is a recruiter and he wanted to meet you. We have been talking about how he could help you get some structure."

"You want me to join the army?" he asks, frustrated.

"No, honey, but he has access to programs that you may be interested in. I would rather see you cause chaos in a legal way. He goes by Seagar. He is over near the bar chewing on a cigar. He loves shrimp, so take these to him and talk to him."

He takes the tray and gives a small huff under his breath. He stands for a second and looks at her. "I will for you, Mom, but I get the final choice. Deal?" He looks into her eyes and smirks.

She smirks back and nods her head. "Yeah! That's a deal."

He smiles and leaves the kitchen, heading into the main party room. As he walks into the room, he stops and starts to look around. He scans the room for the bar and the cigar she mentioned. He spots Seagar walking toward the balcony and quickly makes his way over to him. He follows Seagar out the glass double doors to a balcony that overlooks the main downtown strip, the Washington Monument in the distance.

Seagar stands with his scotch and puts his sunglasses on. The young man walks over and puts the tray forward, offering him an appetizer.

"You must be Chase. Your mother wants us talking. She has the idea I can help your troubled ass out." He turns his head and looks at him while sipping his scotch. "What do you think, Chase?"

Chase shrugs. "I don't know if anyone can help me. Especially you! Why would I listen to you? I'm not a fan of authority."

Seagar grins and starts to laugh. "Because you get the ability to shoot shit 'legally'!" he replies, using his hands to make quotation marks as he says legally.

"Why did you say it that way?" Chase asks curiously.

"The military has many gray areas. As I move my way through the ranks, I will have to manipulate and maneuver my way to promotions. Opportunity is all around us; you take it when you can. I may be in recruiting now, but I plan to be general. I know I will be general." Seagar sips his scotch.

"So how does that help me? What do I have to do? What can I do to change things for myself? I get into fights, steal shit, and cause trouble. School sucks, and I would rather be outside doing things."

Seagar looks at him. "We have a program for teenagers like you. It is like a pre–boot camp for troubled teens. Your mother already talked to me about putting you in it. We have talked about it for a few weeks now."

Chase looks at him, puzzled, and with a little attitude. "How do you know my mom? What are your intentions toward her?"

"I have been dating your mother for a few months now. Not

that you have noticed, with all your disappearing and trouble-making. Basically, you have a choice. You join my program and start life in the military, or you stay gone." Seagar finishes the scotch in his glass, placing it on a side table before walking away.

Chase wakes up suddenly sitting in the plane seat. He remembers the process that got him into the military in the beginning. Seagar dating his mom, recruiting him into the teens program. He has been manipulating Chase's whole life. Chase rubs his face as he swears under his breath. Bull notices it and moves over to the seat across from him. His weapons are detached so he can sit comfortably.

"You good, bro? You were a little vocal while you were resting."

"Must be nice being able to detach from that shit. How are you dealing with all of this shit?" Chase takes a drink from his water bottle.

Bull sits looking forward, thinking for a second. "How the hell did I get here? Why me? I sometimes wonder if I am going to wake up and all this metal won't exist. Reality is that the metal allowing me to walk and do what I can is real. I saved people and this is my reward." He pauses. "Based on your mumbling, I am guessing you and Seagar go far back."

Chase turns and looks at Bull. "I never wanted to tell the team that he was dating my mom when I was recruit-ed. He will use anyone to get what he wants. The man has no conscience. He used my mom and used me. In the beginning I had no choice, because he got into Mom's head and convinced her I needed to go to the military grooming program. I am glad I did, but everything later seemed planned out and I couldn't see it."

"If I remember, I only met him once, and that was

after his presentation at the university when I was studying chemical engineering. I joined the military after that. Figured I could do some good with my knowledge. Sounds like you have some deep-rooted issues with him." Bull looks over at him. "If you have anything you think I need to know, please fucking tell me!"

Chase looks back and nods to him. "I promise, and as soon as we connect back with Surge and the others, we can go over everything."

Boris walks back to them from the cockpit. "My pilot needs to get back to Kraków soon. What's the plan?"

Chase looks up at Boris and thinks for a second. "If Surge and the others cannot get out of Romania, we can't get back to the base in Greece." He stops and starts thinking. "We either have to go get them or all meet back in Kraków. Meeting back in Kraków is faster."

Bull interrupts him. "Why would we go back to Greece? If we are on the run now because of Seagar, that would be like going back into the hornet's nest. Not to mention the fact that Crow and someone are on the run, just like us! Something is not adding up, because we just went from going after terrorists to being in the same position they are in." Bull shakes his head in disgust.

Sabu walks down the aisle to jump into the conversation. "Pawns!" he says quickly. "What if Crow and her brother and Sun were all used as pawns for a greater purpose? Even I didn't expect Azazil to put a knife in his heart. Sun was exasperating and a handful, but he was good at what he did. Killing him was planned and not a reaction. I remember they took his body immediately. Why not leave it if he was expendable? Pawns! We need to go back to Kraków, meet the others there. If Crow wants answers, she should go back to Kraków."

Chase nods his head and agrees. "I'll message Surge,

but if they cannot get out of Romania, we will need to get them out."

Bull shakes his head. "What about these things being created? They clearly have some plan for them. If Seagar is going out of his way to throw us to the wolves, he has an agenda. It is not looking good for us if he does."

Chase puts his hand on Bull's shoulder. "We will figure it out, and I think Kraków will give us the answers. I will message Surge now with the change. Even if it takes longer for us to get to them, we need them. Now that we have the bag and the evidence from those bodies, maybe we can tie things together, especially if we find Crow. Boris! Tell the pilot we need to do a pickup in Romania!"

Boris nods and heads back to the cockpit. Chase buckles in and so do Bull and Sabu. Chase then sends a message to Surge and gets comfortable.

CHAPTER 18

Brug hangs shackled to a brick wall in a dark room. Chains run from his ankles and his wrists to the wall, holding him out in a star pattern. It is a small, dark, cold cell with two lightbulbs dangling from the ceiling side by side. A damp smell fills the air as he hangs from the wall vulnerable. He is groggy and in the early stages of waking from the sedative they gave him. Two SCZ troops stand on each side of him with automatic rifles fully loaded.

The metal door opens, and Azazil and Velnias walk in. They observe him from afar waiting to see if he wakes up. Velnias approaches Brug and starts examining him closely. He starts looking closely at his limbs and then starts looking at his head.

Velnias takes a deep breath in satisfaction. "A perfect specimen for this next phase. When will the other techs arrive?" He turns and looks at Azazil.

Azazil quickly answers. "Seagar confirmed the Greece base is being shut down. Majority of the staff are being sent home; the security detail and certain officers and agents are being diverted to here as well. All movement is under Seagar's orders and is under special operations top-secret clearance. Only the secretary of defense has access to the program's information. The secretary thinks this is linked with the development of the VA PTSD research program. With Seagar's skills at manipulation of things and people, we have open doors and options."

Velnias turns toward Azazil and starts rubbing his hands together. "I want to start on Brug as soon as possible. The chip programming first, then we can go to the upgrading. Make sure Alexis has as many troops as he needs to bring Crow and Sun to us. We do not know how these soldiers from Seagar's amputation program will interfere."

Azazil pulls a cell phone out and starts scrolling through messages. "Tracking shows the jet that Crow took is headed back to Kraków. Realistically, if they enter the air space without permission, they will probably get shot down. Crow has connections in Belarus to help them fly through the Belarussian air space, but Poland air space may be different. We have to be prepared for anything from her."

Velnias moves slowly around Brug, looking at his limbs. "We need her to understand that it doesn't matter what she does, her brother belongs to me now. When I am done with Brug, she will not recognize him. She has protected him all her life, as he has protected her. They would do anything for each other. Alexis needs to make sure she understands the severity of the situation. As of now, I will start the process I have planned for Brug. Do we know anything about what has happened with our decoy? Have we found her? Is she still moving?"

"We don't know yet what she is doing. Alexis will have Bautista track her while they are in Kraków. She left the suite, and the tracker in her head assembly shows her moving rapidly all over the city. She has attacked and eaten the flesh of numerous civilians." Azazil types out a message.

Velnias examines Brug closely. His plans for Brug are

quite extreme and insidious. Suddenly Brug's eyes open, and they look at each other in an intense stare-down. The pair is sizing each other up as they look at each other for a moment. Brug, still groggy from the sedatives, moves his head around. He groans and looks at Velnias with anger for what he has done.

"Where is my sister?" he gets out in a weak voice.

Velnias grins back at him smugly. "As I expected, her skills exceeded expectations, which means we do not know where she is. I will say I was surprised that Sun was part of her escape. How he is cognitively making his own choices and overriding the chip is quite amazing." Velnias takes a struggled breath.

Brug looks at him confused, as he still feels groggy. He wonders how it is possible that Sun is able to do so. Velnias regains his breath and continues his thought. "As my research has developed and I meet my new experiments, the more I enjoy pushing the boundaries. Which is what I am about to do with you. All of this has been to develop the best technology with the best specimen. I am going to enjoy this so much." Velnias pulls out a syringe and removes the cap. "Back to sleep you go!" He sticks it in Brug's neck, sending him into unconsciousness.

| | | | |

The sky is clear as the jet flies swiftly over Belarus. Crow and Sun sit in the cockpit in silence. Crow, still processing the situation, starts to feel an uncomfortable and nauseous feeling in the pit of her stomach. She does not know what happened or why. She needs to be able to communicate better with Sun to get some answers in order to trust him and know why he helped her. *If he is dead and has been programmed, why do what he did?*

She looks at Sun and slaps his shoulder. "I need to get some answers from you. We need to figure out some way to talk. I don't even know if I can trust you. You helped me get away, but why?"

Sun looks at her and nods his head. His face stays the same with no emotion coming through. He motions with his hands in a writing action. She looks around the cockpit for a notepad and pen. A backpack sits in the corner. She hops out of the pilot's seat and grabs it.

As she looks through the backpack, she finds a handgun, a Russian passport from the original pilot, and a notebook. A marker pokes out of a side pocket. She grabs the marker and the notebook and turns to Sun. As she hands it to him, he looks up at her. She can see frustration in his eyes. He starts writing on a page from the book and shows her.

Do dick pic drawings count?

Crow shakes her head. "What the fuck have I started?" She looks at him seriously and starts to chuckle. "Can we first get the serious shit out of the way? Can you remember anything from before?"

Sun starts writing and lifts the page up. *Not a lot! Everything went black at the suite. Then standing in a dark room. A big window in front of me.*

She thinks for a minute. "Did something change when you saw me?"

He starts writing again and raises the page. *Flashbacks!* He starts writing more. *Seeing me teaching you jiu-jitsu as a teenager. When we met, and quick flashes of us.*

"Can you remember anything else from the castle?" she asks, wanting to know so much more. She looks at him intensely, hopeful to jog his memory more.

He writes out more, then pauses. He looks at her and looks back at the page. *There was never a plan to attack the*

Kremlin or assassinate the Russian leaders. They wanted to separate you and your brother. Sun's eyes suddenly show sadness in a small way. He knows more than he is telling her. *They have him!* he writes.

She looks at Sun, not sure what to say. "Why? What are they going to do?"

Sun does not want to write the word, but he knows he has to. *Experiments! Like me, like them!* He pauses, then clarifies who *them* is. *Seagar's AMPD program.*

Crow gets angry seeing that. "We were pawns?" She looks forward as her anger and frustration build. "Son of a bitch!"

Looking out the window and checking the gauges, Crow then says, "We are about to enter Poland, so this could get interesting." She takes the autopilot off and starts to descend to a lower altitude. The radio crackles and a Polish voice requests the jet's heading.

Sun starts writing in the notepad and puts it up for Crow.

We gonna die? He puts the notepad down and writes some more as Crow shakes her head, focused on controlling the plane. He taps her on the shoulder and lifts the notepad up. *I already did that once!*

She starts to laugh and looks at him before raising her hand and flipping her middle finger up at him. "You are one of a kind, Sun!"

A small twitch of his cheek indicates an attempt to smile. He writes another note in the notepad. *I may be dead, but I'm still the asshole you know and love!*

Crow smiles and nods her head in agreement. "Yes! You are an asshole! Thank you." She puts her hand up in a fist toward him. Sun looks at the fist and looks at her, realizing and processing that she trusts him. He returns the favor with his own fist and completes the fist-bump.

As all of this occurs, the radio still crackles with the

request for a destination. As Crow struggles to think of what to say, Sun flips through the notebook to the front. On the third page he finds an itinerary list for the next three days. On the list is a flight for Kraków and a flight number. He slaps her shoulder like she did to him earlier. She looks at him and mouths silently, *What the fuck?* He looks at her with a blank stare and hands her the book showing flight 962 for Kraków on tomorrow's date. She flips the microphone switch on.

"*Lot dziewiec-szesc-dwa do Krakowa!*" she says in rough Polish. She tries again but in English. "Flight nine-six-two for Kraków!" There is a pause over the radio.

The radio crackles and a voice speaks out. "We can continue in English. We don't have you flying in till tomorrow on the flight plan manifests."

Crow takes a breath and does what she does best, manipulates. "Yes! That should have been changed, and we only have two of us on the jet. We have to return it to Kraków before the next charter." She looks at the list and can see it is supposed to leave for Moscow tomorrow evening. "We may have to leave earlier than the evening flight to Moscow tomorrow."

"Okay! Maintain your heading to Kraków unless I instruct otherwise. Over!" The voice disappears. Crow flips a few switches and goes back to autopilot. She starts looking out into the sky. Under her breath, she voices, "I'm coming, brother."

CHAPTER 19

Surge, Kitch, and Salene sit in an abandoned house on the outer perimeter of Cluj-Napoca in Romania. It's a small house with dirt and garbage all over. A few single chairs sit around an old beat-up table. Holes are punched into the walls all over the house near the electrical outlets. Staying in the main farmlands makes it easier to hide. They have no idea if there are more soldiers searching for them. Surge pulls a tablet out of his bag and looks at Kitch. "We need to see what is on the flash drive."

Kitch walks over and pulls it from his pocket. "If I had more time I could have grabbed more. I was lucky to grab that and even see the headgear on the table."

Surge looks at him and starts thinking. "Those soldiers had headgear. The pieces are starting to come together for me."

He takes the flash drive and plugs it in. As the files upload, he looks at his cell phone to see a message from Chase letting him know they are coming for them. Surge types a message and sends it. "Chase and the others are going to come for us, then we are heading to Kraków."

Kitch sits down at the table Surge is sitting at. Salene

walks around listening to what Surge is figuring out. He opens a file named Recondite and several subfiles open up. One is labeled AMPD. He clicks on the file and all of his and Dr. Peck's research pops onto the screen. Details of the enhanced human growth hormone. Specifications of the nervous system connection to the mechanical port designed for the prosthetics. "This is all of our research! Everything we designed and experimented with is in here."

Salene walks over and looks at the screen. "How would they have this? How is that possible? This was a top-secret program that only the general would have access to."

Surge starts looking at other files discovering more information. "These are US Military programs in here. The PTSD program I worked on for a little while. It was designed to help war veterans with severe PTSD to work through the visions and episodes they would have. They developed a head device and programmed chip to input positive thoughts and memories into the brain to override the negative. It was very experimental. But I moved to Dr. Peck's work early on because he needed someone with experience with the nervous system."

"So the device they were developing is capable of stimulating a brain to operate a full body? Sounds like whatever was being done to the vets helped them to discover a way to program a brain. Maybe even a dead brain and control it." Salene grabs a chair and sits down with them at the table.

Surge looks at a few files before he responds to Salene. "The brain is comprised of four sections: occipital, parietal, temporal, and frontal lobes. The head device was designed to stimulate all four parts. If the brain and the nervous system are stimulated at the right levels, it may be possible. But it is clear they have found something that makes it work. Put that with the developments of the AMPD program, and who knows what they are creating. This could explain the bites and torn flesh from the victims in Kraków.."

Kitch suddenly jumps into the conversation. "Hold on! Are you saying the fate of the world could come down to hangry dead soldiers? Well damn, let's load up on candy bars!" He throws his hands up immaturely.

Salene rolls her eyes at him, shaking her head. "I'm sure that we need to look at this a little more strategically. Clearly, as soon as we get to Kraków, we need to find answers quickly. How will Chase and the others reach us?"

Surge keeps looking through the files as he replies to Salene. "They have found help from a few people from Kraków. One is a pilot with a plane. There is a small airport north of here. It is a few hours away, but small enough to avoid any trouble. I am messaging Chase right now. Baia Mare Airport. We should be able to arrive around the same time."

Salene gets up and goes to the rusted sink near the window. She tries the faucet to see if any water runs. Air runs through the pipes and a few clunks through the house sound off. She looks out the window to see a small military truck slowly driving in their direction. "There's a truck coming. We need to get out of here. If Seagar is working with the Plague, he has probably already told them where we are."

Kitch jumps up from his chair. "How about a diversion? You two get the truck ready and running. I can get that military truck to chase after me and give you a head start. It's better if they only know where one of us is than all three of us." He puts his arms up, shrugging his shoulders.

Salene nods in agreement. "He is right. I don't like splitting up, but if they are patrolling and looking, we need to get moving as undetected as possible. What do you plan on doing, Kitch?"

He looks out the window at the garage where the truck has just parked. "We need another vehicle. If I take the truck and run it south, the two of you can grab another vehicle and head to the airport north of here."

Surge looks at him and disagrees. "But if you take the truck, and they see you came from here, they will come and search this place. Salene and I will need to sneak out first, and hope we find a vehicle. You need to give us a five-minute head start to slip out the back way."

Kitch nods in agreement.

| | | | |

On the other end of the message, Chase receives the new location. "Boris, tell the pilot Baia Mare Airport! It is a small airport north of Cluj-Napoca. Surge and the others will be there in a few hours if they leave now. He is also sending me files to download and look at."

Bull opens his eyes from resting. "What is he sending you? They must have gotten something detailed if he is sending you files."

Chase looks at the first file, which details a PTSD program. "It looks like a veteran's program that developed PTSD experiments. Seems Seagar has been a busy bastard. If he is working with Velnias, then he must be taking all of the research our military develops and giving it to them."

Bull stretches his arms out and starts looking at his hands. "A man driven by greed and power will do pretty much anything. I am curious how that meshes with Azazil. The way Seagar manipulates, it would not surprise me if he was keeping things from him." Bull looks at Chase directly. "He did a number on you, I can see that. If that is how he works, the key may be to divide them, or pit them against each other."

Chase looks back at Bull, understanding what he is suggesting. "We need to expect the unexpected with him. We still have no idea who Velnias is or what they are capable of. We must be careful, especially with the more we learn. Perhaps we should look at Crow and Sun as allies."

Bull shakes his head in disagreement. "Until we find them, we have to look at them as an enemy. We don't even know what has happened to her brother. She is loyal to him, and he is loyal to her, no matter what. Bloodlines will trump anything else. We have to be cautious as we approach this."

Chase understands that point and nods. "Once we get Surge and the others, we need to have a plan for when we get to Kraków. I think we need to put you in the square, undercover, and it might be easier to keep you stationary. Sabu and I will try and find Crow and Sun as the others try to track down the flesh-eater. We need to be prepared for anything. We are not the only ones trying to find Crow and Sun. Something tells me we may see more of these things in Kraków. Based on these files, we may see some like us." Chase starts looking through the other files Surge sent him.

| | | | |

Back at the house, Kitch prepares to divert the search party.

He quietly exits the side door and scurries to the garage door. It has been about five minutes since Surge and Salene left and ran along the treeline. The garage door opens and makes a decent-sized screeching noise.

A second military truck driving by stops and two

soldiers hop out. They both have the headgear like the previous soldiers. Kitch jumps into the truck and cranks it up. The engine makes a decent noise as the headlights turn on and the two soldiers stop walking. Kitch flips the radio on as he and the soldiers stare down. After a small pause from the radio, a hard guitar riff starts to bellow into the truck as P.O.D.'s "Boom" starts. Kitch smiles in a devilish grin.

"Oh fuck yeah!" he says loudly. The soldiers raise the rifles they carry and Kitch hits the gas. The rear tires start to spin and he shifts it into gear. The truck takes off straight at the soldiers and they begin to unload multiple rounds into the truck. Kitch accelerates, running straight through the two soldiers. Their guns go flying into the air as their bodies are slammed by the front grill, before disappearing under the truck with a giant thud.

Kitch smiles and yells out a "BOOM!" He takes a sharp left and speeds off, checking the mirror. He can see the two military trucks turn around and make chase on him. He holds at his speed, letting them catch up. He bobs to the music, wanting them to chase as much as possible. As the song screams out lyrics, a large military assault vehicle with a large fifty-caliber turret joins the chase. Kitch looks in the mirror.

"Oh, fuck me! You had to ask!" he says while looking at the radio. The vehicle starts taking shots at the truck and Kitch speeds up. Now in survival mode, Kitch needs to try and lose them. He can see a dirt road ahead to his left.

He quickly takes the turn, sliding the truck, but gathers control. He hits the gas hard, but the assault vehicle follows and maintains ground. The fifty-cal fires several more rounds, nearly hitting the truck. Kitch notices a sign for a rock quarry and takes the right turn for it. He realizes he needs to do something drastic and has an idea.

Speeding up a bit more, he can see the giant quarry's edge ahead. *This may work or it might not, but a risk is needed.* As he gets close to the edge, he turns the wheel and starts to skid and slide. The truck slides toward the edge and he throws the driver-side door open to find the barrel of the fifty-cal.

The truck slides off the edge of the quarry and he leaps up, throwing his arms forward. His wings deploy and the machine guns in his arms start to unload rounds at the military vehicle. He pauses for a second and pulls his right pant leg up. A small compartment in his right calf opens and his right forearm clicks to it. He pulls his arm up and a miniature rocket is attached to his forearm. He takes aim and fires. In a matter of a few seconds the turret and the vehicle are blown to pieces. The other two trucks pull up and Kitch applies his thrusters to fly away from the quarry. But two shots hit his wings and he drops to a wooded area. A group of Romanian soldiers disappear into the woods after him.

| | | | |

As Kitch diverts the search party, Surge and Salene quietly make their way along the treeline. They start looking around and see a black SUV parked behind a farmhouse. They run over to the farmhouse, glancing at the main house. No lights on in the house as they check the doors on the truck. They are unlocked, which seems odd to them. Surge looks through the truck for keys and Salene looks inside the farmhouse.

The farmhouse does not look like a typical farmhouse. Salene can see a small office to her left. She looks in the office, finding a desk. She opens the top right drawer and finds the keys to the SUV. As she is about to close the drawer, she notices a folder with TOP SECRET on it. She pulls it out and opens it to see photos of her, Chase, Bull, Sabu, and Kitch. Files about all of their backgrounds. She takes the file and walks outside to look at the farm. No cows or farm animals in sight. She looks at Surge and tosses the keys to him. They jump into the vehicle and Surge cranks it up. He starts driving and thinks out loud.

"Why did that seem easy?"

She holds the file up and shakes her head. "Probably because all of this area is run by our fearless leader!" She starts looking through the file folder and finds her file on her military background, and files on her last mission. She shakes her head in disgust and anger. "He fucking lied! He knew about everything involved with the bomb run. I am like this because of Seagar!" She looks at another file with Bull. "Seagar was behind all of our accidents!"

Surge follows the dark road, noticing empty farm fields in the area. "Why are all the fields empty?" He looks to both sides but does not see anything. "They control this whole area, it seems. No one is around, and nothing is in the fields. Check the glove compartment."

Salene opens it to see an M9 pistol with two extra clips. A small wooden box sits in the back of the glove compartment. She opens it to see two Cuban cigars nicely protected. Everything Salene believed is suddenly crumbling in her mind. She had so much trust in Seagar and gave so much to what she thought was a real program.

"Can I even trust you?" she speaks out and looks at Surge.

"What? Yes! You can trust me! Everything the doctor and I have worked on was to develop hope and opportunity. Seagar saw the development of what we were working on and wanted to put together the program. The fact that this area is under so much of the Plague's control makes sense. Azazil and his Romanian connections, and Seagar and his connections. They could do anything with no detection, and who knows how many American soldiers could be in their possession in Russia." Surge shakes his head. "I am worried about what else we are going to find out." They keep driving into the darkness toward the airport.

CHAPTER 20

C row and Sun maintain the heading to the main airport outside of Kraków. Sun looks through the pilot's notebook and finds a small paper near the back. On the paper is a list of small air landing strips through Europe. He runs his finger over the list and sees a name for Kraków. He writes down the name of the air strip on a page.

Ladowisko! A small strip northeast of the city.

Crow nods. "I need the headings. Is it operational?"

Sun shakes his head and shows the list to her. They are all abandoned air strips that the pilot could use as last-minute emergency landings. She decides to lower her altitude and try to disappear from local radar. The less attention they get, the better for them. They are approaching Kraków quickly, so they should be able to find the strip.

The Polish man on the radio speaks out. "We just lost your location. Are you there? Do you have a mayday?" Crow flips the radio off and starts tracking her direction. Sun spots the landing strip in the distance to the left. She starts to pilot the plane in a large, swooping arc to get lined up with the strip. The weather is clear and does not cause any issues. She starts a good approach and looks at Sun for a second. "Do you remember how to land? I can't guarantee this!"

Sun looks at her and then writes another note. *I'm already dead! It's your fucking loss, toots!* He turns and looks straight out the cockpit window and puts his hands in his lap.

She looks at him for a second and then focuses back on the approach. "You really are an asshole! Even for a walking corpse, and that's probably the stiffest you ever got." She chuckles to herself.

Sun just sits looking straight and raises his left hand, flipping the middle finger to her. She doesn't respond, focusing instead on bringing the jet safely in. Taking off is a lot easier than landing.

Sun's mind is suddenly going through memories and files. Is it him or the headset? He puts his hand on her shoulder, and even with a blank face he nods to her in reassurance. She feels calmer and Sun takes the levers in front of him. They both feel linked to the jet and it starts to sail toward the landing strip. They start to pull up and she uses the pedals to line everything with the center. Using the throttle knob to lower the power, she brings the nose up a little as it gets closer to the runway. The speed is leveled out and Sun helps her control the approach. He then flips the switch for the landing gear.

"Oh shit, I almost forgot that!" She gets a bit flustered. Sun keeps one hand on the stick and grabs a paper that sits on his lap. He holds it up for her to see. *We're gonna fuckin' DIE!!!!* it says. She tries to not laugh but can't help it.

Together they look forward and the wheels start to touch down on an empty runway. As all the wheels touch, they start to apply the brakes. A large shaking in the rear of the plane begins and she uses the pedals to control the steering. The plane veers to the right toward the grass. Realizing they have no true control of the plane, Crow pushes the black lever inward to kill the engine. She hits the pedals to go right, and as they hit the grass, Sun hits the switch to pull the landing gear up to dig the nose into the dirt. The ground is soft, so it works, but the speed pulls the tail up, flipping the plane upside down. Parts fly all over the place as a large, muddy skid runs through the grass.

No emergency crews rush to the crash, because the strip is abandoned. Crow and Sun sit strapped in the pilot's and copilot's seats. They are not saying anything and have no sense of urgency to get out of the plane.

Sun gives a thumbs-up, but it looks like its thumbs-down.

Crow scoffs. "Fuck off and get me out of this!"

Sun unbuckles himself as he puts his arm around the back of his seat above his head. He slowly slides himself out of his seat to the top of the cockpit. Off in the distance sirens start to scream into the air. Sun moves faster and gets under Crow. He prepares his arms as she unbuckles and drops out of the seat into Sun's arms. He catches her safely without issue. They pause for a second as he looks at her. He still has no facial expressions, but she can see in his eyes someone is there.

"Thanks!" she says, and he puts her down.

They grab everything they need from the cockpit, including the pilot's bag. They move into the main area of the plane, which is crumpled up and destroyed. Seats and debris are all over as the oxygen masks sit on the ceiling of the plane—the floor to them. Sun looks over at the door and starts to release it. Crow looks through the cab, seeing a military briefcase next to some of the oxygen masks. She goes and grabs it while Sun gets the hatch open.

Smoke billows in from a fire from the engine. He turns

and waves to Crow to get out. He hops down and looks around to see the source of the sirens. They can hear the sirens very closely. They realize a hospital must be nearby. The hospital will probably send an ambulance to the location. Crow hops out and looks around to get her directional bearings. She remembers seeing a large building with a helipad on the roof. Realizing it is a hospital, they run toward it with the intention to steal a car.

| | | | |

Detective Bosko drives an unmarked car to the crash location, somehow feeling like this has something to do with the murders in the city. He turns right onto an access road to the landing strip and can see the smoke in the distance. As he gets closer to the wreck, he can see debris and smoke but no one around. He stops the car close to the chaos but not next to it.

Pulling his pistol out of his holster and making his way slowly toward the plane, Bosko stops and stands on the runway to the left of the plane. On the opposite side the door is open. He takes a breath and runs around to the other side with the pistol forward and ready.

He stops and points to the door. "Is anyone inside?" he yells out. There is no response from the plane. An ambulance rushes up and comes to a quick stop behind him. He walks forward and looks through the fire and smoke, lowering his gun and looking around, seeing no one. The fire trucks pull up and they start spraying water on the fire.

The detective starts to look around the crash area and notices footprints. They head in the direction of the wooded area near the hospital. He keeps the gun in his hand and starts to follow the prints.

A few police cruisers pull up to the crash site. Officers

jump out and start to follow the detective. He puts his hand up for them to stop, pointing at one of them to follow him. He signals to the others to go investigate the crash. He stays silent because he does not want to be heard. The officer follows and pulls his gun from his holster.

They approach the treeline and the footprints enter into the woods. The detective turns to the officer. "Stay behind me and watch my back. We don't know who we may be dealing with," he says quietly.

| | | | |

Crow and Sun rush through the woods toward the parking lot. Crow carries the military briefcase with her. It has a large touchpad lock and is pretty heavy. Sun stops and looks at her and the case. He raises his hands, questioning why she is bringing it. She looks back and nods.

"I know it's slowing us down, but we need to know what is in it. This could be leverage for us against Azazil and Velnias. We need an SUV!"

Sun puts his hand up to convey to her to wait here. They reach the edge of the parking lot, which is not extremely full. He rushes out of the woods in the lot and starts looking as he rushes into a somewhat-filled section. He notices a black SUV and glances in the window. He pauses for a second and closes his eyes. Suddenly he can remember all the steps to hot-wire a car. Like a flashback in his head, he can see all of it.

The doors are locked, and at the touch, the alarm goes off. He pauses and starts breaking windows on other cars all scattered in the parking lot. Suddenly ten car alarms are going off with broken windows. He then runs all the way to the far corner of the lot and looks to see a few cars and SUVs. He looks at the oldest and most beat-up one and can see it is unlocked. He tries the door and it opens with no alarm. Getting in, Sun starts to hot-wire the car under the steering column. The SUV fires up and he drives it over to the edge of the parking lot where Crow is waiting.

Crow grabs the case and rushes over to the back door to put the case in. She jumps into the passenger seat and Sun drives off. Car alarms continue to make noise as people start to walk out into the lot checking to see if it is their car.

| | | | |

The detective and the officer emerge from another section of the woods into the parking lot. Crow and Sun are gone, and all that is left is more chaos. The detective walks toward a large group of people checking vehicles.

He approaches a woman looking at her car with a smashed side window. He looks over at a man two cars down with the same. The cars between have no damage and no signs of entry. The other damaged cars are all scattered throughout the lot. He turns around to see if any empty spots stand out. He can see an open spot on the far side of the parking lot. It stands out because it is the only empty spot in a full employee parking lot. He walks over to check the space and see what is on the ground. A small group of older vehicles are there with cigarette butts inside and staff parking stickers in the windshields' corners. He smiles and shakes his head to himself. The other officer walks over and looks at him.

"Sir, what are you smiling about?"

The detective looks at him and keeps shaking his head. "This is how you know you are dealing with professionals. The individual goes to all the expensive and highly secure vehicles. Sets off all those alarms as a diversion. Then comes back here to where the lower-level staff park."

The officer looks at Bosko, puzzled. "But why would they do that?"

Bosko motions for the officer to follow him. He points into the other cars. "Cigarette butts, and unlocked cars. Only place you can go and smoke a quick cigarette on the grounds without being seen. Doors unlocked to be even quicker because no one wants these cars for any reason. Lastly, staff have automatic sensors to let them in and out of the parking deck without paying each time. Quick exit and no dealing with anyone. Go check the security desk and see if they have video of this section. Check the last twenty minutes of video for the staff exit. We need to see who was here." His phone buzzes and a message from Chase comes through.

We will be arriving today back from Romania.

Bosko types a message back.

Land at the closed air strip I suggested. There is a crash site that you need to see.

Chase responds with a simple okay. Bosko walks toward the hospital to check the video.

| | | | |

Alexis Grim and a large plane approach the landing strip where the crash is. The pilot notifies Alexis of the smoke and emergency lights over the PA system. Alexis walks up to the cockpit to see for himself and spots the smoke.

"Change to land at the Aeroclub Krakowski. Give this flight information upon approach." He hands the pilot a paper with a flight and cargo number. "Tell them you are experiencing an issue and ask if we can land on that strip." Most emergency landings must be accommodated.

The pilot nods and starts to radio the aeroclub the information. Alexis knows this and plans accordingly. He goes to the back of the plane, where all the soldiers stand in large cargo containers with them strapped in place. Bautista sits to the side on his own reading through files. Alexis walks over to look at them. "What files are those?"

Bautista closes the folder and looks up at Alexis. "The breakdown from my brother's mission when he got shot. So many gaps in the story. I don't understand what his group was doing in the first place. I had not heard from him in months, and then we get word he was shot in the head on an attack mission on a convoy. There is nothing about why the convoy was the target." Bautista is angry and frustrated.

Alexis grabs the file from him. "I don't know where you got the file from, but you have other things to focus on. Not this!" He starts to walk away from Bautista, but Bautista grabs his arm.

"Have you ever lost your brother? Your best friend? Someone you care about? I just want to know what happened." He looks into Alexis's eyes with agitation.

Alexis pulls his arm away and stands firm in front of Bautista. "I get it, but we have a job to do and I need you focused on that. All I know about it is some guy named Chase was the man in charge of the convoy. As far as I know, he will be in Kraków. Maybe you will get some answers. Maybe he is the one who killed your brother. Let's track this woman down and get Crow and Sun back to Russia."

Bautista agrees and sits back down in his seat. "Am I going on my own or do I have a few SCZ troops with me?"

Alexis puts the file in his bag and turns back to Bautista. "I will give you three. They will be the advanced troops with the prosthetics. If you do run into any of the AMPD individuals, then you will have the troops with you. They are programmed for orders from me and you." He walks off to a separate area of the plane.

A satellite phone case sits against the wall. He grabs it and sets it up to call out. He dials a call and Seagar is on the other line. "My guy is asking about his brother. I told him Chase was involved to get him refocused. You may need some more information to keep him in line. It's messing with his head a lot."

There is a pause over the phone as Seagar thinks for a second. "Let's see how this plays out. If we need to headband him like his brother was supposed to be, then that is what we will do."

Alexis nods his head as he listens. "Yes sir! We are about to land; I will be in touch."

He hangs up the phone and puts the case back against the wall. He starts looking at the troops standing in the secure containers, all lined up in a row like ice trays. He looks at the faces and the eyes.

"Eyes on me!" The troops close to him turn their heads toward him. "Straight ahead!" The soldiers look forward. "These things are going to change my black-market business for sure." He laughs as he walks back to the cockpit for landing.

CHAPTER 21

Dr. Peck opens his eyes and finds himself sitting in his wheelchair back in his operating room at the Greek facility. Surge stands at the sink off to his left washing his hands. On the table is a cadaver with a small generator next to it. Slim wires run from a small device that is hooked up to the generator. The wires are connected to the end of a freshly severed right arm.

Peck starts looking around and wondering if he is dreaming. He was just in Moscow, wasn't he? The sedatives must have him flashing back. This is from when they started the program. Surge still has his hand, and his amputation is what helped them learn how to bond the electrical computer nerve to a human nerve. As Peck looks around the room again, the door opens and his son Lukas walks in. He grabs the computer in the corner and rolls the whole cart over to the right-arm connection.

"Father! What level of charge do you want to start with?" He connects the USB from the computer to the small device. On the screen is a full data display that allows him to apply a charge to the nerves and muscles. The doctor just sits without saying anything. This has to be a bad dream, but he remembers this day. It was the first time they had success without frying the human tissue and nerves. They saw that if they created a port to connect to the body, they could develop the prosthetics to be compatible to the port. He also remembers fighting with Lukas and arguing over the information. It was a few hours later and Surge agreed with the doctor that they had to keep the progress slow and gradual. They weren't to present this to the general yet.

Surge and Dr. Peck always seemed to be on the same page, while Lukas would be to the side holding his opinions. He built up a resentment toward both his father and Surge, and started to pull away, feeling like he didn't have a father.

Dr. Peck looks around again and can see Surge moving next to Lukas. He cannot hear them but can see the tension between them. The doctor starts to feel guilt and remorse for how he dealt with the past. Two days later Surge's accident happened, and Dr. Peck realizes Lukas disappeared around the same time. He shakes his head a few times and starts to wake up.

Another long blackout from the sedative they have been giving him. His wheelchair is chained to the brick wall behind him in a cold, dim room. A steel door is in front of him, and it has a small, sliding metal covering for the viewing window. He shakes his head a little more to gather his senses.

He looks around the dark concrete room and yells out, "What the hell are you doing to me? Where is my son? I want to speak to my son!" He gets his wits and senses clear. The little window on the door opens and two eyes look in. The door unlocks and Velnias enters, walking toward his father.

"You really want to call me *son*? You are not my father! Surge was more of a son to you than I was. You are a man who put his work ahead of his family. Seagar gave me more opportunity to grow and research and do what I wanted to do. He helped us disappear and push the research to where it should have been going—to expand the

PTSD program and how the brain can be revived as well as the muscles and nerves. The things I have just created and done are nothing you could have ever dreamed of. Or you ever wanted to dream of!" Velnias leans down and looks into his father's eyes. "I am not afraid to push the boundaries and unleash new possibilities. You always were!"

The doctor looks straight back at the burned and scarred face and throat of the man who is—or was—his son. "It isn't about being afraid, it is about knowing what boundaries not to cross. This was about developing hope and opportunity for those who needed and wanted it. From that, giving them a chance to continue to serve. Some of that changed along the way. What happened to the boy I raised? What have you become? We started this work to create hope and help people. Now you are creating destruction, chaos, and what seems to be true horror!"

Velnias laughs at that sentiment. "Horror? Look at my face! Hear my struggling voice! Horror happens in life. Unfair things happen in life and we adapt to the horror, push the limits because of the horror. I am choosing to give war a new name. A new face. If that face is horror, then that is what it is! Mother died in the fire in Dubai and I recreated her by pushing the boundary. It worked, and from her came programmable soldiers. Thanks to the PTSD program you did not want to tap into, the headgear worked. It was like the computer and the brain operating as one. All four lobes suddenly working with the data." Velnias begins to circle his father, feeling so proud of what he has done. "I am not God, but I am his vessel, his masterpiece!"

The doctor feels more saddened by what he is hearing. "Why are you keeping me like this? What good can come of you doing this? If you want to kill me, just kill me!"

Velnias sinisterly laughs loud. "Kill you! That is the furthest thing from what I want. I want your brain and I want what is inside you. Every person on this planet has memories and knowledge and skills. I want to push the limits even more and see if we can take knowledge from the brain. Why question someone and interrogate them when you can put the headgear on and take what you need? If I can put programming into the brain, maybe I can pull information out of it! Seagar wants the power; I just want to experiment and see how far I can go! I will tear apart hundreds of minds if it gets me closer to achieving it. Once I figure it out, I will put the device on you and take every thought, memory, and piece of knowledge you have. That is how I will pay you back. Till then, I have been playing and experimenting on Crow's brother. That has become a masterpiece of its own, I must say."

Dr. Peck slumps forward, emotionally destroyed by what he hears. "What have you done to him?"

Velnias turns and looks to the soldier standing at the door. He raises his hand, motioning it toward himself. "Bring him! I want the doctor to see with his eyes my creation. The creation for devastation!" The soldier leaves.

Dr. Peck coughs and clears his breathing. "This is crazy. You are crazy! I was not a good father; I can admit that. But I always taught you the boundaries of science and research. We started in order to help injured vets and maybe start helping the population. The military built it to what we do now. It was never about building weapons and armies." The doctor feels sick by what he is hearing. He wants to fix it but knows it is beyond fixing.

"You may be right! You were not a good father in the end. It was always about pushing boundaries for me. Seagar taught me to see that. He saw my potential and the ideas I had moving forward. I talked to him many times, away from you. He loved the idea and thoughts I had. It is why I left, to start working on all of this. Then the accident happened, and the boundaries were pushed even further. I wanted to see what I could do with Mom, so I tried the PTSD headgear on her and worked on slowly reviving the brain. Once we got her operational, we tested her with actions and implanting orders. We put her into Kraków as a decoy for Crow. We have been tracking her."

Azazil enters the room and approaches Velnias. "I come with news!" Azazil grins. "We just caught ourselves a new guinea pig—one with mechanical wings. Apparently, he was the distraction to help the others get away. My Romanian allies have him in custody. They will send him here. He thinks they are helping him by giving him transport to Seagar."

Dr. Peck looks up, feeling despair and powerlessness. "Not Kitchener! He is young and has his whole life ahead of him." In his mind he knows Chase and the others have no idea he is gone, or that the Greek base has been shut down. Things are going from bad to worse.

Azazil looks at the doctor with no sympathy at all. "He is a cog in our machine now, like many are. You truly don't know how far we have already reached with this. Soon we will be providing this technology and development to armies all around the world. Whether legal or not, we will change the world."

Velnias turns to the open door as a large upright table is wheeled in with a sheet covering it. "You asked about the brother. Well, I needed a strong and capable candidate for this. Pull the sheet away!"

The soldier removes the sheet to reveal a completely different Brug. The headgear is on him, and his whole body is completely torn apart and put back together.

Both legs are fully metal, as well as both arms. He is unconscious and not moving.

"He is what I wanted him to be," Velnias proclaims. "The experience he has, and knowledge, is adapted into his headgear. Our protocols and orders put into his head. A physical specimen with the technical upgrades that can destroy a small army. Now all we have to do is unleash him and see what he can do. Plus, we have a buyer for him once he demonstrates the ability we have created."

Azazil motions to the soldier to remove Brug from the room. He turns to Velnias and takes his jacket off. His right forearm looks metal, but he still has his right hand. "The implant is adapting nicely." He slides a collapsible cover to show a touchscreen. "I can send direct orders to the headgear or implants of my choice."

Velnias nods in approval. "Good! The implants will be ready soon." Dr. Peck looks at them with worry. He wants to ask about the implants, but he knows they won't tell him anything. He pretends to black out in hopes they keep talking.

Velnias looks at him for a second and thinks he is unconscious. "Before anything else happens, we need Grim to bring Crow and Sun back here. Let me know when the flyboy arrives!"

CHAPTER 22

Surge and Salene are making good time, but they have not seen Kitch at all. As they raced away from the quiet town, the plan was to meet ten miles down the main highway. They have no idea he had to ditch the truck or that he got chased by a military assault vehicle.

Salene has the visor down with the mirror open, staring at herself and wondering why this is her path. She looks at her face and then shifts to look at only half of her face. Surge notices as he is driving, wondering what she is doing.

"You okay?"

She keeps looking at the half of her face without the robotic eye. "Just reminding myself of what normal was like. How I used to look. And now I am this!" She looks at her whole face, then closes the mirror and looks straight ahead. "You know, our normal life is gone."

Surge takes a breath. "Is any life normal? We all signed up to be of service in some way for our country. Our lives at some point were never going to be normal, whatever *normal* is. When the idea of the program came up, it was to create opportunity for those to live life and continue to be of service to our country."

Salene understands and nods in agreement. "I get that. As a sniper, I always enjoyed working alone. I would put my earbuds in and play the music that gets me focused. I loved rock bands led by females. My father taught me how to shoot when I was little. He was a SWAT marksman. He was killed on duty when a bank robbery turned into a hostage situation. The robbers were desperate and detonated a bomb after being pursued by my father and another member of the SWAT team. It killed them instantly. I hate change, and since then I've wanted to follow in his footsteps. I ended up joining the military and was the first female to be top of the sniper class and program. I was placed in Afghanistan and was part of major operations deep in the mountains.

"Several months ago, everything changed again. A part of me can't remember how long ago. While I was doing recon on the Turkish and Syrian border, I got caught near a battle between Turkish soldiers and Syrian militia. I never engaged, but suddenly I had a mortar shell go off next to me. I was taking cover and neither group knew I was there. I was able to radio my position before getting hit. Seagar's group was conveniently close. I woke up in Greece like this."

Surge keeps his eyes forward but wants to console her. "I just wanted to help our soldiers. Did choice ever pop into my mind? It honestly didn't. From the moment we enter the operating room, it was save a life and enhance opportunities. Where is the line drawn? That makes me question what I have done. That line never existed in my mind. Not until Chase said something. Till right now, listening to you."

"My superiors told me Seagar wanted the best sniper they had to get into that zone. He knew based on these files I would be selected," Salene replies, angered. "I feel like everything I believed in and that he told me is just a con! How many people has this man hurt or ruined just to get himself a little bit further ahead? How far into our superiors could this go? The secretary of defense? For the first time I feel vulnerable. The fact that you just said that makes me trust you more. Why? I don't know, but I do!"

Surge makes a turn off the main road and pulls into a small airport parking lot. "I hope he is close behind us. I am guessing that Chase and the others are close as well."

Salene looks around and can see security and small groups of employees. "This airport is active. How are we supposed to get through any security with the weapons we have?"

Surge starts to think and looks to the back seat and trunk area. "If this belonged to Seagar or Azazil, maybe there are files and credentials. As soon as they land, I'll act as if you are a prisoner being transferred. Start checking the bags and the back. I will check with Chase on when they are landing."

| | | | |

Chase and the others start to prepare for landing.

The pilot comments over the intercom, "We have been given permission to land. This airport is operating on a small scale. Should I tell them you will depart the plane?"

Chase gets up out of his seat and opens the door to the cockpit. "No, land and pull in, but inform them that we are picking up three passengers." He goes back to his seat and taps Bull on the shoulder to wake him. "Wake up, sleeping beauty! We are about to land."

Bull opens his eyes and looks over at Chase. "I was dreaming pretty good. Couldn't give me five more minutes?"

"Was it a dream worth talking about?" Chase gives him a dirty smirk. "Better not be a Salene dream! I know how you were in the hangar." Chase chuckles a bit as he sits down.

Bull gives him an *eat shit* look. "No! It was not a Salene dream. It was me as a teenager, playing football, running, and laying out big hits. Feeling everything. Feeling normal! Waking up to these arms and legs still feels like a dream, but it's real. Like some of my humanity has been taken from me. I'm grateful to be alive, but what life do I have now, other than being the military asset they deem me to be? I am starting to get what you were saying in the hangar. I just don't think it has sunk in yet. Not till we got out here."

Chase looks straight ahead at the seat in front of him. He thinks for a second. "I have never had any control in my life. Everything I did was to try and control things to be what I wanted. Over time, all my actions got me the opposite—arrested, beat up, losing things, losing friends. Everything I did was selfish. Then my mom gets this military guy to convince me to go into a program. Which led me to boot camp, which led to my service. My mom told me I would do great things and be somebody. That was when I was accepted to boot camp, and she was so proud of me for doing it. I wonder what she would think now if she saw me like this. If I had kept down the path I was going, I would've ended up dead and someone else would be the one sitting here talking to you. Everything feels so out of control right now, but I'm comfortable with that. Maybe I have already accepted it, and now just want to make that difference."

As they talk there is a sudden robotic buzz that comes from behind them. They look at each other and turn their heads to look at Sabu. He's sound asleep; as his chest exhales, the robotic buzz comes from the voice-box mask that he wears. They start to laugh as they look at him.

Chase comments, "I really want to video that!" As he states that a message comes in on his phone. Chase reads it out to Bull. "Salene and I are here. Kitch is missing! To get through security she is my prisoner. Be ready to take off as soon as we board."

"That doesn't sound good! Kitch is missing?" Bull responds with concern. "We may be landing in hostile territory if they are saying that."

Chase agrees and turns to wake up Sabu. He taps his leg and Sabu wakes up looking at Chase and Bull. "Are we landing?" he says in the robotic voice he has.

"We are about to land. Be prepared, we may have security issues." Chase buckles in and the other two do as well.

The pilot comes over the intercom. "We are starting our descent. The tower has instructed us to taxi into the far-left area of the tarmac. Security will be checking the passengers we pick up."

| | | | |

As the plane approaches, Surge and Salene find handcuffs and travel passports and documents in the duffel bag. Surge puts the handcuffs on Salene and looks through the bag for anything he can use for his documents. The bag is full of badges and identifications for US and foreign soldiers and officers.

"We need to take this bag with us." Surge grabs an ID for a high-ranking officer in the Romanian army that looks like him. He puts black gloves on to cover his metal hand. "I hope this works."

Salene looks at him. "It will! Just stay calm and keep it

simple. I doubt they have a huge security presence here. Put these files on top with mine visible."

He does, zipping the bag up then putting it over his shoulder. He grabs her arm and they start walking toward the front door. The automatic doors slide open and they walk into a very empty lobby.

A security guard near the door approaches to help them. He can see the handcuffs and puts his hand near his holster. Surge puts his hand up.

"Prisoner transfer!" He waits a second to see if the guard understands. "English?" he asks in the hopes that he speaks it. The guard nods.

"When are you flying out?" the guard asks as he looks at Salene and her laser-scope eye. He is about to ask more, but Surge quickly answers them first.

"The plane is landing right now. She is to be brought to Kraków immediately. I need to get through security as fast as possible." He flips the credentials out in hopes it speeds up the process. The guard looks and agrees to help them get through.

He escorts them to the security check, where officers wave them through after seeing the badge. No one is in the airport at this time of night. After making it through, the guard returns the badge and escorts them to the tarmac.

The plane has touched down and starts to approach them. As it approaches, three military jeeps with Romanian soldiers come out from behind the hangar to the right. Salene turns and knees the guard in the groin, swinging both arms and knocking him cold to the ground. Surge grabs the keys and unlocks the cuffs she has on.

As the plane moves toward them, the door on the side opens up and Chase stands in the opening with his right arm straight out. As one of the jeeps approaches the plane, a huge stream of fire blasts from his forearm, engulfing the whole jeep into a ball of fire. Screams come from it as the soldiers fall out to the tarmac in balls of burning flesh.

Salene pulls off her jacket and puts her arms up, scoping the other two jeeps at once. As both arms are up, she has an accurate look at each driver. She takes a deep breath and both arms fire at the same time. In a matter of seconds both bullets shatter the front glass and hit both drivers square in the forehead, killing them instantly. Each arm fires again as the passengers try to grab the wheels of each jeep. They are both suddenly struck in the temples, killing them as well. Both jeeps lose control and collide, flipping over several times and killing the remaining soldiers in the back of them.

Surge can see more soldiers running through the airport toward them. Salene and Surge run to the plane to get away.

As the pilot starts to turn the plane around, Chase throws a rope down from the open door. Surge still has the duffel bag over his shoulder, which is slowing him down. Chase yells at him to drop the bag, but he refuses.

The soldiers running out onto the tarmac start firing machine guns at them. Chase gets out of the way, allowing Bull to move into the open space. He clicks his right arm behind him and pulls the rotating mini Gatling-style gun forward. He squeezes his fist and the gun immediately rotates and sprays bullets at the soldiers, reducing them to shredded body parts and puddles of blood.

They get Salene and Surge pulled up into the plane. They shut the door and the pilot ignores the tower's request to stand down. The plane speeds up and takes off down the runway.

Bull unhooks his back attachment and Salene and Surge get settled into seats. Chase and Sabu start looking through the duffel bag Surge brought.

"What is all of this?" Chase asks as he sees the file of him.

Surge takes a breath. "It's all of our files, from before our accidents. Seagar has had us under surveillance for quite a while. We found this in a barn near the castle that blew up."

Bull looks at them, confused by what he is hearing. "What do you mean these were in a barn in a small town? Start from the beginning. What happened after the castle blew up?"

Surge takes another deep breath to compose himself. He had never been in a situation like that before. "After we escaped from the first group of troops coming at us, we found safety in a small house in a large farm area. At first we didn't notice, but none of the farms had animals. Jeeps and trucks patrolled the area. The only way to get out of there was to create a distraction. Kitch drew them away in the pickup truck we had taken. Salene and I went a few farms down to grab another vehicle. It was also empty and had a new SUV. Again, no animals! There was a farmhouse next to the SUV and inside was an office where we found the SUV keys and these files in a drawer. We think it means Seagar had a place near the castle. That whole area is run by the Plague."

Chase looks through the files. "So Seagar is the missing link to the Plague. Which means we need to find Crow, Sun, and Brug in Kraków and figure out who is biting and killing people."

Surge looks at Chase. "The other thing that we found is these soldiers wearing head devices. Kitch even saw one in the castle, and they resemble the head devices the US Military was working on. Years back, before I started with Dr. Peck, I gave input on a program that was helping soldiers with PTSD. I never got fully involved, but I did see the prototype for it. It basically helped input images and positive memories into the brain to replace the PTSD flashbacks they would have. The fact is, it can stimulate the brain to take suggestion and information."

Sabu interrupts. "If they can do that, they can stimulate the whole body? Program it?"

Surge thinks about it. "Technically yes, but that also means they would need the research Dr. Peck and I had for the AMPD program. If Seagar is a part of the Plague, he has been passing the information on to them this entire time."

Chase puts the files down and looks at everyone. "So how does a woman eating human flesh come into this? How does she fit into the equation?"

Everyone sits, not knowing what to say. Surge thinks the hardest about it his mind going through all the information he can think of. Suddenly it hits him. "Protein! The body needs protein to maintain itself. If she was re-animated like these soldiers were, then at some point the body needs to be refueled. The headgear programs the brain to operate and react. The body at some point needs to survive. It will crave and need protein. The body will starve unless it feeds, like any animal." Surge stops and thinks a little more. "What if she was the first? The official guinea pig of the experiment."

"Then we could be looking at hundreds, maybe thousands of these things turning loose on whoever has them," Chase replies. "Or even worse, they know and don't care because they want to create chaos anyway."

Salene speaks out. "When we get to Kraków, we split up into teams?"

Chase nods and looks at the group. "I want Bull in the square undercover. It is better to have you stationary with those big guns attached to you. Focus on finding Crow, Sun, and maybe Brug. They will need to come to the square at some point. Sabu and I will search for the woman. He can spot her better than any of us. Salene, you and Surge will search out the troops and anyone leading them. Maybe use rooftops, and if anything goes down, we have an advantage with your rifles. Get some rest while in flight. We will be in Kraków pretty quickly." Chase gets up and goes to the back of the plane. He holds his file in his hand.

Surge goes to say something, but Bull motions to him not to. They all get settled and rest for what is about to happen.

eagar sits in a hotel room with a full set of monitors and computers. The setup in one corner of the room shows several locations. It is a full suite that the general has obtained without the knowledge of anyone. A US security technician sits watching the screens as another has headphones on listening to an audio feed. Several screens show the view of hidden cameras in the facility where Velnias is working. A fourth screen sits dark, but not because it is not on. Street cameras of the Kraków square are displayed with specifics near the museum and monument. The first tech makes notes on a large pad of times and any important visuals.

The tech turns toward the general and motions for his attention. "General! Grim and a large group of soldiers are organizing and setting up to move into the city," the tech reports, handing the top page from his notes to Seagar as he walks over to look at the monitors.

"Record all feeds with them and let me know if you see any signs of Sun or Crow. Make note and let me know of the exact location. I also want to know if any of the AMPD team show up. Record any activity with them and keep those files separate from the others." Seagar pours his whiskey and walks outside onto the balcony of his suite.

He puts his drink on the table and pulls a cigar out. With his cutter he clips the end and lights it. As he looks out at the streets in the distance, his cell phone buzzes. He checks it and waits for a second. He waits and then answers with no urgency, "Yes, Mr. Secretary. What can I do for you?"

The secretary of defense replies, "Why am I hearing one of the AMPD projects has been found and apprehended in Romania? That he possibly blew up one of the Romanian military vehicles while approaching him? That is the report I was just handed. Can you explain this?"

"Yes! I understand that sounds troubling. I am currently working on monitoring the Plague organization. My intel says they are taking him to Velnias. He was working with the others on that mission." Seagar rolls his eyes as he maneuvers his words around the truth of the situation.

"General, you get a lot of freedom in your projects, and on this one I have given the most freedom. I want hard evidence of these operations and full reports. The president is starting to ask questions regarding the AMPD program's progress, as well as visibility of how it is run. Ethics and all. A lot of money has been pumped into it, and as of now we have no idea what the results are. I expect an update within the next forty-eight hours. That needs to include the current status you have of the Plague. Other agencies are ready to move in on this investigation of them," the secretary firmly communicates.

Seagar starts to scowl in frustration at the thought of the CIA and FBI starting to investigate the Plague. "No sir! That is not necessary; we have the Moscow facility under surveillance and intel that we need. Former

Romanian general Azazil is in the city and running the operation. We know that the main hub is here somewhere. Any changes would compromise the entire mission, and I promise you I have the best working on this."

The secretary pauses for a second. "Forty-eight hours, a full update! Or else I will decommission the program if I have to." The secretary hangs up.

The general picks up his glass and shoots the whole amount. "What a fucking boy scout! I will have his job next soon." He shakes his head and puffs on his cigar a bit more. He looks at his phone and puts it in his right pocket. A buzz comes from his left pocket. He grabs another cell and answers. Azazil is on the other end, confirming Kitchener is being delivered to the facility. Seagar types out a quick message.

He is all yours. Do as you wish. My understanding is you have a buyer.

The general smirks with a little bit of joy and no remorse.

The first tech comes to the door and waits before he interrupts the general. "Sir, you may want to see this!" He turns and goes back to his station.

The general puts out his cigar and follows a few minutes later. As he approaches the monitors, he can see a body lying in the street. The tech rewinds the video to a few minutes prior and a second person is shown biting and eating the flesh of the body. The general looks at it in shock.

"Can you zoom in?" he asks the technician. The tech obliges and zooms as much as he can to show the woman who left Bonerowski Palace a murder scene. The hat she wears covers the headgear, but he can tell it is the woman that Velnias and Azazil released as the decoy.

Seagar walks away from the screens for a moment and wonders if he should tell them what is happening. He can use this to his advantage against them, as he is playing both sides. If the AMPD program is successful, then he can gain more power and move up in leadership. With the development of the headgear and the future technology they will bring, he can profit and put all his money in his safehouse in Romania, untouched and untraced by anyone. His techs are in his pocket, and they move everything the way he needs them to. Government funds from the PTSD program and the AMPD program have built the foundation that the Plague has developed. His manipulating and puppet mastery have put him in control.

He goes back to the monitors and looks at the Kraków views. "Have you seen Crow or Sun at all?"

"No! I have not, but the troops Grim has are moving into the city. A small group of five has separated from them into a different direction toward where that body is. The lead is Bautista from Azazil's independent mercs, and the others are SCZ troops." The tech starts recording the small group.

Seagar remembers who Bautista is and wants him tracked. "Make sure you keep me informed of everything he does. Let me know if he tracks down the decoy and if you see him have any contact with the AMPD group."

| | | | |

Azazil approaches Velnias in his personal chambers where Velnias sits quietly in a dark room, his hands softly draped on his stomach. His hood is up covering his head and hiding his face. He breathes softly but struggled, focused on himself.

Azazil stops and waits a moment before he says

anything, but Velnias knows he is there. He says, "You are concerned. Concerned about Seagar."

"This alliance was never going to last forever. You and I know that only one true leader is needed. We used Crow, Sun, and Brug to get what we wanted. He used his military assets to get what we wanted. Now, you and I get what we want! Do you agree?" Azazil stands just inside of the room wondering what Velnias thinks and waits for a response.

"The three of us were never going to work long term, and we have Russia's support. It is time to clean things up. We have all the files we agreed on. It would not surprise me if Seagar has held information back. Have your contacts in Romania go through the house he has on our settlement. And make sure the winged soldier gets to me as soon as possible. Do we know where Seagar is?" Velnias stays in his seat without moving.

Azazil moves over in front of the chair. "I have had people monitor and follow his movements. He has a surveillance set up in a hotel near here. He thinks he is clever, but if we take that out and make him disappear, we can move forward fully. I think it is time, otherwise he may try to control the situation."

The hood over Velnias's head moves up and down in agreement. "Keep the surveillance on what he has set up. Anything he has, we need access. Everything can be used because of his connections. First, we focus on Crow and Sun in Kraków. Then we lure him out to us."

"Agreed! I will let you know when the pilot arrives here." Azazil turns to leave the room.

Velnias speaks out to stop him. "Do we have access to the Ruslan? How many troops do we have ready? How many can we get into the Ruslan?"

Azazil stops and looks at him. "Are we changing

plans? Wanting to make a statement? Tell me what you want and I will prepare it!"

Velnias gets up from his chair and starts to pace back and forth. "Get the aircraft and prepare it. Load as many troops as we can. Get Evolution One ready for his introduction. We are going to Kraków! I want to get my mother back. Up until now it has been about development and building us. It is time to show what we have done on a larger scale. Prepare to drop some of the troops into the city. The rest will be moved in from landing."

Azazil has an evil happiness on his face. "We are attacking the city?"

Velnias nods his hooded head and responds, "You are attacking the city. Make it happen! Unleash our new asset and see what he can do. I have my own plans here! It is better with you in Kraków."

Azazil wonders what Velnias means, but accepts the order and agrees. "And what about Seagar? Do I need to know anything?"

Velnias uses his left hand and waves him away as he looks at paperwork on his desk. Azazil leaves the room and Velnias sits down. He pulls out a phone and dials a number. After a few rings it is answered and a Russian voice answers. Velnias pauses a second and starts to speak.

"Your administration needs to contact the American secretary of state. Notify them that a General Seagar has orchestrated the abduction of a Dr. Peck and an Officer Kitchener Williams. It appears they have been taken to Moscow. Seagar is suspected to be the unidentified leader of the organization known as the Plague. I am sending you digital files with outlines to his actions."

There is a pause on the other end and then the voice agrees and confirms the files. The phone hangs up and Velnias sits back. He stares straight ahead, slowly breathing. With so much emotion, he is heading to the point of no return. For him it is not about power or control. For him it is about creation and destruction.

There is no going back.

CHAPTER 24

Several hours have passed as Crow and Sun ditch the truck at a parking deck near the Palace. They have been hiding out, but were able to grab different clothes and some rest. The hooded shirts they found in the truck help to cover themselves up. They decided to finally move from the parking deck to the square.

They carry the case in a covered shopping cart and slowly make their way toward the statue as a few small groups of people walk through the square. Crow motions for them to move to the side next to the corner of the museum just diagonal from the Bonerowski Palace. Yellow police caution tape still blocks the entrance and the side street it is on. Crow is curious and wants to investigate what happened. "Stay here. Act homeless."

Sun squats down and sits with his back up against the wall and flips his middle finger out at her. As she walks away from him, she shakes her head. He takes a card and writes the Polish currency symbol for zloty on a card. He holds it up and bows his head to cover his face.

Crow starts walking over to the caution tape slowly as she pulls her hood down. She approaches an officer monitoring the barrier.

"English?" She gives him a smile. He nods a hesitant yes. "What happened?" She looks at him, concerned, manipulating him.

In a reassuring action he puts his hand up. "Nothing to worry about. We have everything under control. The scene and area should be opened up in the next day."

She pouts her lips. "You aren't allowed to tell me, are you? Someone died or was killed in that hotel?" She looks at him flirtatiously. "Be honest! I just arrived and want to know if that's the case."

The officer looks at her, feeling compelled to say something. "The maid and the desk clerk were killed. But that is all I can say about it." He turns and walks away from her. She stands at the tape looking around the entrance. As she is about to walk away, a voice behind her speaks. "We need to talk!" She turns around and a man is standing in front of her.

"Who the fuck are you and why should I talk to you?" Crow is about to turn around and walk away when the man raises his metal hand up. He starts moving his fingers and then pulls his sleeve up to show the metal arm. "I heard about you guys! You here to arrest me? I don't think that is going to happen."

He puts his hand up in a waiting gesture. "No! That is not why I am here. I am here because I think we can help each other. My name is Chase. Alexis Grim and his SCZ soldiers are in the city. My team and I just got here and have been waiting for you to come out of hiding. Is Sun the homeless guy you walked away from?"

Crow starts looking around to try and spot any other people with him. "Why should I trust you? I don't trust anyone but my brother and Sun. Whatever game you are playing, take it elsewhere, or I will signal him."

Chase reacts disappointed. "Which means I'll signal

my sniper on the roof nearby. I've already got Sun covered, too, if that is the route we are going. I am asking you to trust me."

She shakes her head. "No! You will just have to catch me!" She quickly kicks him in the stomach and runs under the tape and down the side street. Chase grunts and quickly follows.

Sun jumps up to pursue, but Sabu suddenly appears in front of him. He throws off his jacket to reveal his shining appendages. Sun puts his arms out and his katana blades slide out from his sleeves.

People start to scatter as the two face off, circling each other. Sun makes the first move as he drives forward with his right blade and swipes with the left. Sabu sidesteps and ducks the first motion and suddenly a flurry of fast fighting activity takes place.

As Sabu uses his metal arms to block, he reaches behind him and two scythe blades appear in his hand to combat the attack from Sun. Sun retreats to regroup and tilts his head, not expecting that. He nods in respect and the two start to circle again. This time both attack, and the blades fly in a flurry of action.

As their fight continues, Crow finds herself running down the side street looking for an exit in another direction. Chase pursues, trying to stop her. As she comes up to the next side street she runs into a woman, colliding massively with her.

Crow hits the ground hard and so does the other woman. The hat the other woman is wearing flies off, showing her face and her blood-covered neck and mouth. She lunges at Crow, trying to bite her. Crow starts to fight her off but struggles to do so. Saliva and blood drip from her mouth as her teeth grind and a groan comes from her.

Crow gets her foot up to push her back. As she does, Chase comes flying in with his metal fist engulfed with flames. With a powerful swing he connects to the side of the woman's head. A sudden snap and crack sound as the woman drops to the ground in a heap. Blood starts to pool out from the mouth and cracked-open head.

Crow takes a deep breath while lying on the ground and looks up at Chase. He turns and reaches out his normal hand to her. She pauses, asking herself why he helped her. She puts her hand up and accepts his gesture. As she gets to her feet she says, "I still don't trust you."

He is not surprised by her statement. "I don't expect you to trust me. Not yet. I want to talk with you and Sun. I am sure we can fill in a lot of gaps and help each other. I know they turned on you." He motions to follow him back. She pauses, but then agrees to do so.

"How do you know that? For the record, Sun can't talk!" She keeps her eye on Chase closely. "How did you find us so quickly after arriving here?" She looks around, wondering if they are being followed.

"Detective Bosco! He was first at the crash site and tracked you to the hospital parking lot. I have to hand it to you and Sun. Both of you are good, but the video surveillance caught you leaving the deck. Once they had an idea where you were, I told them to wait." He looks back at Crow. "I have them on standby right now! I wanted to talk one on one first to gain your trust. We need each other." He shrugs his shoulder in an *it is what it is* way.

Crow's eyebrows rise a little. "We will see about that. But first, you need to answer my question. How do you know they turned on Sun and me?" She is not amused.

Chase stops and stands for a minute. "We looked at the evidence left at the airport in Smolensk. We arrived shortly after, and everything pointed to a circle around one person. Then the footprints showed an individual in the circle helping the person in the middle. The severed heads pretty much gave away Sun, even though our spy said he was dead." He points at Sabu, who is suddenly fighting side by side with Sun.

Asher has shown up and is attacking them with weaponized arms. He is wielding urumi flexible swords, ancient Indian swords made of a razor-sharp flexible metal. Asher uses them with skill and accuracy.

Chase and Crow begin to run toward them. Bautista and his three troops step forward to intervene. Coming from the right, Bautista throws a strong punch, knocking Chase to the ground. "You killed my brother!" He throws another punch, connecting with Chase's jaw.

The three troops block Crow from intervening and grab her by the arms. As all of this happens, civilians scatter and take cover.

Alexis Grim starts to approach from the main square with rows of armed troops following him. He orders the soldiers holding Crow to follow him. They cuff her arms behind her back and escort her to Grim.

A pair of gunshots is heard from a distance and the two troops are struck in the head. They drop to the ground, but before Crow can run, the soldiers with Grim pursue and grab her.

Grim yells, "Contain her! Kill the others!" Troops surround Sabu and Sun and take them with Crow.

Chase looks up at Bautista. "What did I do to you and your brother? I don't understand!" He puts his metal arm up to blast him with fire. He pauses. "I can't do that! I could kill you instantly if I wanted to, but I'm not going to do that. Who was your brother?"

Bautista just looks at him with anger. "The convoy! You shot him in the head. In cold blood!" He pulls his pistol out and puts it up to Chase's forehead. "This is for him, you murderer."

Chase quickly yells out, "Wait! How could I kill anyone when we were ambushed? Then medivac took me to get this arm and leg! We were taking medical supplies to refugees! I never encountered anyone personally!" Chase looks Bautista in the eye, hoping he believes him.

Bautista stands with his gun to Chase, not knowing what to believe. "Seagar told me you shot my brother during the encounter. You were moving weapons, and my brother's contract ops team was to engage them! They were contracted by the US government." Bautista gets ready to fire.

Before he can fire the gun, Chase flames up his hand and grabs Bautista's forearm. He pushes the arm to the side as the gun goes off. Bautista drops the gun as he yells in pain from the burn. Chase then swings his leg around and sweep-kicks Bautista's legs out from under him. He drops to the ground and Chase gets on top of him in a superior position with his metal hand in a fist. The fist is engulfed with flames as he looks straight into Bautista's eyes.

"I didn't kill your brother! And I'm not going to kill you." The flames go out on his fist and he punches Bautista out with his normal hand.

Chase stands up and puts an earbud in. "Salene! You hear me? Bosco? Can you hear me?" There is a pause.

"Yeah!" Salene responds while surveying from the rooftop. "Surge and I can see you and I can hear you. They are taking them toward the monument. Bosco and his officers are being blocked by Grim's troops. They have these troops everywhere."

Chase cracks his neck while holding his hands up, cracking his knuckles. "Let's show these motherfuckers who we are!" He starts following Grim and the troops. "Take good shots and don't overuse your ammo, Salene!"

"Copy that! I'm taking the guy next to Grim first!" She uses her eye to focus in. "Why do the troops' expressions look like that?" She focuses in on a few of them. Their mouths have a weird grin as if they are grinding teeth. "Chase, be careful! If the troops are like that woman, they may have a high craving for flesh." She just chuckles to herself. "Did I really just say that?"

"Yeah, you did! And I will! Have all the civilians gotten to safety?" He keeps his distance but can see soldiers approaching him.

Salene responds, "Yeah! Most are gone. You have troops coming behind you as well. I'll focus on Grim's group."

Chase unclips his fifty-caliber handgun and pulls it out with his left hand. He cocks it and turns as he throws his right arm behind him. As he does, a huge stream of fire roars toward the soldiers coming up behind him. In an instant the soldiers are engulfed in flames and drop to the ground in heaps of burning flesh. He turns back to the main group and fires off a few shots, hitting the two troops blocking him. The bullets pierce through each head.

Alexis walks as the troops guide Crow and the others with him. "You created a lot of problems getting away in Smolensk. Especially with that case being on the plane. That case was for a separate deal I was supposed to drop off. You two really fucked up my schedule! Made me look bad."

Crow scoffs at him. "Like I give a shit about your schedule. You always look bad! What happened to my brother?"

Alexis just laughs with amusement. "Wow! Everyone has brother issues! I never had a brother or a sister. So I don't give a fuck about yours! All I care about is doing my job and getting paid." He turns to Crow. "Your brother is with Velnias and," he throws his thumb up, pointing at Bautista behind him, "his brother got shot in the head by flame boy over there! This is how things are going to go. These soldiers under my command are taking all of you back to Moscow to Velnias and Azazil." A shot from a distance goes off suddenly and the troop next to Grim takes a bullet to the head and drops to the ground. In dramatic fashion Grim screams out. "What the fuck? Who shot that? It was that sniper bitch, wasn't it? She is quite a hot shot, isn't she?" He is feeling really pissed off.

Sabu looks at him with a calm demeanor. "Don't worry! We need you alive, dipshit!" his robotic voice quips arrogantly.

Grim shakes his head and laughs. "Shut your robotic piehole. For a cyborg, you are a bit of a dick! My troops will make sure I stay alive. It is in their programming. Serve and protect the leader who controls and orders them. It is a nice feature of theirs."

Sabu looks at Grim. "These things can turn on you. They *will* turn on you! What about that woman who killed the employees at the Palace? She bit them and tore flesh from them."

Alexis looks at Sabu, not believing him. "I guess that was our decoy. She was basically a guinea pig. If what you say is true, then this whole city is fucked. I have one hundred and fifty troops in the city, so if they turn, then everyone will die."

Sun takes a step toward Grim but turns his head to Crow as the troops block him. He looks at her and bows his head slightly. He can see Chase running toward them in the distance. He looks at Sabu for a second and winks. He turns his focus back to Alexis and his two blades slide from his sleeves. Two more shots go off and hit the two troops in front of Sun, and he lunges toward Alexis. A few more troops respond as Sun tackles Alexis. Crow pulls her pistol from behind her and fires a few shots as she moves to her right toward the museum and the seating area.

Sabu throws his arms up and fires multiple blades from his forearms as he follows her. Sun furiously fights against four soldiers who are protecting Grim. He swings his arms and blades with quick swipes. The soldiers avoid his attacks and suddenly have him surrounded. Grim retreats away as more troops approach with rifles in hand. With so many SCZ troops everywhere, the options for escape are getting smaller.

Sabu and Crow stand against the wall. Her gun is raised and his arms are in a defensive posture. They both look around but cannot see Chase anywhere. He has disappeared, and Sun is surveying his options.

Grim's voice suddenly shouts out from a distance. "Nice little effort! Not much changed. What now? Some bruiser going to show up with big machine guns?"

As Alexis shouts that, Bull walks out from behind the monument. Both arms and Gatling-style guns are in position. "Damn right, motherfucker!"

As he opens fire and causes the SCZs to scatter, the sound of a motorcycle revving is heard where Bautista was lying knocked out. Chase has grabbed a motorcycle and comes flying around the corner of the museum and straight down the square. As he gets closer to the soldiers, he lifts his feet up on the seat.

Sabu runs from the wall and grabs a table from the seating area. He breaks two legs off of it and, holding the two legs, props it on his back and crouches down, creating a ramp. Chase rides the bike straight at the table and steadies it with one hand. He hits the table ramp and is in the air heading toward the large crowd of SCZ troops.

As the troops fire their weapons, Chase lets go and pushes off, sending the bike hurtling at them. He throws his prosthetic out and sends his fire stream at the bike, engulfing it. Suddenly a large motorcycle fireball flies into the crowd of SCZs, wiping them out. Chase lands and front-rolls to a safe stop, looking back at Sabu with a grin.

As Chase motorcycle-bombs the crowd, Sun fights his way out of being surrounded. Salene helps by taking two out with a couple of headshots. More SCZ troops move in, but suddenly they begin firing their weapons at random all over.

Screams come from all over the square as random civilians try to find safety. A handful of SCZs start walking toward Grim with guns in hand and a different look in their eyes. He is frustrated with what is happening and not sure what to think of it.

"Serve and protect me!" The order is ignored and one of the troops grabs his left arm. Grim pulls his gold-plated handgun out with his right and puts a bullet in its head. He pushes them off and starts to run, but takes a bullet in the calf from Salene. She then fires a few more shots to kill the troops near him.

Bull runs over to him. "Just keep your ass down. If you haven't noticed, your protection detail wants to eat you like a drumstick."

SCZ troops descend on the city. The largest group is still in the square. Chase is getting low on his fire bursts, and Salene can only take so many shots at a time. Bull puts his gun to his back and picks up Grim to get him out of the square.

Sabu and Chase start to fall back as the troops continue to move in surrounding them. There are so many of them that they cannot handle it. Several random civilians in the square are attacked and being bitten and ripped apart.

Crow fires gunshots from behind the table she has in front of her. The soldiers move toward her quickly. She needs to run for it to get to the others. She darts to her left as Sun starts to move toward her, swiping his swords and taking out whatever flesh-biting troops he can.

The others are defending themselves and cannot get to her. She fires shots into troops' heads as they get close, but she is running out of bullets and trips as she tries to get away.

Several troops grab at her as she pulls herself under a table. She pushes her arms out to keep them away. Teeth bite into her forearms and she screams. Sun can hear her scream and starts pushing even harder. Sabu gets loose and runs toward her. His metal arms protect from the bites as he punches and kicks.

Sabu gets to Crow from the side and grabs the troops biting and ripping her arms apart. Sabu fights and struggles, pulling the SCZs off her, and continues fighting off the ones approaching. Her arms are mangled badly and a part of her right arm dangles from the elbow. Her left arm bicep is gone, and much of the bone of her forearm is showing.

Sun gets through the crowd and looks over at Sabu and Crow with an intense look. Crow finds him with pain in her face. It feels like everything is slowing down as she realizes what he is doing. The moment is frantic with action and violence, but for her it feels like it is eternity. Sun puts his arms up and presses the blades to the wall. His lips move in a small motion, mouthing, *Go!*

She starts shaking her head. "No!" He clangs the swords against the wall, getting the attention of the bloodthirsty mob. Sabu grabs her and holds her in his arms as they move to get away. In his arms, she looks back to see Sun swinging his blades furiously as the mob surrounds him.

Crow watches him throw himself in harm's way for them to get away. Suddenly he is gone from view and waves of emotions hit her. She cannot believe he just sacrificed himself like that. *Why would he risk himself for me? He was already dead, so how could he make a choice like that?* She is in so much pain from the bites and torn flesh of her arms. As her mind wanders and she begins to feel weak, she can hear sirens and passes out.

A small police van pulls close to the square and Detective Bosco jumps out. He waves for Sabu to come to him. He looks around and can see Chase firing a rifle and running toward the van. Bull comes from another direction carrying Alexis in his arms.

The detective directs them to get in the van. As they climb into the van, Chase remembers Bautista was unconscious. He looks over to where Bautista was lying, but nobody is on the ground where he left him. He runs over to see a pool of blood.

Random gunshots keep firing off. Chase turns and runs back to the van. He looks down the square where the crowd of troops are. They are dispersing and scattering around the square. There is no sign of Sun, and Chase jumps into the van.

They drive off leaving behind violent remains of blood and death.

CHAPTER 25

I t is a dark, rainy night in Prague and a young woman in dirty wet clothes runs down a side street alley. Looking for shelter, she checks back doors and windows. She turns and looks behind her, feeling like she is being followed. The woman keeps going deeper into the alley. Only small spotlights provide visibility on the sides of the building. The rain lightens, but she is soaked to the bone. She checks inside a dumpster for any clothes or items of use, but doesn't find much and turns to head out of the alley. Two male figures stand near the entrance she came in.

One of the men speaks out. "You okay, honey? We can get you a place to stay. Just come with us!"

"No thanks! I'll be fine on my own. Was just looking for something I lost." She plays it off and goes to leave the alley. The second man walks forward and blocks her from leaving.

"Oh, come on, doll! Let us help you out. You may even enjoy it." He looks down at her with a predatory smile. He puts his left hand up, placing it on her arm. The first man comes over and stands behind her. They try to grab her and she starts to struggle. She throws her head back, hitting the one man in the face. The man in front of her throws a hard punch, hitting her in the jaw. She drops to her knees and moans out in pain.

The man behind her gets up with a bloody nose, angry and swearing. As he grabs her arms, he notices a figure behind his partner. The light behind the figure casts a dark silhouette. He starts walking toward them and the guy with the bloody nose lets go of the woman's arms.

"You have a problem, punk?" He throws his arms up wide as if welcoming a challenge. The running figure jumps in the air and throws a strong side kick into his chest, sending the bloody-nosed goon to the ground. The second thug turns toward the figure only to receive a spinning back fist to the jaw, knocking him out cold.

The young woman looks up to see a young Vietnamese man look down at her with his hand out. "I may be an asshole, but I don't treat women like that. Call me Sun. If you need a safe place, I have one near here." She accepts his hand and he helps her to her feet.

She shakes her head and spits out some blood. Then she cracks her neck and looks at him. "I can handle myself. Thanks for the assist." She goes to walk away, but Sun steps in front of her.

"I like your confidence. What you don't know is these two have been my competition for quite a few years. The moment I saw them follow you, I knew I needed to follow them." He puts his hands up for her to wait. "They are black market dealers. Weapons, drugs, women. You would have been long gone into the system they run."

She huffs at him. "Oh! You saved me so I can be in your system? How nice of you, asshole!" She shoves him and starts to walk away.

"I can teach you!" he says out loud. "Something about you tells me you are a survivor. A hustler, living on the streets and doing what you have to for survival. I can teach you to fight. I sell weapons and technology. Sure, I throw some drugs or women in here and there. But not like those two." He pulls his handgun out and puts a silencer on it.

She stops and turns to hear more. As he is about to cap both goons just as they start to wake up, she stops him. She looks in his eyes and takes the gun out of his hand.

He looks back at her and asks, "What is your name? What should I call you?" He grins.

She looks back with a stone-cold face. "Call me Crow." She turns and puts a bullet in each man's head without hesitation. She looks back at Sun with an evil little grin and hands the gun back. Then she turns and starts to walk away.

"Why Crow?" He finds her answer interesting.

She stops for a second. "They're very intelligent, calculating, and they never forget who wrongs them. Let's go! Take me to your place." She starts walking and Sun smiles and follows.

Crow starts to come to as she has a flashback of Sun. Chase carries Crow in his arms as she bleeds from the bite wounds on her arms.

Surge helps the detective break into a closed emergency clinic. The detective turns the lights on as Surge rushes through a door to the back looking for supplies. Crow, feeling weak, groans in pain. Bull walks in carrying Alexis in his arms.

Surge yells out, "Bring her back here with the case!"

Chase carries her back and Bull puts Alexis down in a chair and follows. Salene puts the black case with the keypad down and stays at the door as lookout. She grabs weapons clips from her utility pack and switches them out in her forearms. The detective watches in awe, unable to believe what he is seeing.

Chase enters a room and Surge motions to put her on the table. Surge observes the damage to her arms and puts tourniquets on both arms.

"I need the black case they had with them," he says to Bull. Bull leaves and goes to the front, where Salene and Alexis are with the case. The detective follows, not wanting to see what is about to happen. Bull grabs the case from the floor and Alexis laughs.

Bull looks at him and pauses a second. "You find something funny?"

Alexis looks back at Bull with a straight face. "Yes! She

gets the arms that Velnias was considering giving her. Instead, the military program that was tasked to bring her to justice is making her one of them. I do find that funny!" Alexis smirks at him

Bull looks back at Alexis with an uneasy feeling. He holds the case and pauses, wondering if they are doing the right thing. He heads back to the room and enters as Surge preps her and the room for what he is about to do. He puts the case down and looks at Surge.

"I hope you know what you are doing." Bull takes a nervous breath.

Surge comes over to it and punches numbers into the keypad. A small beep sounds, followed by an unlocking sound. The case suddenly opens and inside are two ports and two specially built AMPD arms. "I don't know if I can make this work here."

Chase looks at him with confidence as he puts pressure on the wounds to try and slow the bleeding. "You can do this! What do you need?"

Surge shakes his head. "I need a specific level of charge to bond the port and the open wound of the limb. The nerves of the arm and the fibers in the port bond with a charge and they become one with the nervous system. It is not cauterizing the limb, but forming a bond with a subtle heated charge. Too much charge and the connection fries. All of the equipment in Greece is what I need. They are set to the levels."

Chase looks at him and says, "Well! If you don't do something, she will die. If we do this, it can give her a chance for something."

Bull suddenly shouts out, "A defibrillator! You can control the level of pulse or shock on the panel. Right? Could that work if we got the ports in place?"

Surge starts to nod. "Yeah! If we are careful, and we

would have to shock the ports flush with the paddle. I still have to figure out the level." He looks at Bull. "Go find one if you know what it looks like." Bull runs out of the room and starts going through the clinic.

Crow opens her eyes, looking at Chase. "Why are you doing this?"

He looks deeply into her eyes. "Because I learned a little while ago, everyone deserves the chance to live. Sometimes it's not perfect, but second chances are a gift when they present themselves."

Surge walks over. "You have so much nerve damage, I can't save your arms. I can give you what was in the case. Do you want that?"

Crow looks at him. "What happened to Sun? Did he get out?"

Surge looks back at her. "Sabu is out looking for him. If he survived, Sabu will find him. Just relax! I have to amputate."

She chuckles and coughs. "Oh great! I get to be a super cyborg like you guys." She fades out and closes her eyes. Surge checks her heartbeat with a stethoscope.

Chase yells out, "We need that defibrillator!"

Bull rolls in with a defibrillator. "It's the only one here. I hope it works."

Surge looks at Chase. "There is no time to put her under. We have to do it now or it's going to be too late."

Chase nods and looks at Crow. Crow opens her eyes and looks back at him. "Just fucking do it!" Chase searches for something she can bite on, finding a belt. Surge and Bull start to strap her to the table to keep her still.

Chase says out loud, "We need a bone saw!"

Surge looks at him and shakes his head. "No! I have my own saw! I will use a scalpel to cut the flesh and tissue." His index finger twists and shows the scalpel. He carefully cuts one arm down to the bone, then puts his hand up and pulls his four metal fingers at the knuckles back. An opening from his palm clears and a compartment in his palm shows. A small, circular saw blade comes out and the blade starts to spin.

Surge takes a deep breath and starts to cut through the bone of the first arm. Blood starts to spray around the room, and in a second he is through the bone and has the first arm off. He quickly moves to the second arm and repeats the process. As Crow is biting down on the belt Chase gave her, she feels dizzy and lightheaded. She suddenly passes out during the process.

In a matter of moments, the second arm is cut and gone. Surge grabs towels and wipes his hands off, putting his metal hand back in place. He uses the alcohol from the counter to wipe around the wounds. He motions Bull to give him the ports from the case.

Bull locates the two ports on the top layer of the case. He grabs one and hands it to Surge nervously. Surge starts to line up the side with electrical fibers with the open wound. He gets the port into place and puts his hand out for one of the paddles. Bull hands him the defibrillator paddle and Surge looks at him while grabbing it.

"Set it to two hundred volts!" He places the paddles flush with the metal port and waits a second. "On the count of three, hit it! One . . . two . . . three!" Bull hits the charge switch. The port is shocked to the arm and Crow groans.

Surge motions for the other port and Bull hands it to him. Lining it up carefully on the other arm, Surge pauses and checks the port before setting the paddle on it. He takes a deep breath and motions to Bull for the shock. Crow grunts and shifts around as she bites hard on the belt in discomfort. Her forehead shows sweat.

Surge walks to the case to see the glass syringe nestled in protective foam. He pulls it out and prepares the needle. Pinching the skin on her stomach, he plunges the needle in and pushes the solution into her body until half of the vial is in. Surge removes the needle and covers the puncture with some gauze. He goes to her deltoid, pinching the skin there as well, and inserts the needle, injecting the remainder of the vial into her.

"Set it for one hundred volts and wait for my signal," he tells Bull. He puts the paddle back on the first port, motions to Bull, and the shock is delivered. The paddle is carefully removed and placed on the second arm. Tension fills the room as everyone waits to see if it works.

Surge takes a deep breath as he says softly to himself, "God, let this work!" He motions to Bull and the shock is applied again. Crow is lying on the table weak and almost unconscious. Surge treats it like a battle situation for a combat medic. "I need an IV bag hooked up immediately." Bull scrambles out into the hallway to find one. Chase continues to make eye contact with Crow to keep her calm.

Surge grabs a heart rate cuff from the cabinets and wraps it around Crow's arm. "I never told you about the solution we inject during the process, Chase. A part of the research was the healing of the nerves while creating the bond. We started working with human growth hormones and enhancing it to a higher level, needing the healing process and tissue generation to be quicker. Ethically, we were breaking rules and laws from the Drug Administration and Center of Disease Control regulations. From an experiment factor, we gained a lot of ground in making this process work."

Chase looked at him, conflicted. "Which we never asked for! All I can do is find acceptance in what I am now. Control is an illusion, and acceptance is the solution to the illusions. I just want to make a difference, and you gave me the opportunity to continue that. However, I cannot say I have a normal life now!" Chase looks at Surge, then back at Crow right as she passes out.

Chase takes the belt out of her mouth as Surge re-checks her pulse, which is still high. Bull comes in with an IV set up and Surge hooks it up to get more fluids into her. Surge checks the ports and the bond with the hope that the connection worked.

Crow starts to wake up and looks over at him. She looks at her arms to see they are gone. She starts to groan in anger and begins to cry.

Chase, standing to the side, leans in and wipes away a tear. He puts his hand on her shoulder. She looks up at him, wanting to hold his hand. She continues to cry a bit more and then screams as loud as she can.

Bull can't watch as she processes the emotions. He walks out, not knowing what to say or do, and heads down the hall to catch his breath as his anxiety and emotions kick in. He throws up on the floor while thinking about what just happened.

Salene looks down the hall and sees him. She heard the scream and wanted to check on the situation. Seeing Bull throw up on the floor caught her by surprise. "You okay, big guy?"

He sees her and feels embarrassed. He starts to nod like he is, but she knows he is covering up his feelings. She puts her hand on his shoulder, and without saying anything she makes him feel at ease.

"I never allowed myself to process what happened," Bull confesses. "Watching that just brought it all up. Is this a gift? Or are we just possessions? I refuse to be owned!" He puts his metal fist into the wall to let his frustration out.

Salene agrees with him and nods. "At first I wanted to be everything I could be for Seagar and the military. But we were used and put in this situation. No matter what the details are, we were manufactured. We cannot change what we are, but we can decide *who* we are. When we leave here, it needs to be with the goal to finish this."

Bull keeps looking at the hole in the wall. "What do we do afterward? It isn't like we can go back to our normal lives back home."

Salene steps in front of him and blocks the hole. "We deal with today first. We deal with these SCZ things and Seagar and the Plague. We all have issues with Seagar's actions, which is why we need to do this together. Come help me guard the front. The detective needs to go deal with the troops in the city."

CHAPTER 26

Sabu moves along a small side street near the square. Through the city the sounds of screams and gunfire is heard. A beautiful city is now turned into a horrific war zone. He continues to circle the square quietly without being noticed. SCZ troops wander aimlessly in the area, getting closer to Sabu. He stops to study them and how they move.

They maintain control of the assault rifles and the movements of their extremities. At the sight of a human being, they race after them like a wild animal hunting its prey. He can see a young man in his late twenties trying to get across the square. Suddenly two troops start chasing and one stops to take a shot with his rifle. The bullet strikes the man in the back and he falls to the ground. The two raging soldiers converge on him and start to tear him apart.

Sabu is shocked watching their control followed by their uncontrollable thirst for blood. Like a sudden switch to hunt is triggered. Maybe Surge will understand how they are like this. He needs to get back with the group but does not know where they are. As he starts to head back the way he came from, he can hear a loud and large plane overhead. A large Russian military plane flies over and figures begin to jump out of the back of the plane. It seems like five at a time jump and in a repeated pattern. Sabu loses track, but the sky fills with parachutes floating into the city.

The city is under siege and it seems like nothing can stop them. Sabu needs to be careful getting back to the others. With no sign of Sun and raging soldiers everywhere, Sabu is in a vulnerable position. In a matter of minutes these paratroopers will be falling right on top of his location. They could even have him surrounded, so he makes a run for it.

A small group of soldiers notice him and start to give chase. Some gunfire comes at him but he is able to dodge it. He throws his left arm up to his side at the chasing soldiers and makes a fist as several projectile blades fly through the air, taking out two of troops. Three more continue toward him and are so close they drop their guns to engage physically. Sabu pulls his arched blades out from behind him.

In a spinning motion, one blade takes off a head as he throws his right leg up in a front kick at a second soldier. His foot extends, making crushing contact into a soldier's sternum. He swings his left arm as the blade detaches yet another head. One soldier is left behind him. In a smooth and quick motion, his hands adjust the blades and he swings his arms behind him and upward just in time to thrust into the troop. He lets go and steps forward to a side position. Sabu then throws a super kick with the help of the pistons, making his kick so powerful it tears the head right off the body. Sabu grabs his blades and looks around. More troops are converging, but he runs into a dark side street and disappears.

| | | | |

In the clinic the group gathers as Crow lies in the other room resting. Salene tends to the gunshot wound in Alexis's leg which she gave him. The bullet exited the flesh cleanly. She patches him up while he looks at her with disdain.

"Why didn't you kill me? You are too good a shot to miss like that."

She looks into his eyes with a cold and straight face. "Who said I missed?" She smiles and wraps it with bandages. She then takes a black marker from her pocket and draws a hand with a middle finger pointing up at him.

"Nice! So why keep me alive? I could turn and fuck your situation up if I wanted. Even with these handcuffs on." He shifts and wiggles his arms cuffed behind him.

She gets up and steps back a few feet. "Well! You are in just as bad a situation as we are. They attacked you, so that makes you expendable. Fight with us and get out of this shit, or just tell us what you can about Velnias and we will keep you alive in here. If you decide to not tell us anything, then I will shoot you in the face. Fair enough?" She gives him a nice big *I will fuck you up* grin.

He looks up at her unamused. "I guess I will join with GI Hoe then." He flicks his tongue at her in an obscene way.

She looks at him and huffs. "You disgust me!" She turns and walks away down the hall.

Chase walks into the room to check on Crow. She is lying on the table with her eyes open staring at the ceiling. He walks quietly up to the table so he doesn't startle her. She turns her head and looks at him.

"What the fuck am I supposed to do now? You took my arms! Sun is gone, and my brother? Who knows. I am alone! Do I trust you or not? I don't know anything about you. As far as I know, you have been looking for me so you can turn me in." She looks back up at the ceiling.

Chase grabs the rolling chair and sits next to the table where she can see him. "I woke up in a hospital bed missing my arm and leg, wondering what happened. I was just running a convoy of medical supplies and then suddenly we got attacked. Through all of this, I have stepped up and done what I was asked to do. We found out we never really had the choice to begin with. It was all our general. He manipulated and set up everything the way he wanted. Ever since I met him as a teen, he manipulated everything."

She turns her head to him. "When my brother was pulled into the German military, I had no one, nowhere to live, so I travelled and survived. Then one night two thugs tried to rape me in an alley. Sun was apparently following me. After that night he introduced me to the world he lived in—arms deals, sales and negotiating, and a lot of fighting and jiu-jitsu. He always looked out for me, even as rude and crude an individual as he was. He was always there if I needed him. Nobody ever really saw that side of him, just me."

Chase understands what she is saying. "I know what that is like. It was just me and my mom for a long time. I never made it easy for her. Then she started dating a military recruiter. Suddenly I was in a pre–boot camp program and he was breaking her heart. I was not there for her when she needed me. I felt guilty about that. She went through a hard time. Eventually she worked through it. Our relationship changed, and it all started when he was in our lives. Now he is our general." Chase sits for a second as emotions roll around in his head. He takes a deep breath as Crow lies still looking at the ceiling. "When we figure out how to get out of the city, we can regroup and find Sun. We are going to need to leave here soon. Sabu is checking the square right now, and it sounds like more soldiers are entering the city. How is your strength?"

She takes a few breaths and looks over at him. "Just fucking peachy! Was I given something to help my healing? It is freaking me out not seeing my arms. The weird thing is my mind still feels them."

Chase touches her shoulder. "Yeah! I know what you mean. I am guessing whatever else is in the case is what we will attach. Alexis said it was going to a buyer. Maybe Surge can help us figure that out." He looks at her, hoping she feels more comfortable, then gets up to find Surge leaving the room. Crow looks back at the ceiling with a calm demeanor.

Chase walks into the front room where Salene, Alexis, and the detective are. The others are searching the clinic for supplies. Chase walks over to them to hear the conversation. Alexis looks over at Chase.

"What's up, pretty boy?" Alexis teases. "Are you the big savior of everyone?"

Chase looks at Alexis with a straight face. "Who was that case going to? Why is it so important?"

Alexis smiles and shifts his body to be more comfortable. "Not sure why it's relevant. Cases like that have gone all over the world the past few days. You *are not* one of a kind!" He gives Chase a big grin, showing his gnarly teeth. "With that said, the case we have just happened to be for a woman I know. It's lucky for Crow she took it." Alexis stops talking and looks out the window. The others wait to see what else he might tell them. He takes a minute to think. "I will tell you what I know, but I want to go free after we get out of here. I need your word!"

"Why would we give you our word to let you go? We need to keep you in custody. Besides, you would be better off staying with us if you did tell us everything. You don't have many options," Salene says, breaking it down for him.

He looks around at Chase and Salene and the others in the room. "Velnias has another deal with someone else. I don't know who. All three of them working together was also the three of them using each other. Seagar provided military technology and access to funds. Azazil provided and developed an area in Romania that could be controlled. He also provided soldiers for experiments. Velnias is the knowledge and ability. Without him, there were no experiments or SCZ soldiers. I don't even know who he is. A hooded, druid-like person with burns and a breathing issue. Look, I need to disappear, because I sold the case without them knowing. I saw an opportunity to make some extra cash, but then Crow and Sun fucked that up."

Chase looks at Salene with concern. "Whatever we do, we have to deal with a three-headed monster."

She shakes her head. "No! We need to get the city under control first. We can't just leave with all of these *things* running all over." She looks over to the detective who has been sitting quietly. "How much help can we get from your officers?"

The detective shrugs and shakes his head. He is considerably overwhelmed. "I would have to call for all officers to fall back to assess the situation. Based on the radio chatter, the soldiers are everywhere. Now they're parachuting in from some plane that just flew over."

Chase looks out at the van they arrived in. "Can you at least help us get reloaded? Salene needs bullets for her clips. I need flammable liquid. The clinic has nitrogen I can use for my flamethrower. We need Bull to check his bullet count and Surge to get armed with whatever the detective has available. Alexis, if you are not going to help us, then you are just in our way. If you want to leave and hope to survive, then go ahead." Chase points to the door.

Alexis looks at Chase, scared. "What? I meant after we get out of here. If I go out into the city by myself, I won't survive."

Chase walks over and gets in his face nose to nose. "If you fight with us, you may not survive. I don't trust you here with Crow by yourself. So you are part of our plan whether you like it or not."

Bull walks into the front from the back hallway. Surge follows him in and pats Chase on the shoulder. "We can get you the gas from out back. We shouldn't spread out and take them on individually."

Alexis pipes in condescendingly. "Use your brains and herd them into the square. Put them all in one place, then maybe we can control the situation more. I may be an asshole, but I do know strategy. It comes in handy."

Bull looks at the van out front and smiles big. "I have an idea about how we can use the van. We just need to hook up some of the PA speakers from in here to the van. Pipe out loud music while we drive through the square. Between all of us we should be able to take them out in a mass attack."

Chase nods his head and feels pumped with the idea. "I like it. Detective! Can you get a few men here to protect Crow? Surge! I need you with us." He looks at Surge, feeling apologetic. Surge nods, knowing that Chase is asking him to be involved in the fight, something he is not fully comfortable with. Chase turns to Alexis. "You had the idea. You drive!"

Alexis looks at Chase like he's crazy. "Fucking drive what? You think I am going to park that van in the square and wait for my demise? Fuck that!"

The detective walks forward. "The vans have an

escape hatch in the bottom. Park it at a manhole cover. You can slip out and have access to the sewers."

Chase puts his arms up. "That's all I trust you to do! I don't expect you to save my life if I needed you."

Alexis agrees with a head bob and puts his fist out. "All right! I still need my gun!" Chase agrees and they hand over the gold-plated Magnum. Bull and Alexis start grabbing the small speakers as the others prepare.

CHAPTER 27

Seagar starts looking at the video feeds with his techs. He watches as Azazil and troops leave the Moscow facility. Velnias stays behind and starts to move around the complex. The tech wearing headphones takes them off.

"We have an issue, sir!"

Seagar looks at the tech. "What is the problem?"

The tech looks at him, concerned. "We have lost all sound in the complex. Everything is getting glitchy."

Seagar is getting mad at what he is hearing. "Well, fix the problem. That is why I have you. I pay good money for you to make sure I have all the access I need." As he voices his displeasure, all the monitors go black and shut down. The techs frantically start checking plugs and switches.

"Sir! We just lost everything. We are completely down!" The tech grabs a laptop sitting on the coffee table. He fires it up and starts going through signals and codes. "I am being locked out, sir! Does anyone know we are here?"

Seagar is getting even more frustrated and angry. He starts grabbing his uniform jacket and items to make a quick exit. Suddenly there is a knock at the door. "Who is it?" he calls out.

"General Seagar! This is Agent Morozov from the Federal Security Service. We need to speak to you about an urgent matter." The voice stops and waits for his reply.

Seagar has no choice but to answer. He stops and looks at the techs. "Let them in. I need to grab my files for them in the other room."

The techs look over at him, confused. The sound tech disconnects from his headphones and walks to the door and looks through the peephole. Agent Morozov stands with his badge up. Four military officers are behind him, as well as Russian police officers. The sound tech unlocks the door and allows the agent and officers into the room.

As the tech is about to speak, the officers realize that the general is trying to escape. Two officers quickly grab the techs and handcuff them while Agent Morozov breaks into the bedroom. He looks around, but Seagar is nowhere to be found. He speaks into his earbud.

"Seagar is running for it. Lock down the building and make a perimeter for a full block. Coordinate with the Russian military and the International Military Security Council. He needs to be brought in for investigation." Morozov walks back into the main area of the suite and looks at the monitors.

The two techs sit in chairs handcuffed, wondering what is going on. Four more men walk in and start collecting data from the computers and monitors. Morozov looks at the two techs. "Where is he going? What was your escape plan?"

The first tech answers quickly. "We have just been monitoring a facility in Moscow. Seagar wanted us to monitor the main airport. He told us that it has a separate section that Velnias and Russian operations are working out of."

Morozov looks at him, confused. "Uncuff them and give them back their weapons!"

The two techs look at each other, confused, and both mumbling out loud, "What weapons?"

One of the officers brings two pistols and hands one to each of them. He steps back out of the way. Morozov looks at the two techs and raises his hand. The other four officers pull their guns and begin to fire, killing both techs instantly.

Morozov radios to the remaining officers. "We have two dead suspects! American techs, and it looks like General Seagar is on the run. Notify the American Secretary of Defense of the situation. If all evidence is correct, General Seagar is now a war criminal." He cuts out the radio and motions for the officers to start collecting everything in the suite.

| | | | |

Before Agent Morozov enters the suite, Seagar climbs out of the bedroom window and drops down to the balcony below. The room is empty, and he is able to get in because the balcony door is unlocked. Luggage sits on a chair inside. He grabs it to check if there is anything he can use. Dumping everything out, Seagar puts his military jacket and files inside.

The jacket propped on the desk chair looks to be his size, so he grabs it and a ballcap from the desk before heading to the main door. Seagar looks through the peephole to make sure it is clear, then he opens the door, leaving with the luggage.

Just as he finds a door to the stairwell, two officers exit the elevator. He quickly goes through the door, but it slams shut behind him. The officers hear it and start running to the stairwell. Seagar darts down the stairs as the two officers follow. He is ahead by about a floor and a half. One officer stops and reaches for his side pouch. He pulls the pin and drops a flashbang grenade. It is timed perfectly and lands just ahead of Seagar, going off and sending Seagar back into the stairs. He yells out in pain and discomfort.

The second officer reaches him, grabbing hold of Seagar. The blast disoriented him enough that the officer is able to restrain and cuff him easily. The officer who dropped it radios for backup, informing them that they have him in custody. Seagar is disoriented and has no idea what is happening. The one officer grabs the luggage from the staircase and they take him downstairs to the remaining officers.

Morozov greets him and puts him in the back of a black, unmarked sedan. The agent jumps into the passenger side of the car while a different agent sits in the back with Seagar. The car speeds off and the remaining officers enter the hotel as a coroner van pulls up.

| | | | |

At the airport facility, Velnias runs papers through a shredder next to his desk. A USB connected to his laptop downloads files, automatically deleting them once they are completed. He slowly moves around the room with brief stops to breathe.

Pulling out a book of matches, Velnias lights the whole book then drops it into the trash can of the shredded documents. He takes the USB out before tossing the laptop into the flaming trash can.

He rolls his sleeves up and starts to pick at his burned forearms. The burns start to peel up and he removes it all to reveal healthy, unscarred skin. He peels off his palms and fingerprints and throws all of the skin into the flames of the trash can. He then starts to pull all of the burnt skin and scars off of his face, showing an undamaged face. He throws all of face burns and skin into the fire. Velnias reaches into his pocket, pulls leather gloves out, and puts them on. He grabs other items and throws them into the fire.

Once everything seems to be ashes, Velnias grabs the fire extinguisher to put out the fire. He grabs the suitcase sitting near the exit and opens the door. He walks out into the hall and slowly down to the back side of the building. He exits through an emergency access door and stands outside in a backway of the airport. He looks around for security cameras and does not see any.

He walks over to a dumpster a few feet away and puts the briefcase down. He pushes the hood back and starts taking off the druid-like outfit. He tears away any leftover burns on his neck and face to show more healthy skin.

A device attached to the front of his throat and mouth used to control his breathing and voice is removed. He pulls a trash bag from his pocket and dumps everything into it. He lifts the dumpster lid and tosses the full bag in.

Velnias now stands next to the dumpster in a full suit, clean-shaven. Dark hair and brown eyes show a completely different look—a younger, thirty-something, approachable man standing in a dark alley.

He waits a second before the sound of a high-performance V12 engine comes from a distance. Around the corner, a black, priceless, eye-popping luxury sportscar pulls up. Velnias opens the door and gets into the car sitting back. There is no driver. He shuts the door and the car starts to drive itself. He pulls out a cell phone and types out a message.

Seagar is in custody! Kraków is under siege! Release Dr. Peck and the pilot!

He puts the phone away and gets comfortable as his vehicle drives into the night.

| | | | |

On the tarmac of the airport, Russian authorities approach the main hangar where Velnias operated out of. A small group of ten in full combat gear get close to the large hangar door. The lead officer reminds them it is a rescue mission and to stay sharp. Two break off toward a side door to the left while another two break off to the right to circle around. The remaining six move straight at the hangar doors. They stop and all get down on one knee with rifles raised.

A moment later the hangar doors begin to open. The other officers have not entered yet. As the doors open wide, a man sits in a wheelchair with another chained to a chair. The officers run over to check on them and see Dr. Peck and Kitchener Williams groggy and barely coherent. Kitchener has metal restraints to prevent him from using his wings or weapons.

Paramedics are on standby and are ready to quickly tend to the two. As soon as the troops confirm the identity, they motion for the paramedics. One medic runs to Dr. Peck and starts to check on him. Both medics look for any severe injuries. They are dehydrated with some bruises and scars, but nothing severe shows. A black sedan also arrives, and Agent Morozov gets out and quickly goes to check on them. Dr. Peck is starting to come to.

"Where am I?" He shakes his head and reacts to his throbbing headache.

Morozov puts his hand out to calm him. "It is okay, Dr. Peck. You are safe now. American military representatives are on the way to get you. We have General Seagar in custody, and you and Airman Williams will be heading home soon."

Dr. Peck looks at the agent, confused. "I don't remember anything! Last thing I remember, I was being put on a plane and brought here to Russia by Seagar. After that I can't remember what happened. I feel like something is missing. I remember a dark shadowy figure, but nothing else." Dr. Peck feels frustrated and angry.

Kitch looks up and around. "How the fuck did I get here? Where is *this*? Did someone say Russia? I was in Romania causing a distraction and ended up in the woods. My head hurts like a motherfucker!"

Morozov stands back up after crouching to Dr. Peck. "Seagar is in custody. We have tons of evidence for his actions and manipulations. The International Military Security Council will be working with the old process known as the Hague for war crimes. General Seagar, a.k.a. Velnias, will be under trial in front of the world."

Dr. Peck looks at the agent in shock. "Seagar is Velnias? That can't be—"

Kitch looks at the agent with anger. "What do you mean war crimes? What did he do and how is he Velnias? He wasn't the one creating these things. He wasn't even in Romania." Kitch is frustrated and wants out of his restraints.

Morozov puts his hand up, trying to calm him down. "I understand your anger! We have accumulated evidence and information about his actions creating the situations that injured you and put you into your current state. He has also been orchestrating major scientific developments that are morally questionable. The IMSC is moving forward to make sure none of the developments have become compromising globally."

Dr. Peck feels sorrow and frustration. "That would

mean my research and program with the American government is under investigation?"

Morozov doesn't agree, but also does not dismiss the question. "Time will tell regarding your program. I am not really sure of much else regarding that. I do know that you are safe and will be picked up soon. They will take both of you back to the US for debriefing."

Dr. Peck shakes his head. "I need to go back to Greece to the facility. To see the others and make sure they are okay. If they want to close the program and facility, they need to do it the right way. Other than Seagar, I know more about it than anyone. I am going back to my offices. I think Kitch would agree with me."

Kitch nods and stands up as he is released from his restraints before stepping back from everyone. He shrugs and his wings deploy. He moves his arms and legs and feet. He feels good and smiles. "Yeah! I agree! We have more work to do, and obviously this IMSC group needs us over here. This isn't over! Where is my team?"

Morozov doesn't react to Kitch and his flair. "They are in Kraków. There is a major disturbance in the city. Communication says they are in the center and with some of the local police. Your secretary of defense can tell you more when you speak with him. He is working directly with the IMSC."

Kitch steps forward. "Are they getting military assistance? Get me there so I can help! They need me!" As Kitch gets set to apply his wings and thrusters, a couple of the armed agents lift their rifles to prevent him. He pauses and puts his arms up, displaying that he is stopping.

Morozov puts his hands up in a calming action. "No one can enter the city. These troops that were produced have overrun the city. Shooting people, biting people, eating flesh. Until we know more, no agency is approved to enter. Polish military have a large perimeter set up around the city. No one can get out without confirmation of no contamination. The city will be under lockdown for the near future."

Dr. Peck looks at him like he's crazy. "Fuck that and fuck you! We want our people out of that place and we *will* make that happen! Let me know when the American plane gets here." He turns his chair around and wheels away.

Morozov just watches and says nothing.

CHAPTER 28

Gunshots and screams fill the air of the city of Kraków. The detective stands at the door of the clinic keeping watch as Bull and Surge set up speakers on the police van. Two officers have arrived to stay at the clinic to watch over Crow as she recovers. Surge walks back into the clinic and heads to the back.

Chase walks over to him. "Surge! Are we all set? We need to move out as quickly as we can and send Alexis into the square."

Surge looks back at him. "I need to check Crow one more time. I know we need to leave, but we also can't afford for anything to happen to her. She has information we need. Let me check her, and then we can go!"

Chase agrees and steps back to let him in. Surge walks back into the room and sees Crow as she was before, lying on the observation table looking at the ceiling. "How are you feeling? I wanted to check on you before we head out."

Crow looks at him. "You sound like you don't want to go. You sound scared!"

Surge shrugs. "That obvious? I have been a medic and scientist. But never a combat specialist. I helped create this technology, but I would be too scared to use it. I do love giving others the chance to use it."

Crow turns back at the ceiling. "I used to be scared like that. Then situations forced me to step up. But my brother was by my side always. He got through and over things. It's why I called him Brug."

Surge looks at her, curious. "You called him Brug? Why? What does it mean?"

She chuckles. "It is the Danish word for bridge. He is always strong and supportive. I wanted something different and found that. It just fit him. He always liked saying it meant Big Raging Ugly German." She pauses for a moment, thinking. "Everything I have done in my life has been about survival. I am a fighter and always will be. If I had arms, I would fight with you. I know you may not believe that."

Surge looks over at the case and nods. "I actually do believe that, and if anything was to happen, you need to have a chance." He walks over to the case and removes the layer that separates the ports from the arms in the bottom. He looks at them then at her. "I remember creating different models and ideas for prosthetics. How this case ended up with Alexis, I don't know. Whatever the reason, these were meant for you. I think it's fate so let's put them on you so if anything happens, you can survive it." He pulls one arm out and connects it to her right side. Then does the same with the left.

Crow starts moving her fingers in amazement. Surge smiles and starts to leave.

"Wait! What do I do now?"

Surge turns and looks at her. "Stay here and rest." He smiles at her and turns and leaves the room.

Crow lies back down and watches her metal fingers move. As she thinks about how sharp the nails are, they suddenly project out like claws. She giggles and smiles with subtle joy and a little deviousness.

"Well that's a fun surprise!"

| | | | |

Surge walks back out to the front area where everyone stands ready. The two officers walk back in position outside of Crow's room. Surge looks at Chase and nods that he is ready.

Chase looks around at Bull, Alexis, Salene, Surge, and Detective Bosco. "The goals: Find Sabu and Sun, if he is still alive. Lure those things to the square! Unleash hell till there are none of them left, or we die trying! That is what I am going to do. If you are not one hundred percent with me, then stay here and hope they don't come. Alexis, the deal is set. Run that van to the square! Exit under it and go to the manhole cover closest to you. Take out as many as you can. We will cover you and support you. You are free to go through the sewers." Chase puts out his hand and everyone follows, putting hands on top of each other.

Salene suddenly speaks up. "We do this for us and the civilians in this city!"

Alexis claps his hands together and starts walking toward the door. "All right, then, let's get this shit going!" He turns and looks at Bull. "The sound system is set?"

Bull gives him a thumbs-up. "All set! Now we just need to feed the noise or music through to draw them to the square."

Alexis gives a big shit-eating grin. "I got that covered! If I don't see you assholes again, go fuck yourselves." He pauses and looks at them. "Good luck!" He turns and gets into the van.

Bull looks around at the others. "Maybe he isn't a complete despicable scumbag!"

Salene shakes her head. "No. He is a piece of shit. He just understands the situation! He has just as much to lose as we do. He realizes how expendable he is."

Alexis sits in the van, taking a deep breath and connecting his cell phone to the van's system. He cranks the van up and looks into his phone's music. He scrolls down to a band named Skillet. A song called "Finish Line" pops up.

He starts to drive, and after a few seconds a hard-rock guitar riff screams out of the speakers and blares through the city air. He speeds up the police van. The SCZ soldiers start following the noise and shoot at the van. Dodging bullets while driving through the streets toward the square, Alexis can see the music is working.

The others start to follow, running along the sidewalk. They can see the soldiers following and shooting at the van. The detective goes to fire his assault rifle, but Chase stops him. He looks at him and shakes his head.

"We don't want to draw them away. If we engage them up close, we'll stay hidden better in hand to hand. Or we can take them out from behind quietly. Save the ammo!"

The detective agrees and lowers his rifle. Chase looks at Salene and points to a building in the distance that has balconies halfway up. He then looks at Bull and points at him and the detective. He motions with his hands to go straight to the square then turn left and move down to the monument. They need one on each corner behind the monument. The van will be in that open space. Bull nods, understanding Chase's hand gestures and signals.

Chase looks at Surge. In a low voice he tells him the plan. "We need to try and locate Sabu and get to the other side of the museum building. If Bosco's officers can block the far side of the square, we can hit them from all sides. Then we pray it works."

Surge nervously agrees and starts to follow behind Chase. They can hear the gunfire and rock music ahead as the van turns slightly left to go into the square.

Alexis is taking on heavy fire from the troops but pushes forward. Two tires are suddenly flat and the van begins to slow. The engine has been hit several times and it is almost dead. As it pushes forward, not too far into the square, it suddenly dies. The others can see and rush forward to help him.

Before the van gets surrounded, Sabu comes running from a dark alley to the van. Alexis can see him and opens the sliding door for him to jump in. As Sabu runs, his feet push off, giving him added thrust into his steps. Alexis starts shooting at several troops coming toward the van. A handful of SCZ troops gets in between the van and Sabu. Sabu fires blades from his forearms, hitting them. He dodges some bullets and then plants both feet and jumps. His piston feet deploy and send him into the air as he flips and twists to land behind the troops but facing them. With both arms out, he fires an array of blades from his arms then jumps back into the van. Alexis slams the door shut.

Sabu looks at him, confused. "Thanks?" his mechanical voice offers hesitantly.

Alexis shakes his head. "Don't get sappy! I am out of here the moment I have a chance. Chase and I have a deal." Alexis starts looking at the few weapons in the van he can use. He grabs an assault rifle and clicks in an ammo clip. He grabs two more clips and puts them in his pockets. The music still bellows loudly into the air, drawing the violent troops to them. Random shots hit the van as Sabu and Alexis stay still and low.

Chase, Surge, and Salene move toward the building Salene will use for a higher position. The detective and Bull quickly move down the far side of the square toward the monument. A few random troops are close to them. Bull approaches from behind. He pulls out an eight-inch bayonet and stabs the first troop in the back of the head, then quickly snaps the neck of the next. The detective keeps a close watch for any other troops approaching them. They quickly make a run for the statue and get to it quietly.

Chase and Surge stand watch as Salene starts to punch hole grips into the outer wall. She tests out a few and discovers how strong the amped-up arms are. She starts to scale the wall of the building using the hole grips.

Surge has a nine-millimeter pistol with a silencer ready and Chase has a police-issue AK-12 assault rifle in his left arm and his amped-up flamethrower right arm ready. Surge notices on the far side of the square police officers are starting to create a line to block any escape. Chase looks up and finds that Salene is almost to the balcony on the fourth floor.

Surge surveys the area and can see Sabu in the police van with Alexis, and it is suddenly getting pounded by gunfire and swarmed by the SCZs. He looks off to the distance and can see Bull and the detective getting into position at the monument. He continues to look around as Chase watches Salene get into the balcony.

Suddenly a woman starts to scream off to the right of them. Three troops are grabbing her and trying to bite on her. She pushes and fights to get free but can't. Surge reacts quickly and starts to fire, hitting all three, allowing the woman to get away. But her scream has attracted attention and a number of soldiers start to pull away from the van. Some move toward where the woman was attacked, while others head toward Surge and Chase.

Chase starts to fire his assault rifle eliminating about a dozen troops before they can attack. Salene up in her balcony perch takes aim. She fires a few shots at troops attacking the van. She starts to scan the square from above with her mechanical eye. She whistles down to Chase and Signals him with three fingers up. Then with both hands makes round circles with her metal fingers.

Chase sees it and nods that he understands. He looks at Surge with a big smile. "We just might be fucked!"

Surge looks at him with another nervous look. "What the fuck do you mean? Way to help me feel good about things!" He shakes his head and switches from the pistol to the assault rifle.

Bull and the detective are set at the monument and start to add to the attack. Bull clicks his Gatling-style guns into place and starts to unleash a barrage of bullets. Dozens of soldiers get mowed down as Bull unleashes hell on them.

Detective Bosco unloads in the direction of the van to give Sabu and Alexis a chance to get out. The side door slides open and Sabu jumps out with his blades in hand, slicing limbs and heads off with quickness and ease.

The multiple-direction attacks start to confuse the troops. They start firing weapons all over and in many directions. The police officers to the far side of the square start to move forward in two straight lines of twelve. They are spaced out and staggered so the second row has space to shoot. Most of the SCZ troops are central to the square.

In the distance there are still gunshots and screaming in the city. This also adds to the confusion for the SCZs, which fire scattered shots. The distant gunshots create a problem for them, which Chase and the others begin to take advantage of.

Sabu twists and turns through the crowd. As he moves, he can see Asher approaching the lines of police officers. Asher raises his arms and his whip-like flexible blades unravel. With a couple of quick motions and turns, he whips his arms forward. One blade slices through an officer's arm and the other slices the neck. He continues to throw the blades with ease as they slice through other officers left and right. He goes to throw his left arm, but as he does, Sabu blocks it with his arched blade. They stand firm, looking at each other as they square off. The police officers move back and reposition as a one-on-one fight ensues.

Asher pulls his blocked sword back and takes a fighting stance with his left leg forward. Sabu stands with his left leg forward as well.

The two circle each other, sizing the other up. Sabu wonders how much the head device will affect instinct. A few seconds pass and suddenly they are both lunging at each other in aggression.

Sabu blocks the whip-like weapon and uses his right leg to front-kick and push him back. He swipes across with his right arm, but Asher avoids it. Sabu steps back and resets his arms and blades.

Asher moves forward with a staggered attack of his arms, then rotates and repeats the action as Sabu retreats backward waiting for his opening.

Sabu abruptly tosses his blades at Asher, creating a confused reaction. Asher stops to process what is happening. Sabu drops down and rotates himself in a backward sweep-kick motion.

As he moves, he positions himself to go to a full handstand and spins until he is behind Asher. Asher is too slow to react as a blade jets out of Sabu's right foot. The blade then plunges into the lower skull, where it connects to the brain stem. He pulls his foot back and Asher drops to the ground in a heap as blood pours from his mouth in a pool around him. Sabu returns to his feet and picks up his blades off the ground.

Salene continues to pick off troop after troop with her shots from above. Chase and Surge hold firm below with the assault rifles. Bull and Bosco are doing the same near the monument. Alexis is now on the roof of the van and he continues to shoot the assault rifle as the speakers continue to blare heavy guitar riffs and metal music. SCZ troops continue to come toward the music while bodies pile up.

The plan is working, but Chase has a bad gut feeling.

On the far side, the police officers regroup and position to start moving forward to the main fight. As they set up in a row, they are about to move forward when a loud, blood-curdling scream comes from the far end of the line. They all turn and scatter as they see a huge, enhanced, amped-up Brug with metal arms holding an officer in the air with his right hand holding the officer's forehead. He begins to squeeze and the officer's head is crushed. Brug looks over at the other officers as they stand in horror. Brug gives a snarling grin, and there is complete power in his eyes. He raises his metal left arm and makes a fist then starts to laugh evilly as machine -un rounds fly from above his forearm. The officers scatter more but are destroyed by the high volume of rounds. Brug throws the dead officer to the ground and looks toward the van.

Alexis stands on the van and notices Brug in the distance. He watches for a second to see him reach over his left shoulder to pull something forward. He realizes Brug has a small rocket launcher attached to his body. In a matter of seconds, a small rocket hurls through the air at the van. Alexis jumps off and lands hard on the ground as the van gets blown to pieces.

Salene can see Brug from her perch and takes aim with both arms. Her scope zooms in to see he is looking right at her while the launcher moves in front of him. He reloads as she takes her shots, but he starts moving, never taking his eyes off of her location. The prosthetic arm attaches to a rotating plate, which connects to the body, allowing the launcher to move from back to front. Brug pauses, and then the launcher fires a rocket right at Salene's position.

Chase sees it and screams at her to jump. The rocket hits as she jumps from the balcony, but the explosion sends her out toward the crowd of soldiers. The troops catch her fall, but she is surrounded.

Chase runs toward her with his flamethrower ignited and aimed at the troops ahead of him. Salene fights them off and fires random shots to create space. Surge follows Chase, shooting to his left and right to protect him from being attacked from the side.

Sabu attempts to run at Brug while Bull and Bosco turn their attention to Brug. The crazy and destructive Brug raises his right arm and starts firing machine-gun rounds at them while watching Sabu run toward him.

Sabu fires blades from his forearm, but Brug's arm blocks some as the few that get through barely faze him. Sabu lunges and jumps up to kick Brug in the ribs, but Brug swats him away. Sabu goes flying to the ground and rolls to a stop in a heap.

As Brug takes over the situation, Alexis spots a manhole cover. He remembers a pry bar in the van. But with the van blown up, he has to look around to see if it's on the ground. He luckily spots it ten feet away from him on the ground. He pulls his pistol and starts shooting any soldiers near it, then runs to grab it. He stops and looks around to check who is where. Alexis wants nothing to do with Brug and runs for the manhole. As he gets to it, an SCZ goes after him. He raises his gold-plated gun and puts a bullet into the forehead of the flesh-eating minion.

Alexis uses the pry bar to get the heavy iron disk up and open. He keeps his eyes open to gauge others coming for him. He wants out of the situation as soon as possible. The opening is big enough for him to get into. He slides himself into it, finding the metal ladder that leads down. But he notices Brug moving in his direction. He starts to rush, and as he gets into the hole, he shifts the disk over until it drops into place. He quickly scurries down the ladder into the sewer tunnels under the city. The smell is awful and he gags a little.

He pulls out a small flashlight and scans around to decide a direction. He slowly moves down the tunnel a few hundred feet. It is quiet and creepy on his own. He stops suddenly, thinking he heard a groan. A little freaked out, he scans around again. He hears a voice.

"Grim!" It's a weak voice and it groans with pain. Alexis looks around to see Bautista slumping against the sewer wall. He is covered in blood and has scars on his face and arms. Alexis moves toward him and starts checking him.

"What happened to you? How bad are you hurt?" Alexis looks at the wounds. They are not deep and mainly surface scratches. He is relieved to find Bautista and have someone with him. "Can you move? We need to get away from this area."

Bautista nods and gets up on his feet. He stretches and moves his body, testing how it reacts.

Bautista looks at Alexis and pats him on the shoulder. "I'm not too bad! I found my way down here after I came to. I wanted to stay out of the chaos. You go ahead and lead the way." Bautista holds his ribs and points to his right.

Alexis agrees, and with his gold-plated gun in his right hand and the flashlight in his left, he moves forward. He scans the tunnel with the flashlight. Everything looks clear, and he turns to see Bautista standing with a gun pointed at his head. A silencer is attached and is an inch away from his forehead. Before Alexis can say anything, Bautista pulls the trigger multiple times.

Alexis's head sprays blood, skull, and brain matter into the dark tunnel behind him. He drops to his knees and slumps to the side. Bautista takes the silencer off and puts his gun away.

He searches Alexis's body and grabs the flashlight and the gold-plated handgun. He takes papers from Alexis's pocket, then stands back up and looks down at the body.

"As of now, I work alone. *La Calavera!*" He pulls a black-skull military mask out and puts it on before disappearing into the sewer tunnels.

CHAPTER 29

D r. Peck and Kitch sit on a small military jet on the tarmac at the Moscow airport. Two agents prepare a tablet for a video conference with the secretary of defense. The first agent, a muscular Black woman with curly hair, walks over to Dr. Peck and hands him the tablet.

"The secretary should come through in a minute. He needs to ask you some things regarding General Seagar. If you need anything, let me or my partner know. I'm Agent Kennedy, and this is Agent Bardsley."

Her partner walks over and nods to them before saying, "We should be leaving in about twenty minutes. Once we get back to Washington, you can give a full debrief. Right now the secretary just needs a few details. The situation is pretty bad internationally now that we know the general was running the Plague." Agent Bardsley hands Kitch a glass of water.

Kitch and Dr. Peck look at each other before Kitch responds. "What do you mean Seagar was running the Plague?"

Agent Kennedy responds, "The Russian government informed us that they found you, and that through certain channels of underground weapon sales and espionage they had evidence that Seagar was pulling the strings. Azazil was assisting in the process. We also know the situation in Kraków has become an international incident. As of now, the IMSC is not allowing anyone into the city until it is deemed safe from a humanitarian standpoint."

Dr. Peck interrupts her. "That doesn't make sense, though. If they created a way to reanimate the brain to use dead soldiers, then anything they are doing would have to be programmed."

Bardsley understands what the doctor is saying and interjects. "The problem is, you have hundreds of soldiers in the city destroying it while biting and feasting on people. How can that be normal? How can that be programmed?"

The doctor thinks for a second. "Can the two of you help me convince the secretary to go back to Greece with the rest of our team? The only way to understand it is to look at my data and findings. We also need to know what Chase and the others have found out."

Kennedy and Bardsley look at each other. Kennedy nods, agreeing with Dr. Peck. "Chase and the rest of your team are currently trapped in downtown Kraków. We believe they have been able to stop some of the soldiers that have caused damage. Right now it is unclear what will happen, or *why* this is happening."

The doctor sits for a minute, thinking quietly. Kitch is bit more animated and wants to get to Kraków. "You need to take us there. I need to get in and help. I can't just sit here."

"You have to, because right now our orders are to keep the two of you safe and get all the information you have," Bardsley says firmly. "I get it! I would want to be by my team's side as well. At this moment, we wouldn't even get to them in time to make a difference. Trust me and my partner. We will help you to get to Greece first. That makes the most sense."

The tablet starts to beep and the secretary appears on screen sitting at a desk. "Dr. Peck! Greetings from Washington. Are you okay? How are you feeling?"

"I don't remember anything after the jet. I just know Seagar was with me and injected something in my neck. I have flashes of a dark room like an interrogation room. I don't know what else to tell you, Mr. Secretary. We need to go back to the facility in Greece to figure it out." The doctor takes a deep breath.

"I need you to come to Washington for a debrief. The government and my two agents here are to oversee the dismantling and collection of all evidence from your facility. This is an international issue, and now the IMSC is getting involved to prosecute General Seagar as a war criminal."

Agent Kennedy moves into the field of view. "Mr. Secretary! With so many questions unanswered, maybe we should keep them with us at the facility." She looks over at Bardsley. He motions his head in agreement. "Put Bardsley and I in charge of them. They can report to us and we will report to you. Once we have all of the evidence and findings we need, we can shut it down."

The secretary starts to shake his head. He doesn't like the request, but knows he needs to do something. "Are you suggesting the whole AMPD team return with you to the Greece facility? We just moved all of the security staff and onsite personnel out of there. All that is left is a few techs and maintenance staff. The next move was to send in agents for collection, which is what you would be in charge of."

"Yes! Once the Kraków situation is under control, they will come back with us," Kennedy says confidently.

The secretary thinks for a minute and opens a file in front of him. "Whoever makes it out of Kraków alive is to report to you. As soon as we can make contact, I want to speak with them. You will report everything directly to me. This situation is of high priority, and I will deal directly with the International Military Security Council on my own."

Dr. Peck speaks up before the conversation ends. "Mr. Secretary! Be aware that what is happening may not be biological. It may be a case of programming!"

The man sits at his desk, trying to understand what that means. "Are you saying whatever they have done to these soldiers was on purpose? Even the flesh eating?"

"Yes! Think about it! If you create something, you have to find a way to fuel it and give it nourishment. It sounds like a form of cannibalism. You need to give us time and space to truly figure this out. I'm basically saying back the fuck off and let us do our job!" the doctor says with authority.

Agents Kennedy and Bardsley's eyebrows rise in shock. Kitch just chuckles as the secretary tries to figure out what to say. He clears his throat and closes the file he had opened. There is a look of displeasure on his face. "Okay! Agents Kennedy and Bardsley, you are the official liaisons for the AMPD program. You are to report all activity and projects to me. Dr. Peck, I am putting you in charge of the team and research. You report anything and everything to them. I will pull the plug on this at any time if I feel the need to. I want you to check in twenty-four hours from now." Before anyone can say anything else, the secretary shuts down the connection.

Bardsley looks around at everyone, confused. "Did he just make us babysitters?"

Kitch chuckles and speaks up. "No! The proper word is liaisons. It means the same thing!"

Bardsley looks at him, unamused, and Kennedy rolls her eyes.

Dr. Peck puts his hands up to ease their minds on the situation. "I promise we will work with you. We will research and investigate things together. Please trust me." He puts his hand out and both agents accept the handshake. "I guess we need to go to Kraków then! I hope the situation is not as bad as it sounds."

| | | | |

Crow continues to lie on the table. Her mind goes through all the good memories she had with Brug. She worries about him and is scared of what may have happened to him. She can hear the gunfire and explosions in the distance.

She doesn't want to be lying here. She wants to be involved to let out her anger. She misses Sun because he kept her focused and alert. Ever since the first time they met, she has felt at ease. No one ever knew it, and she made sure that people did not know it. They always had a bond, and now he may be gone as well.

One of the officers peeks in to check on her. She stays still and closes her eyes. Her metal arms just lie at her sides. It is a surreal feeling not to feel, but know, her fingers are moving. She opens her eyes to the ceiling again.

With one quick thought she decides to get up, but she is still strapped down, meaning she has to use the new hands and arms to unstrap herself. As she thinks about it, her new arms suddenly begin undoing the straps. She looks at her right arm, amazed at what she can see. She thinks of flipping the officers the bird and her middle finger rises to position.

The belts are undone and she gets up to a seated

position. She looks at her nails and they jet out like claws like before. On both arms there is a section that wraps around the wrist area. The sections has numbers and appears like a dial. She uses her right hand to adjust the left arm's dial. She can hear a slight hum from her hand, although it is very subtle. She touches her thigh with her finger to feel a slight sting and shock.

"Oh, Doctor! Why did not you mention this? Naughty boy. Excuse me, officers, can you help me?" she calls out. She adjusts the two wrists to a moderate volume. The two officers walk in to see her sitting on the table with her legs dangling to the floor. "I was hoping to move around, but was afraid of not being strong enough. Can you spot me as I get to my feet?"

The two officers agree to help her. They position on each side with arms ready as she moves to get on her feet. She shifts to her feet and suddenly grabs each officer's forearm. In an instant, the two officers stiffen up as volts of electricity surge into them. Both make twisted faces as they drop to the floor twitching. The voltage was moderate, so they should be okay but subdued for now. Crow smiles and adjusts the voltage down.

"Wow! That was perfect. Thank you, boys!" She walks out of the room as the two lie on the floor continuing to twitch and grunt.

CHAPTER 30

C hase and Surge get to Salene, who is hurt from the blast and fall. Surge gets her in his arms and he retreats back as Chase uses the flames to push the troops back from them.

Bull and the detective are getting Brug's attention with gunfire as Sabu tries to recover from the hard hit. He can see the van has been destroyed, and with no music, the soldiers start to scatter all over the square. He turns to see Brug moving toward him. He raises his arms and fires numerous blades at Brug with no effect. Even with the gunfire from Bull and the detective, he isn't slowed down.

Bull stops firing the machine gun and motions to the detective to stop. The detective looks at him funny, wondering what he is doing. Bull moves his arms behind him and clicks his Gatling-style guns in place. His arms are now free from them and he walks out from the memorial and puts his arms up in the air.

"Hey, big boy!" he calls out to grab Brug's attention. "We know you got the big guns. How about we deal with this one on one? Heavyweight to heavyweight." Bull starts walking toward Brug, expecting him to accept the challenge.

Brug pushes the launcher on his shoulder back and punches his metal right hand into his metal left hand. He looks over at Bull and snarls in response to the challenge. They are suddenly moving quickly at each other and cock back their right arms in anticipation.

Bull comes to a quick stop and uses his left arm to block the huge punch Brug throws. Bull throws a hay-maker punch and connects to the jaw. Brug's eyes go wide as he shakes it off and looks at Bull. Brug grabs him by the throat. Bull looks at Brug with amazement.

He won't give up, though, and grabs Brug's hand with his left and turns to his left with a twist. He pulls Brug to gain leverage on the arm, but Brug counters and swings his right arm up and makes contact with Bull's chin, knocking his hand loose and moving him back.

Brug starts throwing a barrage of punches and body shots. He throws a massive punch that knocks Bull to his back. Brug raises his right arm and takes aim, but the detective sends off shots from his assault rifle, hitting Brug's arm and grabbing his attention. Brug starts firing at the detective as he jumps behind the monument.

Bull rolls out of the way and gets to his feet. He regroups with Sabu to the side of the museum building. Chase starts to head toward Brug with his flamethrower active. He fires shots at Brug from his rifle and misses. Brug sees a fire hydrant to Chase's right and takes a few shots, hitting the valves and opening up a high-pressure release of water that hits Chase. Brug is walking closer to Chase and the water. The remaining active troops are either attacking Chase or shooting at Bull and Sabu.

While Brug is distracted with Chase and the others, Surge carries Salene from the crowd of blood-craving troopers. Chase motions for them to head back to the clinic as he creates a distraction with his flamethrower.

As Surge has Salene in his arms, she fires off a few shots behind them at a few random followers.

After a few minutes they are in the clear. Surge is feeling out of breath and slows down. He moves over to the building wall and puts her down to check her. She groans with pain as she shifts her body to lean on the wall, placing a hand on her side, indicating a possible broken rib.

Surge puts his hand on the area and touches gently. Salene jerks her body at the light touch. He motions to her to take a deep breath, and she does, but groans in pain. "It hurts pretty bad!" Her breathing is labored.

Surge shifts her legs straight and tries not to move her too much. She looks at him and smiles at how attentive he is to her. He looks back at her with a smile. His eyes connect with hers, but she gets flustered and self-conscious. She looks down, feeling ugly because of her prosthetic robotic eye. She doesn't want to look at him. With his good hand, he touches her chin and raises her head. As he is about to say something, a female voice comes from behind him.

"Am I interrupting?" Crow looks at Salene. "Are you okay?" she asks with sincerity.

Surge turns to see Crow standing in the street with her fully functioning prosthetic arms and a face that says, *I want to fuck some shit up*. She starts moving her fingers like she is cracking her knuckles.

Salene looks up at her. "Yeah. I will be okay. Go help the others if you can!" She looks at Crow with trust.

Crow turns and starts walking quickly toward the square. Before Surge can warn her about her brother, she is already heading down the street.

Moving at a quick pace, Crow turns the dials on her wrists up and her claws jump out. A couple of random

SCZs come at her as she gets closer to the square. The gunfire gets louder and the first trooper gets close. He raises his rifle, but she swats it away with her left arm and plunges her claws into the chest of the soldier. The electricity enters his body and fries the chip and components of the headgear. She pulls her claws out and the body collapses to the ground.

The reaction from the soldier gives her an idea. She starts looking at her arms closely to see what else she may be able to do. She notices holes in her wrists in front of the dials.

As she does, two other troops are getting close. They raise their rifles, and before they can shoot, she points her wrists at them randomly to see what happens. Both arms shoot out taser cables that connect in the chest below the neck of each soldier. Suddenly a violent electric charge surges through the cords and into the bodies, shocking their systems and frying them. Crow pulls the cords back and they retract into the forearms.

She walks up to the bodies and grabs one of their assault rifles. She checks it and cocks it ready. Looking up, she starts to run toward the square, firing the rifle at random troops and surveying where everyone is. She can see the water flowing from the hydrant. Many of the troops stand in the pooling water. In the distance she can see a large figure with their back to her. He is firing hundreds of rounds in different directions.

Crow can see the opportunity based on what she just tried with the cables. She has the dials on full and drops the rifle to the ground. She puts her arms forward and yells out to Chase. "Get out of the water!" She fires the cables into the middle of the pooling water.

Chase can see her and fights his way out of the standing water to get to Bull and Sabu.

The cables hit the water and stick into the ground. The electric surge flows into the water and starts to shock everyone and everything touching it, including Brug, who is in the distance with his back to Crow. SCZ troops start to drop to the ground as the surge of electricity fries the chip and headgear.

In the distance Brug turns as the high voltage shocks his entire body and his eyes roll back in his head. Brug does not have the same headgear that all of the others have. Burn marks start to show through the skin at six different spots on his head. He drops to his knees and slight groans come from him.

Crow realizes it is Brug and pulls back the cords from the water. She stands at the edge, not knowing what to do. Her mind is suddenly a barrage of visions and memories. Did she just kill her brother? She runs through the water to get to him as his body slumps to the ground. She starts to cry and screams in horror at what she just did. She gets to his body and gets down on her knees in the water. Continuously muttering "No!" and "Oh God!" she grabs his metal hand with hers but can't feel his touch, and that draws even more pain and suffering in her. She looks at his face and head, noticing the burn marks.

Chase walks over to her as Sabu and Bull watch for any SCZs still moving. He puts his real hand on her shoulder to comfort her. She drops her head and sobs with heavy tears, putting her arms around his neck and her head on his chest. The detective slowly walks over from the blown-up monument holding his arm, which may be broken.

Chase looks around, surveying what just happened. He doesn't understand why they would put so many troops in the city to cause chaos. Bull looks at him and can see he is uneasy.

"Chase! What's wrong? I can see the wheels in your

head turning. This isn't the end of it, is it?" Bull looks around and can hear random gunfire in spurts.

Chase looks at Bull with a worried face. "This was a test. I feel like this was to see how they perform. What reason would they have to drop this number of troops in Kraków? Other than we were in the city."

The detective stands next to Chase with his phone in his hand. "Our headquarters just got confirmation that agents for your government are coming to get you. The doctor and a young pilot from your program were recovered at an airbase near Moscow. As of right now the city is on lockdown. They are trying to patch your secretary of defense into me as soon as they can." The detective keeps checking his phone.

Chase turns his focus to Crow. He gets down on his knees next to her and puts his hand back on her shoulder. "You didn't do this! It is not your fault. I promise we will help you make this right."

She lifts her head off her brother's chest and looks at Chase. "You are going to help a known world criminal and arms dealer seek revenge on the people who did this to her brother?" She looks at him in disbelief, not trusting his words.

He nods his head and puts his hand out to her. "I give you my word!"

She pauses and doesn't want to believe him. As Chase puts his hand out, the detective's phone rings. He looks to see it's the patch from the US secretary of defense. The detective answers and hands the phone to Chase.

Chase pauses and looks at Crow. He mouths the word *speaker* to the detective, who obliges and puts the phone on speaker.

Chase speaks out and greets the secretary. "Good evening, Mr. Secretary!"

"Good evening, First Lieutenant! I have been told you neutralized the threat in Kraków?" the official voice speaks out.

"Yes sir! We have, and we obtained a lot of evidence and information to process," Chase answers eagerly as everyone stays quiet.

"Have you taken the fugitives Crow and Sun into custody? Are we able to process them with General Seagar?" the secretary asks with anticipation that they are.

Chase pauses and looks at Crow. "No sir! We have not! We believe Sun may be dead and Crow has evaded us. She is in the wind, and we have no idea where she may be." Chase smiles at her. Crow doesn't know what to think.

The secretary reacts in an upset tone. "That is disturbing news. I have two agents on the way to pick you up and take you back to Greece. I am apprehensive about keeping this program running, but your doctor seems positive that it is necessary. I told him I expect a check-in within twenty-four hours. Take any evidence you can from the scenes in the city."

"Yes sir! I am planning to keep Sabu here in Kraków to help the local authorities with the last few random troops. We also want to confirm whether Sun is dead or alive." Chase feels uneasy on the phone.

"Fine! I do want him to stay in the background. No media attention or exposure to the civilians. Everything stays as top secret as we can."

Chase tries to respond, but the phone clicks and the secretary is gone. He stands and looks at Crow and puts his hand out to her. "If we take Brug with us, we can determine everything they did to him. We can also make sure you are okay!"

She brushes his hand away. "Why would you take a known fugitive back to a government facility? To put me in custody! That does not sound like something I want. I appreciate you telling them I am gone, but finding Sun is my priority. I feel like that is what I need to do."

Sabu steps forward and puts his hand out to her. Crow looks at him and is not quite sure what he is implying. "Let me help you," he speaks out in his electronic voice. "You can trust me."

Chase agrees and responds to Sabu. "You can trust *us*. This seems like just the beginning. We need you and you need us. Work with us! Maybe we can find all the answers we are looking for."

Crow looks at Chase and looks around at the destruction and chaos that has happened. All her life has been about survival, and now whatever choice she makes will be about survival. She agrees and puts her fist out. Sabu nods his head and returns the fist-bump.

Bull stands to the side and looks around before he notices movement at some café tables that are scattered. He takes a few steps forward to see a German Shepherd slowly moving. He walks over and kneels down to greet the dog. The dog starts to move toward him but struggles. Its left hind leg appears to be broken. Bull moves forward a little more and puts his hand out. The dog sniffs his metal hand and looks at him. Bull softly pets him and the dog licks his metal fingers. Bull moves up to the dog and uses his arms to brace him and pick him up. He walks back over to the group and looks at Chase.

Chase looks at Bull and the dog. "Is he hurt?"

Bull turns and shows the hind leg. Chase can see the wounds on the leg as the dog's eyes stare at him. Chase can't help but smile. "The dog comes with us, but you are in charge of him when he is fully recovered."

Suddenly Bull has a huge smile on his face. He looks at the dog and the dog looks back, then licks Bull's nose.

Chase looks at Bull in amazement. "That's the first time I have seen you smile like that."

"I have always been a dog person!" He smiles again so big.

Chase receives a message from the doctor notifying them that they are on the way. The two message a few times confirming the return to the Greece facility. Chase also confirms they have Brug's body, but does not mention Crow or the prosthetics.

He turns his attention back to the group, only to see Crow and Sabu have already vanished. He smiles and looks around the square and into the sky. He looks at his arm and thinks back to that ditch he was lying in. He knows this is only the beginning.

"There is more to be revealed!" he says to himself softly as he starts walking back to Surge and the others.

Acknowledgments

Thank you to all my friends and network in Atlanta, Georgia, for supporting me and inspiring me. I could not achieve this without you.

I also want to thank my father, Nicholas, and my brother, Jason, who have been by my side through everything.

About the Author

Thomas Hraynyk is Canadian-born from Oshawa, Ontario. At forty-three, he is accomplishing a long dream of publishing his first novel.

Through many obstacles over the past five years, he has persevered and worked hard to get to this point. After his son was born, his fiancée tragically passed away, leaving him mentally and financially bankrupt. While living on his friend's sofa, he began the process of starting over, which included asking for help when feeling suicidal. Working through all of that, he found himself wanting to write again and started looking at the story he had started years ago.

Over the past two years, he has committed to making it happen and learning the process. Thanks to the support of his family and friends, he focused on showing his son and anyone who has suffered loss, depression, addiction, and mental health issues that you can achieve your goals.

Never give up on yourself and believe in yourself. Life is not easy, and things can happen in heartbreaking ways. You can get through it.